APRONS & VEILS
BOOK ONE

The Finding of Miss Fairfield

GRACE HITCHCOCK

Published by Valmont House Publishers

GraceHitchcock.com

Names: Hitchcock, Grace, author.

Title: The Finding of Miss Fairfield / Grace Hitchcock

Other Titles: the finding of miss fairfield

Series: Aprons and Veils; book 1

Identifiers: ISBN 979-8-9858217-2-7 (eBook) | ISBN 979-8-9858217-1-0 (Paperback) | ISBN 979-8-9858217-3-4 (Hardback) | 979-8-9912707-3-1 (Large Print Paperback)

Subjects: Christian Romantic suspense fiction

All scripture quotations, unless otherwise noted, are taken from the King James Version of the Bible.

This book is a work of fiction. Names, characters, places, and incidents are either products of the author's imagination or used fictitiously. Any similarity to actual people, living or dead, organizations, and/or events is purely coincidental.

Author is represented by The Steve Laube Agency.

More From Grace Hitchcock

Aprons and Veils Series:
The Finding of Miss Fairfield
The Pursuit of Miss Parish
The Enchanting of Miss Elliot
The Vanishing of Miss Victoria
The Courting of Miss Cady
The Making of Miss Matthews

Best Laid Plans Series:
To Catch a Coronet
To Kiss a Knight
To Win a Wager

American Royalty Series:
My Dear Miss Dupré
Her Darling Mr. Day
His Delightful Lady Delia

Heiresses of Adventure Series:
Miss Blaire in Blackwell's Island
Miss Wylde in the White City

Novellas:
Hearts of Gold, a Historical Romance Collection
"The Widow of St. Charles Avenue" in Second Chance Brides Collection

For Declan,
A dream long since dreamed.
Mama

"For God hath not given us the spirit of
fear; but of power, and of love, and of a
sound mind."

2 Timothy 1:7

"If I were loved, as I desire to be,
What is there in the great sphere of the earth,
And range of evil between death and birth,
That I should fear—if I were loved by thee?"
~ *Lord Alfred Tennyson*

CHAPTER 1

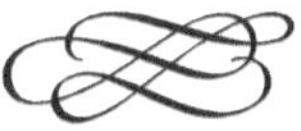

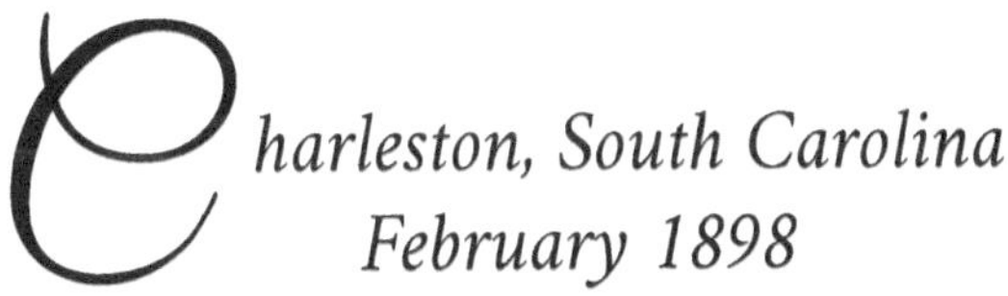

Charleston, South Carolina
February 1898

SOPHIA FAIRFIELD'S heart skipped at the sight of Mother holding a damp handkerchief to her eyes as Father and his business partner, Prescott Payne, stood before the floor-length windows facing Charleston Harbor with their heads together, speaking in low, somber tones over the crackling of the fireplace. They halted their whispering when they caught sight of her standing in the second-floor East drawing room doorway, her reticule dangling from her fingertips with her box of new poetry, papers, and pencils propped on her hip. "Mother? What's wrong?"

Mr. Payne stepped forward, his emerald eyes capturing hers in a most disconcerting fashion. Grinning down at her, he ran his hand over his neatly trimmed gray beard. "My dearest Sophia, I've spoken with your father and mother, and they have wholeheartedly given us their blessing to wed."

Sophia's stomach dropped, her limbs aching to bolt from the parlor as the grandfather clock in the corner sounded the noon hour. Her gaze darted to Mother's elated face. Sophia had only accepted Mr. Payne's suit last month as a courtesy to her father, intending on ending things once Mr. Payne saw that they were ill-suited for one another, given he was over twice her age, but he had apparently not understood her subtle hints for him to cease his efforts. *Or not even cared, given he sought my father's answer instead of my own.*

"Is my darling bride-to-be speechless at last?" Prescott held his hand out to her, inviting her to join him.

Bride-to-be? The box slipped from her grasp, the items scattering about the floor. She dropped to her knee to retrieve them, but Father crossed the room and seized her arm.

"Leave it for Belle." He waved forward the petite maid standing beside the tea service.

Sophia sent her friend an apologetic smile as Father drew her away into the gilded parlor. Though a small room, gold leaf adorned the crown molding and the ornate medallion with the gold and crystal chandelier in the center of the room that illuminated the platinum wall coverings that perfectly matched the opposite West parlor room. Mother had to have a matching set of French chandeliers of her own after her visit to her sister's in New York.

"I have already accepted his hand on your behalf, daughter. You will wed as soon as you choose the day. We were just discussing the arrangements right before you returned home from your little shopping expedition on King Street."

Perhaps I can reason with Father when Prescott departs? But one glance at the pride radiating from her father, she knew it would be hopeless and she would never have the courage to stand against him. Like every time before, she would wilt beneath his crushing will despite her best arguments. She glanced down at her ring finger. She had been fortunate he had never pressed her into a marriage before now . . . but she supposed being the seventh, homeliest child of nine had something to do with it, and now that her youngest and prettiest sisters had wed at Christmas, she should have suspected she was next.

Mr. Payne captured her hand and slid a gold ring with a ruby cushioned by a pearl on either side onto her shaking finger. "What a lovely bride you will be, my dear. I am a fortunate man indeed to have found three women in one lifetime whom I have loved." He kissed her fingertips, his bushy mustache brushing against them and making her jerk back her hand. He narrowed his gaze for a half second before laughing.

Her? A lovely bride? She had been told far too often to keep her bangs trimmed and tidy to hide her high hairline and scolded more often than not for reading too late as it made her eyes habitually shadowed. No one in this family had ever accused her of being a beauty, except perhaps her youngest sister Jane. But Jane was the sweetest of the Fairfield daughters. Maybe it was because of her plainness, Sophia had never thought she would be required to marry. It would have required too much financially of her father to make a good match with a handsome suitor. She worried her bottom lip. Prescott, though twice her age, had retained his charm and could have had any of the society widows. *What has Father offered him to lure him into a match?*

"My second wife was a widow, so I have forgotten how you young brides can be with your wedding nerves," Mr. Payne said to her, conspiratorially elbowing Father.

Mother had the decency to blush while Father joined in the bawdy laughter, slapping Mr. Payne on the shoulder.

She swallowed back her protest over

their assumption that she would marry Mr. Payne, but she could not broach the subject while *he* was in the home. She would have to do battle in secret. She had never stood up to Father's demands before, but her parents had not set their sights solely on marrying her off before. She studied the ruby and all that was tied to it. She twisted it around her finger.

Mother grasped Sophia's hand and admired the gem before turning her bright smile up at Prescott. "It is magnificent. Well done, Mr. Payne. We will make the announcement at Sophia's birthday dinner party tonight. My daughter's engagement to Prescott Payne on her twenty-fifth birthday will be a surprise and delight to all who attend. I would love for Sophia to have a June wedding, but it is rather far away."

Sophia gripped the back of the settee to ground herself. *Please Lord, give me the courage to speak with my father and be victorious just this once. I cannot lose when there is so much at stake.* Now that her siblings were married, she was supposed to have this time to herself—to enjoy being the only daughter in the Fairfield house, to spend her days studying and tutoring her nieces and nephews, as well as the dear girls at the orphanage.

"Two months will be more than sufficient to plan a wedding fit for American royalty," Prescott replied, dismissing Mother's suggestion without so much as an apology. He snatched up his burgundy planter's hat and cane from the settee and turned on his boot's heel to face Sophia. "I must depart to dress for our engagement party, but know that I am counting the minutes until we wed, my sweet girl."

Then you will be counting forever if I have my way. She managed a weak smile, willing herself to be silent until they were alone. For if she did indeed lose this battle, she did not want Prescott to think of her as a spineless woman, even if everyone else in this family thought it was true. She waited for the downstairs front door to close behind him and crossed the drawing room to the window, watching the happy couples and families in carriages passing below her on East Bay Street. She closed her eyes against the sight, silence greeting her ears. She ached for the days when the house was filled with the sounds of her siblings running up and down the stairs, laughter filling the home—no matter how much they teased her for her looks and her nose always being stuck in a poetry book.

"Don't you think it is a little soon for me to consider marriage to Mr. Payne?" Sophia looked tentatively up at her father. "Not that I am not honored by having a gentleman in such high standing interested in me, but we hardly know one another."

"It certainly is not. For some reason, he considers you attractive even though you are practically an old maid and well," he motioned at her with one hand.

"Ernest." Mother cleared her throat. "What your father means is that he's far more established than any other suitor you have ever entertained."

"At fifty-five, one would hope for establishment, but I've only entertained the suitors my sisters rejected who only wanted to call upon me in order to become better acquainted with Father and his shipping industry," Sophia mumbled, running her fingertip over the wavy glass, longing to be out of doors, even if it was freezing, to be away from his oppressive gaze. At least on the portico she could breathe and pretend not to be trapped by her parents' expectations.

Father sighed and gently grasped her wrist, turning her toward him. "You are trying my patience with your protests, my dear. You must admit I have been more than indulgent of your sisters' choices in suitors, and your lack of interest in suitors in the past, but you cannot stay in my household forever. And if you will not pick a gentleman who suits your fancy and who actually wishes to marry you, I will."

Mother rested a staying hand on Sophia, quieting her protest. "Sophia, you know Prescott could have his pick of any widow in Charleston and yet, he has chosen you, and we couldn't be happier with the match."

She lowered her head, her cheeks flaming with suppressed anger at her helplessness. "I am well aware of that fact, but you see, I didn't choose him. *Father* did. And how on earth he could expect that I would be happy with a man better suited to be my aging uncle than my husband, I'll never know."

Mother gasped. "Sophia Bird Fairfield! Such an outburst is not to be borne. Apologize to your father at once."

Father held up his hand, the diamond in his gold ring on his little finger shimmering. "No, she's right. I was the one urging you to accept my friend as a suitor in the first place, and I'm the one who has accepted his hand for you." He took Sophia's hand in his with a tenderness she had not felt in years. "I've always had your best interests in mind, which sometimes means I have to make the difficult decisions for you. As a little girl, you trusted me to take care of you, but after that bout with scarlet fever that weakened you, I had to be, what appeared at the time, callous in my choices for you." He stroked her cheek with the back of his hand. "All I ask is that you trust me again, Sophia, and know I will do what is right for you."

"I do trust you, but am I never to have a voice? Or would you have me follow your will on this as I have done for everything else in my life because it's easier than disagreeing with you?" She bit her lip at the hardness returning to his eyes. Sophia's will waivered as it always did in the face of his disapproval, and he knew it.

"Your siblings have all made marriages of advancement. This would not only make me happy, but I've spoken with your brothers Elton, Thomas, *and* Robert. They all agree that Prescott is a most advantageous match for the family. As my business partner, and a gentleman of great means in his own right, I know Prescott has stature among not only all of Charleston, but nationally. He will take care of you in the manner you are accustomed to and will give you all that your heart desires." He gave her a little smirk. "I imagine he would provide you with a library full of every poetry book you have ever dreamed of possessing."

Mother nodded, placing her arm about Sophia's petite waist. "And more importantly, Prescott expressed to me how much he adores you."

"We have only been seeing each other

for a month . . ." Sophia shook her head, incredulous at the news. She could count on her right hand the weeks he had called upon her. "No, it hasn't even been a month because he was out of the city for a week, so how on earth could he possibly *adore* me?"

"Sometimes, it only takes a day." Mother smiled up at Father. "It only took a moment for us to fall in love." She stroked Sophia's cheek, tucking a stray flaxen lock behind her ear. "A love for Prescott will come. Trust us. Just give it time."

SEATED in the middle of the massive mahogany dining table with Mr. Payne on her left, Sophia felt on display in her copper silk creation from Worth with its daring neckline, which Mother had insisted upon. And seeing as Mother would broach no argument, Sophia defiantly had her bangs braided back to reveal her high hairline, despite her mother's expressed disapproval.

Sophia glanced to her right where Mother was making small talk with her dinner guests across the table, her siblings and their spouses sprinkled throughout the group of close friends. Sophia struggled to keep her expressions from reflecting the dread she had been attempting to mask all evening in the flickering light of the Girandoles, their four candlesticks further illuminated in the convex looking glasses.

Smoothing her silk skirt, she attempted to slow her racing heart and focused on the melodies of the string quartet. Mother hated lulls in conversation, so she always had soft music flowing through the foyer from the downstairs parlor during dinner parties, which sometimes made for a noisy dinner, but for once, Sophia did not mind as it gave her time to collect her thoughts. How had this afternoon gone so differently than she had hoped?

When she had broached the topic of becoming an English tutor for the other young ladies of Charleston, as well as continuing her work at the orphanage, both her parents scoffed at her offering—even though she had been the one to teach her nieces and nephews how to not only read but enjoy the study of poetry. While her parents saw her tutoring in the orphanage little more than wasted charity, Sophia knew she was making a difference as two of her charges, who were aging out of the orphanage, obtained positions as English teachers.

If she wasn't allowed to tutor, what other choice did she have? According to her father, she needed to have her own home at once—to be provided for as a gentlewoman. Without the option of a position, she was left with no other choice. *Lord, give me direction. Send me someone else! Or give me a way out of this marriage.*

"You are radiant this evening, my darling."

His deep voice awoke Sophia from her reverie, and she looked to her intended. He was a well-preserved gentleman for his age and if they had time together, perhaps she could indeed become friends with him even if the thought of sharing a life with him made her stomach turn. "Thank you, Mr. Payne."

"I believe it would be appropriate now

for us to address one another by our given names. After all, we are betrothed," he grinned, his eyes sparkling in the candle-light that further shadowed his crow's feet.

"Very well, Prescott." She took a substantial bite from her sweet potato roll to avoid saying anything else. The sweet bread caught in her throat, and she released a series of strangled coughs that had her reaching for her water glass and her mother shooting her a scowl.

"I wish you did not feel so nervous around me, *Sophia*." Prescott chuckled, returning his attention to his mushroom soup.

"Nervous? Why ever would you think that?" Sophia cleared her throat and took a spoonful of soup but missed her mouth slightly. She snatched up her napkin and dabbed her reddening cheek.

His hand slid over the tablecloth and encased hers. "Because, besides almost choking on your bread, I can feel your hand trembling." He smiled. "A sweet trait for a bride-to-be, but as your future groom, I would like a bit more from you than a chaste kiss on the hand."

"More?" Her voice cracked. *What is he asking?*

He leaned toward her, his eyes rolling appreciatively over her gown. "A kiss at the end of the evening is more than proper . . . and I do not mean on the cheek." He slowly ran his finger over her wrist in small circles. "You have no need to fear me. I will be a good and gentle husband to you."

A kiss. Simple to a man with two wives before her, but she had always longed to share her first kiss with a man she loved. She carefully withdrew her hand and dipped her head, sensing Prescott stiffening beside her at her silent refusal.

Father rose from the head of the dining room table, clearing his throat and lifting his glass. Prescott caught her hand under the table and Sophia's cheeks flamed as she once more slipped her hand away and folded them demurely on her lap. They were not married yet and she had no such intentions of allowing him *any* liberties, no matter his disapproval. *You can do this, Sophia.* She glanced across the table toward her childhood friend, Beatrice Hawthorne, and sent her a small smile, wishing she had the chance to tell Beatrice before the announcement even though she had no intention of following through with the match.

"Ladies and Gentlemen, may I please have the honor of your attention?" Father clinked his glass with a spoon. "I have asked you here tonight, not simply as a gathering of friends and family, but in celebration of a long-anticipated matter." He smiled down at Sophia and Prescott, sending murmurs throughout the dinner party. "Most of you know, the Payne family and the Fairfields have done business together for many years and tonight, our bond deepens. Tonight, it gives me great joy to announce the engagement of my daughter to Prescott Payne."

The room erupted with applause and cheers. Chairs scraped against the oak floor as her sisters and friends rushed to wish her well and congratulated Prescott. Despite her tumultuous heart, she smiled and accepted their warm wishes, endeavoring to catch the eye of Beatrice, but her friend remained seated, her gaze fixed on her crystal glass with heated cheeks. Sophia thought she could detect tears glistening in Beatrice's eyes, but before she could reach her, Prescott threaded Sophia's arm through his and led her up the curving stairs to the entertaining rooms, only pausing once they were in the center of the East drawing room. The Persian rug had been rolled up and stowed away, allowing for dancing. With a nod of his head, he signaled the quartet, who must have taken the servant's stairs during the announcement to meet them.

He bowed to her as they began to play a waltz. "May I have this dance?"

Feeling all eyes trained on them, Sophia curtsied, allowing him to take her into his arms. His gentle touch upon her waist brought forth a sigh from a group of ladies as Prescott guided Sophia past, her skirts whirling as he effortlessly moved them about the floor in perfect time, his eyes never leaving hers. His attentiveness almost made her think they had a chance of happiness, if this was somehow the Lord's will. But as the music faded into silence, Prescott led her off the dance floor and the spell vanished from his eyes as guest after guest came up to reiterate their happiness of the couple's coming nuptials.

Jane drew her into an embrace, her blue eyes bright with unshed tears. "Dearest sister, I am ever so happy for you both." She rested her hand on her abdomen. "Marriage is such a boon, and children are a blessing that fills one to overflowing with joy." She kissed Sophia's cheek, whispering, "I know you are uncertain of the whole business, but truly, I think you will be happy."

"Thank you, Jane." She squeezed her sister's hands as the next couple pressed forward. She longed to have a talk with her sister, but if she approved of the match, she might inadvertently give away Sophia's true feelings on the matter. No. It was best to keep her feelings tucked away.

But with every well-wisher, Sophia's

heart grew heavier. *Lord help me to get through tonight. Give me direction.*

"Sophia." Beatrice hissed, tugging her arm from behind.

Sophia was about to excuse herself from Prescott, but found he was so engrossed with a fellow businessman, she could easily slip away without notice. She grasped Beatrice's arm and accepted the silk shawl from her ever-attentive maid, Belle. Sophia smiled her thanks and guided Beatrice out onto the portico, inhaling the gentle breeze from the bay rustling through the magnolia leaves and palmetto branches. She leaned against the thick rail, drawing in the lights dancing in the harbor from anchored vessels. Perhaps there was a captain in need of a ship's boy? She was scrawny enough. Or perhaps a handsome captain who needed a bride and wouldn't mind if she wished to spend her time teaching and reading?

"I should have been told." Beatrice crossed her arms against the chill.

She reluctantly turned away from the ships and the wealth of imagination they offered her. "Please forgive me for not telling you sooner, Beatrice. I would have . . . if I had known of my family's intentions."

Beatrice pinched the bridge of her nose, scowling. "Didn't you just tell me three days ago you were going to dismiss him?" She motioned toward Prescott and his ring on Sophia's finger. "And now you are to marry him in a matter of months. What happened?"

Sophia drew her silk shawl over her arms. "What I always feared would happen. My entire life I have been groomed to be a wife. I am not allowed to work. I cannot even travel alone without a maid to accompany me and even to travel *with* a maid, I must have my father's blessing, which he never gives." She met her friend's gaze. "I'm trapped by society and my father's rules. I have no other option because, in my father's eyes, I'm his frail little girl that needs to be looked after by a strong, wealthy man."

Beatrice shrugged, pulling at her gloves to return them to above her elbows. "I could've told you that, but I knew the only way you'd realize the truth was for something like this to happen, or better yet, you'd actually fall in love." She nodded toward Prescott. "But I thought if you didn't become madly in love with Prescott, I wouldn't have minded so much as I would've enjoyed consoling him."

"Beatrice! Some things should not be jested about."

"I am not jesting. I would be honored if he came to call on me. He's everything you could ever want in a man," Beatrice sighed as she gazed hungrily at Prescott. "If you'd only open your mind, you'd see what a good man he is and that he's been trying so hard to capture your hand this entire month. You cannot do better than Prescott Payne, and I suggest you take your focus off of yourself and your *feelings*. We aren't all as fortunate as you to have a wealthy suitor. So, try not to make any impetuous decisions, Sophia. Think of your family and your future." She glanced across the room, "Now, if you'll excuse me, I need to make my own future secure."

Stunned, Sophia followed her friend inside and leaned against the fireplace mantel as Beatrice wove through the crowd to Mr.

Steward's side, an elderly single gentleman of seventy with considerable means.

"My stepfather is the most favored man alive to have captured another angel for a bride," a deep voice murmured behind her.

CHAPTER 2

Sophia turned and met the towering gentleman's eyes before alighting on his muscular frame and dark hair. She had certainly never seen him at any of the parties she attended over the years since her debut. *And did he just call me an angel . . . in reference to Prescott as his stepfather?* The flitting illusion of being rescued was doused at once. "I am guessing you are Prescott's stepson, Carver Ashton?"

"His much younger and much, much handsomer stepson."

"And much humbler too." Sophia laughed.

He grinned, his bronze eyes sparkling.

"May I have this dance? I'm certain if the bride-to-be is found to be avoiding the dance floor all night, people will begin to suspect she is not in love with her groom."

Her smile faded as she felt heat rush to her cheeks at his assumption of her loving the man. "Well, sometimes there is more behind a person's decision than . . . love." *And it may not even be her decision.* She placed her small hand in his outstretched one.

"Quite." Carver pulled her into his arms for the waltz. "Tell me, how *did* my stepfather manage to capture the heart of such an exquisite lady?"

"He is a close friend of my father's." *No, really?* She swallowed at the obvious statement, but she had never met anyone quite as striking and she was finding herself at a loss for words.

"Ah yes, of course. I suppose proximity does have a hand to play in the game of matrimony. But I must say it is a pleasure to finally make your acquaintance. Lately, Prescott has spoken of little else but the pursuit of your hand, a hand he had never mentioned in previous months."

I'd hardly called it a pursuit. He circumvented me and went straight to my father. To avoid inadvertently saying something she would regret, she snapped open her fan. "I heard from Prescott that you live in Louisiana?"

"Yes, I've been exploring some exciting investment opportunities in New Orleans. I am still heavily invested in our family's shipping company, but I want to withdraw my assets to build something of my own. I don't necessarily want to be tied down to Charleston for the rest of my life. The world is too vast. I want to travel and know life before I settle down and I think I have found the way to do just that." His voice rose in excitement as they twirled about the room.

"I envy you, Mr. Ashton. I'd love to travel to new places and experience life outside of this safe little trunk my family has placed me inside. My father wouldn't even allow me to take a grand tour for fear something may happen to me. Even touring the rest of the states is out of the question for him." She shook her head and sighed. "But what wouldn't I give for a chance to see the West."

"Really? Not many women would wish to leave the comforts of home to travel into the unknown." His eyes shone with approval. "Prescott has found himself quite the bride. But, sadly, I doubt that you will be doing much traveling once you two are married."

"No?"

"Prescott is not the travelling sort. He usually sends me on his errands, near or far."

"Which would explain why I have never met you before," she interjected, her cheeks warming again at her admission of noticing his absence.

He nodded. "Now that I have finished with my classes at Tulane University and have some experience under my belt, Prescott thinks I am perfect for *representing* the company. However, he would never allow me to run it on my own, even though I am twenty-six and more than capable, which is part of the reason why I wish to venture out on my own so badly, but not in the shipping industry," Carver admitted as the music faded and he finished their dance with a bow. "I hope I didn't bore you too much?"

"Not at all," Sophia reassured him, allowing him to escort her from the floor. *It's refreshing to be treated like I have a mind.* "If not shipping, then what is your dream?"

"I wouldn't want this coming back to my stepfather."

"I assure you that I will not speak of it to him."

He grinned. "Maybe someday soon then. May I bring you some punch?" He raked his fingers through his hair, lifting back a stray lock of his dark brown hair from his forehead when Prescott appeared at his elbow.

"You didn't tell me that your stepson would be joining us, Mr. Payne."

"I hardly knew it myself, Miss Fairfield." Prescott finished off his glass and set it on a passing footman's tray. "If you will excuse us, Carver, I must speak with my bride-to-be." Without waiting for a reply, he guided Sophia out onto the portico, the cool air stinging her shoulders.

She rubbed her arms, missing the shawl she had left on a chair and waited for him to speak, but when he leaned toward her with desire sparking in his eyes, her stomach turned. Surely he did not think he would win a kiss from her now, especially with the upstairs guests in plain view.

He brushed a golden curl from her face, tucking it behind her ear in a practiced manner. "I am going to miss you."

Sophia's heart thudded. *Is he going to release me?* "Miss me? Whatever do you mean?"

His brows lifted. "I'm departing in the morning to go on an extended business trip. Your father didn't tell you?"

She shook her head. *Why would he? He arranged all of this without my knowledge or my permission.*

Prescott chuckled. "Typical Ernest. It is because of the business trip that I desired to announce our engagement so quickly, so no one else could lay claim to my beautiful bride." He sighed, shaking his head. "Still, I wish he would have told you like he promised me he would. I have to leave for the next couple of months of our engagement."

Hope soared in her heart. A couple months was all she needed to convince her father to release her from this farce of an engagement. Perhaps she could even find another man better suited to her. Carver's handsome face flitted through her thoughts, but she instantly dismissed him. *Your would-be stepson as a replacement suitor? Father would laugh in your face.*

"But I am certain you will be busy enough planning the wedding and won't notice I am even gone." He rubbed his thumb over her palm.

Hardly. She cleared her throat, trying to appear apathetic, for if she was to convince him it was safe to leave her, she needed to appear somewhat open to the arrangement. "What kind of business trip?"

Prescott gently squeezed her hand. "Don't worry your pretty little head about that now. Just focus on planning our wedding."

Sophia gritted her teeth into a smile.

"You will at least write?" *And give my father proof of how ill-suited we are?*

His eyes brightened at this. "I would write you every day if I thought the letters would get to you, but the post is highly unreliable where I will be traveling."

"Oh." Sophia looked down at her ruffled hem to hide her relief.

"But remember that the entire time I am away from you, I will be wishing I could be by your side." He lifted her hand to his whiskered lips and kissed it. "Until that day, I will see to it my stepson acts as your escort in my absence."

That is exactly what she needed—a handsome gentleman squiring her about with no hope of being rescued by another more suited to her. "Won't Mr. Ashton have other work to do besides taking care of me?" *Like his work in New Orleans?* Even though she had only just met the gentleman, there was no way she would tell his secret wishes to his stepfather.

He shrugged. "He will do whatever I tell him. And your safety is more important than any of his little hobbies down in New

Orleans. You can be certain he will take care of you until my return." He pulled her forward. "Now, about that kiss."

She ripped her hands from his, spun on her heel, and charged into the East drawing room, cringing at his chuckle. *Let him think I am playing coy.* As long as it kept her first kiss safe for a little longer until she formed a plan.

"WHAT DO you mean that I am to look after your bride-to-be for the next six weeks?" Carver hissed to his stepfather, his fist enclosing the glass of punch. "You cannot expect me to drop everything in the New Orleans port office. I have deals on the brink of—"

Prescott motioned for him to keep his voice low and nodded at the guests passing their corner of the East drawing room. "The deals can wait. It is quite fortunate that you came before I had to summon you. As always, you will do what I say because it is *I* who is in control of the company and our family fortune. And *I* am the one shoring up our future by marrying Miss Fairfield."

Carver thought of her sparkling blue eyes looking up at him as they danced, her golden hair curling about her rosy cheeks. If he wasn't so drawn to her, it wouldn't be a problem to stay, but as it was—Carver shook his head free from the disconcerting feelings rising in his heart. "I couldn't possibly."

"I will pay you handsomely for your sacrifice. Consider it a bonus."

It wasn't the money, but as he could hardly admit that without divulging his attraction to the lady, he sighed. "When do you leave?"

"Tomorrow. I've already informed her that you will act as her escort until our nuptials."

"Thank you for telling *me* about your little scheme." Carver tugged at his white neckcloth, ready to be free from it, along with the pomp and circumstance of Charleston high society.

Prescott lifted his glass to a comrade

across the room. "Go find her. She is probably off sulking in that little library of hers."

"I thought she didn't know you well enough to feel sorry for your absence." Carver scoffed at Prescott's postulation as he adjusted his cuffs.

"She doesn't. But the annoying maiden seems to thrive on attention, attention that I cannot give, nor wish to give . . . at least, until our wedding night." He chortled, reaching for a second glass from the nearby footman.

Carver grimaced, disliking his stepfather's lack of affection for Miss Fairfield. A kind lady like her deserved respect at least. She did not deserve Prescott's wandering eyes, nor his callous view of women. How was Carver supposed to hide his opinion of the real Prescott from such an innocent as Miss Fairfield? Why wasn't her father protecting her when he certainly knew of his partner's taste?

Prescott lifted his glass in the direction of the hall. "Get on with it. I don't want a sullen bride on my hands when I return.

Make her fall in love with the idea of me, won't you?"

That would take a miracle. Carver set aside his punch and stepped into the hallway. He glanced through any open door as he went, searching for the library, when he spied a glow coming from a door left ajar. The familiar scent of leather-bound books greeted him as he nudged open the door to find her before a crackling fire in a wing backed chair, her feet tucked up under her dress. She was engrossed in a crimson book with gold lettering. He crossed the room to her side. "What are you reading?"

She started, clutching the book to her heart as she swung her feet to the rug. "Mr. Ashton!"

"Forgive me for startling you, but Prescott sent me in search of you."

"So, your task has already begun, has it?" She gave him a despondent smile. "I'm sorry for delaying your business dream."

"There could be worse ways to spend my time than with an intelligent woman." *Not to mention beautiful.* He held out his hand. "May I?"

She bit her lip and reluctantly handed the book to him. "I'm not certain you would be interested in *The Poetical Works of Lord Alfred Tennyson.*"

Carver closed the book and recited, "'*If I were loved, as I desire to be, What is there in the great sphere of the earth, And range of evil between death and birth, That I should fear—if I were loved by thee?*'"

"You know Tennyson?" Her thin lips parted in surprise.

"Well, not personally, but I must confess I have a fondness for poetry." He gestured to the wall of books. "So, who is the lover of literature in your family, or did you come by your passion on your own?"

She smiled fondly at the bookshelves. "My grandmother. As a child, I used to crawl onto her lap, and she would read me story after story. She died when I was thirteen, but before she passed, she made certain I had a list of literature to keep me busy until my thirtieth birthday. Tennyson wasn't on her list, but I didn't think she would mind if I deviated slightly."

"What a wonderful, thoughtful thing for

your grandmother to do for you. Is Keats on your list?" He leaned toward the books, scanning the titles.

"She made a note for me *not* to read him until I was in love. She thought Keats might make me too romantical for my own good if I read it any sooner." She rolled her eyes and laughed.

He lifted *Sonnets from the Portuguese* from the shelf, smiling at the well-worn volume and the annotations in a feminine hand filling the margins. "There's nothing wrong with being a romantic."

"Why? Do you spread your coat over puddles so a lady might walk without soiling her shoes?" She smiled up at him, the teasing light in her eyes softening her words.

"Chivalry will not die as long as I am alive," Carver declared with a flourished bow.

"Does Prescott share your fondness for reading as well?" Miss Fairfield trailed her fingers across the spines of familiar titles on the shelf next to her.

"Prescott?" Carver threw back his head

and laughed at the thought. "Besides the business section of the paper, no. I'm afraid Prescott doesn't do much reading and I also *never* promote that I enjoy poetry. My stepfather would harass me relentlessly." He looked pointedly at her. "A fact which now has me worrying that I have confessed my darkest secret to his future wife. As far as Prescott knows, my only hobbies are pugilism and shooting. So, this will be our little secret, yes?"

Miss Fairfield appeared to be swallowing back her laughter, but she nodded in agreement. "Have no fear on my account. I'll keep your secret safe. But I must ask that if Prescott isn't a great reader, what does he do in his spare time?"

"We both enjoy boxing lessons."

"Boxing? I thought gentlemen preferred fencing over using their fists?"

He shrugged. "I suppose most do, but my father preferred the sport to any other and it was something that we did together since my boyhood. In fact, my father met Prescott while we were boxing and began inviting him over to our home." He sighed. "And that's how my mother met him. Two years after my father died, when I was about fifteen, she married Prescott and we continued to box together until Mother passed and he eventually became too busy. I continue the practice as it reminds me of Father."

She grasped his hand for a moment, her slender fingers wrapping about his. "I am so sorry for your loss."

He nodded, unable to voice his true pain on the subject. Though it had been years since he had last heard his parents' voices, he could yet if he only closed his eyes. "Thank you." He cleared his throat and reached for a book from the bottom shelf that appeared to house newer editions than the rest of the library.

"So, are you any good at boxing?"

Carver chuckled, the heaviness of the moment shifting. "Not at first, and while I will not be stepping into the rings with any champions, I can go toe to toe with the best of them."

She rose, took the book from him, and set it on the oversized chair by the fireplace.

"I suppose we must get back to the party before people notice I am gone—no matter how much I am enjoying our conversation."

"As am I." Remembering his missive, he cleared his throat and added, "I know quite a few stories that aren't circulated about Prescott. Stories which I am certain he wouldn't appreciate being shared, but since I find them highly entertaining and he won't be here, that's what you get when you leave your future wife in the hands of your stepson."

Miss Fairfield pressed her gloved hand to her mouth, hiding her smile. "You know, I think you are completely right. You must tell me *everything.*"

He laughed and held the door for her. "Then I shall tell you all over a cup of coffee. You *do* like coffee? Please don't tell me you are one of those ladies who only allows tea to pass their rosebud lips?"

"These rosebud lips drink two cups of coffee a day, Mr. Ashton."

"Thank goodness. Because I don't think escorting you about the city would have worked otherwise."

Her giggle spilled out and he couldn't help but join her laughter.

"And please, call me Carver." He had not laughed this much in months. His task was going to be far pleasanter than he anticipated . . . a fact that was rather disconcerting.

"Well, if I do, you must call me Sophia."

He took her hand in his and pressed a kiss atop it, loving the feel of her petite hand in his despite his mind reminding him with every breath that she was not free, and she *certainly* wasn't his.

CHAPTER 3

After a sleepless night filled with dreams of being chased by Prescott Payne, Sophia donned her simplest gown and curled up on the settee beside the parlor fireplace with her new book of poems, intending on only taking breaks for meals, when a deep voice sounded in the hallway. *Carver?* She leapt off the couch and dashed to the looking glass, pinching her cheeks and lips to bring a bit of color into them. But no amount of pinching would hide the dark circles about her eyes. She pulled her short, curly bangs free from her braided coiffure and folded her hands before her skirts.

"Sophia, I'm so glad you're home!" Carver tramped inside the room, hat still in hand, much to the following butler's consternation. "I was worried you had already departed for your morning calls. You do have a pair of skates, don't you?"

"Mother left to do the rounds without me. And did you say, skates?" She asked, her smile escaping at his unfettered excitement.

"Yes. You know, those shoes with wheels that you use to glide on the paths like this," Carver replied, skidding across the hardwood floor on one foot.

Sophia laughed, shaking her head at his antics. "Of course. I have an old pair of Plimpton roller skates, but I haven't used them in years."

"Well, send your maid to fetch them out of hiding because with everyone out calling in their carriages, this is the perfect time to skate about Marion Square."

"On the flagstone path? Won't that be rather . . . dangerous?"

"Where is your faith in me? My stepfather said to keep you happy and when I think of what made me happiest as a boy, I think of skating in that square." He took her hand in his, pulling her toward him and the front door. "Say you'll come. I cannot go alone."

She blinked against his scent of sandalwood and leather and focused on his warm eyes, but that led her to his strong nose and clean jawline. Could he be any more striking? She glanced down at her dress, regretting her choice in the sensible gray at once as it did nothing for her complexion. She sighed. It did nothing for anyone's complexion, but she had ordered it for when she attended the orphanage so she would not stand out from the other teachers. Spying a vase filled with fresh rosebuds from the hot house, she broke off three buds and tucked them into her low coiffure, hoping the pink would draw the eye to her pink cheeks. "Lead the way, good sir."

Snatching her chapeau from the hall tree, she pinned it into place. She accepted his hand and stepped into his gig built for two that would leave precious little room between a couple and as Carver's arm pressed against hers, she couldn't keep her heart from skipping. *He cannot be your hero, Sophia.*

"So, I found you reading another book of poems. Is reading your passion?" He flicked the reins, sending his dappled mare into a trot.

She gripped the side of the gig as they made a rather daring turn onto Meeting Street, the wind whipping her chapeau's feather into her mouth. She smacked it aside. "I am not allowed to do much else with my time besides riding and stolen moments playing lawn tennis."

He frowned, slowing his horse to yield to a pedestrian. "Mr. Fairfield does not appear to be that controlling of a gentleman."

"He hides it well." She pressed her hand to her lips at her confession. "Promise me you won't tell him?"

He gave her a half smile. "Your secret is safe with me. But tell me, what would you do if you were allowed? More lawn tennis?"

"I'd do everything from traveling to riding a mule down the Grand Canyon." She breathed, slouching against the tufted leather seatback and running her hand down the polished railing, admiring the craftsmanship.

"Really? I respect your bravery. I've seen sketches of the mule rides and I'm not certain I would have the stomach for that!" He turned the horse down a less busy street that would still direct them toward Marion Square and snapped the reins. "But I understand a bit of having a controlling figure in your life."

"Oh? But didn't your mother and father leave you any money?"

"When my mother married Prescott, she handed over the entirety of our fortune to him. She trusted him to see to that he honored my father's wishes regarding my inheritance, but Prescott wishes for me to become a self-made man and I will only come into my inheritance when I am thirty. Until then, I work for a living and that living, along with my inheritance, unfortunately, is controlled by Prescott Payne." He cleared his throat as he pulled the carriage into the lane alongside Marion Square and halted the horse. "My apologies for speaking ill of your intended."

"No need." She pressed her lips into a thin line against her reply that Prescott was most certainly not her intended. Her father may *intend* for her to marry the man, but she would find an escape, one way or the other.

He lifted his hand to her, sparks tingling between their fingertips as she grasped it and descended. She nearly stumbled when he broke their connection to gather the skates in his arms.

He nodded toward a park bench. "Let's sit there and fasten our skates."

She glanced at him, admiring his profile as they crossed the path. Carver dropped the skates and jerked her to him.

"Whatever are you doing?" She gasped against his chest, his scent filling her head.

"Me? You were the one who nearly strode into a gaslight pole." He grinned down at her before releasing her.

She sucked in a breath through her teeth, praying he had not noticed her distraction had been *him*. Attempting to focus on Carver as nothing more than a friend would prove much harder than it had seemed last night when she made her resolution. There was no way any attraction toward Carver could end well in the eyes of society with him being her fiancé's stepson.

He took her hand and helped her take a seat on the bench before he sank down beside her and picked up his skates. "You've been awfully quiet. Did I offend you by, um, holding you?"

"Not at all. I have a lot on my mind and it's a little colder than I thought it would be." She set her teeth to chattering to prove it.

"Would a story of Prescott help distract you? I'm not certain how much I can tell you that you don't already know with your being his fiancée and all."

She stuffed her hands under her skirt in an attempt to warm them. "Pretty much anything you can tell me would be helpful. We only courted a few weeks and the next thing I knew, I was engaged without ever saying yes and he was gone."

"I see," Carver replied, his brow wrinkling as sounds of children's laughter grew.

Watching the two little boys and girl

chasing their escaped puppy across the green, she bit the tip of her tongue to keep herself from spilling her true feelings on the matter to him. After all, she had only just met him and shouldn't trust him . . . should she? *He doesn't seem to have a great love for his stepfather.* She straightened. She had known Carver for all of two days and her romantic heart was making her ridiculous. What she needed to be doing was making a viable escape plan—on her own as it didn't seem she would be meeting any eligible men with Carver as her guardian. She glanced at him. *But with Carver as my guard, would any other catch my attention as he has?* She shook her head. *Stop it. Nothing can happen.*

"I am guessing that you do not love my stepfather?" He grunted as he finished tightening the straps of his skates.

She twisted her lips and met his gaze, silent.

"So, this is an engagement of convenience?"

How could she tell him what was on her heart without insulting his stepfather? How could she tell him that she had thought of all the different ways she could end this engagement? But she was a coward at heart. She knew if she did not come up with a plan quickly, she would most likely end up marrying Prescott. "I always thought I'd at least have the chance of getting to know my future husband, but it seems even that wish is too much to ask for my father. Save for what you tell me, Prescott and I will be strangers until our wedding day."

"Ah." He shifted uncomfortably. "I, uh . . . don't know what to say to that."

"Forgive me. I've made you uncomfortable. I have yet to learn to keep some thoughts to myself." She cleared her throat, searching for a new topic. "The other night you told me you enjoy boxing. And as you live in New Orleans, did you happen to see the bout between Gentleman Jim and a Mr. Sullivan that took place seven years ago? My brothers have still not ceased discussing it."

"You want to discuss the boxing champions?" His face lit up.

Sophia hoped her smile was convincing.

Anything to distract you from my honest comment about your stepfather.

"Well, I was in New Orleans at university when the greatest boxing match of all time occurred," Carver responded, his eyes bright with the memory. He paused. "You're sure you wish to hear about this fight? It was violent."

Sophia wrapped her hands around her knee and leaned back. "Quite. Everyone treats me like a delicate flower, and it makes me wish to box something myself, so I can relate to the thrill of a good punch."

Carver's mouth gaped before he threw his head back and laughed. "You are positively shocking, Miss Fairfield—Sophia," he corrected himself.

"I doubt Prescott knows what he is getting into." Sophia laughed softly, quite liking the sound of her Christian name from his lips. "My parents think I possess far too many shocking opinions and could benefit from Prescott's strong guiding hand."

"Ah yes, Prescott," he replied, his smile faded. He glanced at her skates still piled before them. "Maybe we should talk more about Prescott, and I'll take notes on your stories to give to him."

"How romantic."

Carver knelt before her and slowly lifted the hem of her gown a few inches to expose her boot, gently taking her ankle in his hand before securing the leather strap of the wooden skate. And, just for a moment, he held her foot in his hand before switching to the second skate. "What tiny feet you have."

Very aware of him touching her, she focused on the carriages passing on King Street, rather than the feel of his hands upon her ankle. Well, attempted to focus.

He stood and held out his gloved hand to her. "Ready?"

Sophia placed her hand in his and allowed him to tug her to standing, the motion gliding her forward on the grass. "This isn't so difficult. I must be better than I remembered." She released his hand and took a step to join him on the flagstones. Her right foot swept forward, sending her reeling backwards.

Carver grabbed her waist and jerked her up to him, his hard arms encircling her, pulling her so close that his lips brushed her forehead for a moment. "Whoa there, little lady. I have you."

I wish you did have me. I wish I wasn't to be Prescott's— "Thank you." She released a nervous laugh. "Are you planning on holding me while we skate?"

"My apologies," he murmured and slowly released her waist, but kept a firm hold on her hand as he glanced about, no doubt thinking of the matrons and their daughters who were taking calls and could spot them in such an intimate position from their carriages on King Street. "Though, I best hold onto your hand, lest you break a leg. Stay with me and you will eventually be able to do it on your own." He held both of her hands as he skated backwards, urging her onward before he tripped and was forced to skate forward and merely pull her along with one hand under the boughs of the tree lined path.

She squealed, her skates accelerating beyond her control. "Slow down, Carver!"

"Miss Fairfield, we are going approximately the pace of a very fast snail." He grinned at her struggle for balance.

"Very droll, *Mr. Ashton*." She rolled her eyes but maintaining a scowl while attempting to remain upright was too difficult, and she couldn't help but giggle at herself.

"Come on, you can do it. Give a little shove off your strongest foot."

Sophia drew a deep breath, released his hand, and pushed, sending her into his hard chest, knocking her chapeau from her head, the pin ripping a few hairs out. Grunting against the pain, she disentangled herself from him and bent to fetch her hat, forgetting her skates.

"Allow me—" Carver grabbed her elbow to stay her, but momentum was the victor as Sophia's skates slid out from under her, wrenching him down top of her.

Sophia's face flooded with warmth at the touch of his nose against hers, their lips so close that if she lifted her chin, they would meet. Her heart pounded as she turned her head away and attempted to scoot out from under him.

Carver chuckled and pushed himself up to standing. He extended his hand to her. "I think the lesson here is not to get too sure of ourselves before letting go and then smashing into innocent bystanders, shall we?"

Sophia laughed and slapped her gloved hand into his as he assisted her to her feet.

"That was quite the tumble!" Beatrice exclaimed as she strolled to their side in a darling fur trimmed crimson half cloak with a matching fur muff. "She is a handful, isn't she? Where's Prescott when you need him to save you, eh, Mr. Ashton?" She laughed as her brother James trotted up behind her, her eyes burning into Sophia's hand that was wrapped securely in Carver's.

"Prescott, on roller skates?" Carver shook his head, chuckling under his breath. "He would flop on his stomach in a split second."

"Carver, give me a moment with sweet Sophia. I might be able to teach her a thing or two. While Sophia was tucked away last spring with a cold, I became quite the avid skater while out with my suitors." Beatrice took Sophia's hand from Carver's without waiting for an answer.

Carver looked to Sophia, and for a moment, she thought she could read a hint of agitation.

"Just don't let her take another tumble, Miss Beatrice. I promised her mother and my stepfather to keep her safe while he was away." Carver turned his attention to James. "Bet you five dollars I can beat you to the end of the square!" Carver shot down the path with James running alongside and though Carver was quite proficient on his skates, James was already passing him.

Beatrice threaded her arm around Sophia's and turned her bright, piercing green eyes on her. "And what, pray tell, are you doing?"

Sophia tilted her head. "What on earth are you talking about?"

"You are *flirting* with your fiancé's stepson. Do you have no shame at all?" Beatrice fumed as she increased her speed, her hold on Sophia loosening. "What do you think society is going to say about this little outing? I was in the carriage heading down King Street when I spotted the two of you, arm in arm. Hardly the *matronly* pose you should be adopting."

Sophia tried to keep up with Beatrice's angry clip, but her balance was wobbly at best. "Please slow down, Beatrice. I have no idea what you are talking about." She protested, even as she felt her cheeks heat from the falsehood. She *had* been enjoying herself too much—innocent as their outing was.

"Oh, please." Beatrice rolled her eyes. "You've always gotten everything you ever desired as a sickly child, so why shouldn't it be the same way now when you are a grown woman? You already have one rich gentleman. Leave the other for the rest of us."

CARVER RACED his childhood comrade to the other side of the square, desperate to put some distance between himself and Sophia. This was supposed to be a simple task. Take care of his stepfather's fiancée until his return. But the moment he laid eyes on her at the dinner party, something had sparked within him and as much as he attempted to remind himself that she was not free with stories of his stepfather, he couldn't help but wonder what it would have been like if *he* had found Sophia first. She was nothing he imagined his new stepmother would be —she was all smiles, wit, charm, and cleverness.

However, it was his stepfather who held the fortune, who first made the merger with Fairfield Shipping. Until his stepfather had mentioned a specific Miss Fairfield weeks ago, Carver had never heard of a Sophia Fairfield. She had simply been known to him as one of the many Fairfield daughters. It was his curiosity that caused him to leave New Orleans to surprise his stepfather . . . and now that he had met Sophia, he almost wished he hadn't, not if he couldn't control his growing feelings for her. Prescott spoke of her as a business deal and mentioned that she was pretty in her own right but spoke nothing of love. And judging from his conversation with Sophia, she felt next to nothing for Prescott, which made him feel only slightly less guilty for his attraction.

He reached the end of the square a minute behind James and glanced over his shoulder to see Beatrice striding across the green to them—without Sophia. Carver spotted her near the edge of the path. She had almost shuffled to the bench when she smashed face first into a bed of flowers. Wincing, he shot down the path toward her as she tucked her wrist under her arm and adjusted her skirts before unsuccessfully struggling to stand.

"Sophia!" Carver skidded to a halt, kneeling at her side, taking her injured wrist in his hand, and gently removing the kid glove. "Why did Beatrice leave you?" He glanced over his shoulder to Beatrice and motioned her to join them, but she either didn't see him, or pretended not to see him signal her. *Isn't she supposed to be your friend?*

"Please don't cause Beatrice any discomfort." Sophia slid her hand out of his and attempted to pull on her glove to conceal the cuts, grimacing. Leaving the ruined glove off, she patted her hair with her fingertips where only a single rosebud remained, dangling by its stem.

"Allow me." He gently untangled it and discreetly slipped it into his pocket. "That looks like it might need stitches." He rubbed his forehead between two fingers, berating himself for leaving her. If he could control his attraction to her, she wouldn't be bleeding. "Your mother is going to kill me."

"It doesn't hurt too badly. I'll wear gloves and take my meal in my room tonight. Mother won't know until after my hand has a chance to heal a little."

He gently assisted her onto the bench and took her hand once more, turning the palm up to inspect her wound and hissing through his teeth at the blood trailing down her palm. He retrieved his handkerchief and pressed it over the wound. "We need to get you home. I'll fetch the gig."

"Please, nothing is broken. It's just a little tender. Let's skate a bit more. I don't want to end our fun on account of me taking a little spill, especially now that I feel like I am *finally* getting a handle on it." She lifted those wide eyes up to him.

"A little spill? Is that what you'd call it?" He chuckled, grasping her elbow, and helped her to her feet. "I will let us keep skating on one condition. You are not to leave my side the entire time you are on those wheels. Agreed?"

Her feet wobbled and she gripped his arm tighter, sending a charge through his veins with such power he prayed she did not sense it.

"Agreed."

"And you have to wear this cap as your chapeau is beyond help." He pulled his wool cap from his head, slipped her hatpin out of her bun and whisked away her fashionable, yet crushed, chapeau. In doing so, her golden hair tumbled to her waist. He swallowed and plunked the cap on her head, pulling it down to her ears. "I won't have your death on my head. If you fall, it will at least protect that pretty head of yours."

Sophia giggled, adjusting the cap to cover her ears as he tossed the chapeau onto the bench. “An unusual request, but my if it isn’t quite cozy.”

He nodded, liking the jaunty look his cap lent the usually prim and proper Miss Fairfield. She tucked her bangs into the cap, leaving only long tendrils framing her cheeks and her hair streaming behind her. He quite liked seeing her so unencumbered from her heavy fringe. “Those hats you ladies wear are fashionable, yet anything but practical.”

She sighed. “True. Beatrice will never let me live down this fashion debacle, but at this point, I really don’t care as long as I get to keep skating with you.” She leaned heavily on him as they ventured out onto the path.

After an hour of skating, she eventually was able to skate on her own, but by that time, Carver didn’t wish to tell her because that would mean not having the excuse to hold her close, and he couldn’t think of another time when he would have the chance.

CHAPTER 4

Sophia blew her nose for the hundredth time. She tossed the used handkerchief into the wicker basket beside her and leaned back on the settee, pulling the knitted blanket up to her chin and moaning. *I can't even go skating without catching a cold . . .* This did little to aid in her argument to Father that she was a strong woman who didn't need to be coddled by a man. Her eyes fell on the vase of greenhouse flowers that Carver had brought her two days ago when she had fallen ill, and she smiled. *Well, at least I don't have a fever anymore.*

"Back already?" Mother's voice floated into the parlor from the hallway.

Sophia's pulse pounded at the guest's familiar voice. She scooted her legs off the settee, set aside her book, and arranged the blanket over her pale blue skirt to keep warm, but also to hide the wrinkles. She ran her hands over her hair, brushing her bangs into place and smoothing the escaped wisps. She tugged on her blouse to be certain it was free from creases and pinched her cheeks, hoping their rosiness would distract from the crimson hue of her nose and shadowed eyes.

"Well, I did promise my stepfather I'd visit a few times a week, so here I am."

Sophia slapped her cheeks one last time and demurely folded her hands in her lap, her heart giving a strange flutter in anticipation of seeing Carver.

For yesterday's visit, she was too weak to do much conversing, but Carver had brought her a stack of new poetry books from her favorite corner bookshop on King Street and spent the afternoon reading to her, his speech never stumbling over the complicated verses. After a few hours under his thoughtful care, her heart was very much in danger.

"She is in the parlor. I'll show you to her, but I am afraid that I must excuse myself again as I have a prior engagement," Mother answered, their footsteps sounding nearer.

Mother swept through the doorway in a cloud of burgundy brocade. "Mr. Ashton is here for a *short* visit. Please do not exhaust yourself. I'll send the tea in before I depart. And before you protest, coffee is not healthy for you at the moment. Herbal tea will open your lungs. We want to make certain you are well enough for Beatrice's party tomorrow."

"Thank you, Mother." She gave Carver an apologetic shrug. "I tried."

"Never you mind on my account. I already had my pot of coffee this morning. But today, I thought you might enjoy something a little more relaxing and less dangerous than skating or walking into gaslight poles," he said with a small bow as their eyes met. "Or even poetry."

Sophia stifled a giggle and instantly regretted it as it turned into a violent sneeze. She covered her nose with her hand and desperately looked around for her fresh handkerchief, which had magically disappeared. *Where is it?*

Carver slid his handkerchief from his pocket and handed it to her, averting his eyes to afford her some privacy. "God bless you."

"Thank you," she murmured into the cloth, her cheeks flaming. *That's an image he won't get out of his mind for a while.*

"I've got quite the game for you," Carver announced, settling on the divan across from Sophia, leaning back on the cushions as he crossed his legs and arms.

"Oh?" She attempted to discreetly dab her nose, but there was no way to be dainty about it.

"Yes, a little game that I like to call, *Five Questions to Become Better Acquainted with Your Fiancé*!"

Sophia shook her head, her laughter dying at the thought of Prescott and his return creeping closer with every passing day and she *still* hadn't a plan that didn't involve marriage. If only she had a maidenly aunt in the country in need of a companion, which seemed to be the solution for every desperate heroine in her novels. "Clever. Well, let's have some tea then and get started." She smiled her thanks to Belle as she rolled the tea cart beside the settee.

Belle curtsied and moved behind Carver's divan on her way to the door. She sent Sophia a wide-eyed look and grin that acknowledged Sophia's comment this morning about Carver's handsome looks that sent heat scurrying up Sophia's neck as she reached for the tea.

"A spot of tea will always add pleasure to a cold day," he replied as Sophia poured him a steaming cup of rose hip tea.

"Sugar?" She paused with the tongs poised over the sugar cubes.

"Four please," he stated as she began plunking the cubes into his teacup. "Though you best make it five."

"You are essentially having tea with your sugar."

"Life is short and, let's be honest, tea is better with sugar, especially when it smells rather medicinal in nature." He cleared his throat and rubbed his hands. "Shall we begin?"

She worried her bottom lip, attempting to think of anything to ask. "What's his favorite color?"

"Really? You are going to waste your very first question on what his favorite color is?" He snorted. "Priorities, Sophia!"

"It *is* important. What if I wanted to buy him a wedding gift and I didn't even know what his favorite color was?" Sophia crossed her arms, frowning. "If we are going to play this game, you cannot mock my questions, no matter how simple they may sound to you. I have my reasons for asking."

"Well, I suppose you would just have to guess on that one." Carver took a tentative sip. "Yes, five lumps *was* definitely the right decision . . . rose hip tea tastes like the way my grandmother's perfume smelled."

"That explains your mocking. It was to cover the fact that you don't even know the answer yourself." She tossed her throw pillow at him, which he easily dodged.

He rolled his eyes. "Men don't really sit around and talk about their favorite colors." He paused, tilting his head. "Wait . . . do women?"

"Of course we do as it relates to many things, especially while shopping." She smiled at his astonishment. "Mine is yellow, like the color of a golden finch."

"Mine is cornflower blue, like your eyes."

Sophia clutched her teacup, attempting to keep her color down and hide how pleased she was at his compliment. With her sisters always about, she was hardly ever given notice, much less praise from a gentleman caller. *He is not a caller.* Her grip tightened on the teacup, her knuckles whitening over the painted blue roses. "What is the first thing that Prescott does when he returns home after a long day at the office?"

He scratched the top of his head. "You keep asking difficult questions. Well, if Prescott still follows the pattern he set during my youth, the thing is, he usually doesn't get home from the office until after eight o'clock every evening. When he does, he just shuts himself in his study, reading his newspaper and has his dinner brought to him on a tray. He was quite the recluse, even when my mother was still alive." He cleared his throat. "After she passed, he brought me to his club for dinner one night a week—as if that completed his duty to me."

"Oh." She dropped her gaze and took a sip of tea to disguise her sorrow for Carver's boyhood. While hers had been filled with laughter and light with her siblings, his had been spent alone.

"Next!" Carver announced, breaking the somber mood.

Taking his lead, she decided not to press him further on the subject of his mother's marriage to Prescott. "Well, even though Prescott is an eremite at home, do you think there is a chance at all that he might learn to enjoy traveling once married?"

Carver grimaced. "I'm afraid not. That dandy has sent me on every business trip that has ever been required of *Payne and*

Fairfield Shipping Company. He would rather catch pneumonia than to hop on a train or ship to travel to anywhere that isn't to the office and back to the family mansion."

"Until the moment he becomes engaged to me." She muttered, her confusion over the man growing. *Not that I am complaining. I wish he could stay away for a year.*

Carver reached for her hand, mistaking her confusion for despondency. "The only reason Prescott is going on this business trip currently is because it is for the biggest customer the shipping company has landed in ten years, and your father essentially *begged* him to go. So much so that Mr. Fairfield even put it into the contract for your —" He stopped short and reached for his cup of tea, gulping it.

"Contract for my what? Why would a contract have anything to do with me?" Sophia pressed the back of her hand to her cheek, the room suddenly too hot with the mention of a contract.

He cleared his throat with a cough and lifted his empty cup to her. "It isn't my place to say, but please, ask your next question."

"What could my father possibly have that Prescott desires to be written into a contract?"

"You mean, besides his beautiful daughter's hand in marriage?"

"I am under no false impressions of my so-called beauty." She gripped the teapot and poured him a second cup, adding the five lumps of sugar. Was there another reason Prescott decided to wed her? "Does he have any interest in getting to know me at all before we get married?"

"I—uh, there is no telling how long this trip will last." Carver ran his hand over the back of his neck.

She nodded, handing him the filled cup in its saucer. "He doesn't. That's good to know that his declaration of love was a complete falsehood." *As I suspected.*

"Sophia—"

She rose, dropping the blanket to her feet in her haste, avoiding Carver's piercing gaze. "If you don't mind, I think I would rather not talk about Prescott anymore."

He rose with her, remorse in his chocolate eyes. “As you wish. What would you like to do?”

“I’d like to take a walk.”

“But your cold?”

“Will be gone in a few days. I simply must get out of this house, with or without you.” Sophia marched to the closet in the hall that the servants used for the house’s winter garb, pinned on a hat and slipped into her cloak.

“Your mother is going to be furious with me.” Carver lifted his coat from the hall tree.

“My mother doesn’t need to know.”

CARVER TROTTED down the stone steps after her, his hand encircling her petite wrist, turning her to him. “I sincerely apologize that the game distressed you.”

She shook her head, tears brimming. “Of course it didn’t.”

He leaned toward her, brushing his thumb under her thick lashes. At her widened gaze, he dropped his hands, at once recognizing that he was being far too intimate. He cleared his throat and shoved his hands into his pockets. "Then why are you crying?"

"I know you meant well, but this truly is all a game to Prescott and my father, and I do not wish to play. Don't they think I have dreams of my own?"

Carver clenched his jaw. He had been so caught up in trying to speak only kind things about his stepfather to keep his mind from wandering back to Sophia, he had neglected to remember that this situation was not ideal for either of them. "My stepfather is a fool for ignoring you."

"I do not wish for his attention." She dropped her hand from his. "Perhaps I am still too weak for a walk."

He couldn't allow her to return home in worse spirits than he had found her in. "Would you rather a carriage ride?" He gestured to his gig, the scrawny stableboy holding the reigns looking bored and cold. "I'm sure it would do the horse good to get moving in the cold air and Isaac would like to go back inside," he added, shifting his shoulder into her, nudging a small smile from her. "It's too beautiful of an afternoon not to take a drive . . . and let's be honest, your mother's meeting will last at least another hour, and I know you have no desire to be home alone with your thoughts at the moment."

Sophia lifted a single brow. "And how on earth could you know how long Mother's meeting lasts?"

"Because my mother used to attend the same meetings and I always ducked out of the house to avoid all the chattering ladies."

She laughed and slipped her arm through his and allowed him to guide her across the drive into his gig.

Carver dug into his pocket and tossed the stableboy a coin. "Thanks for looking after her."

Isaac lifted his cap to them, flashing his shock of red hair, and trotted back into the carriage house.

He helped her into the seat before joining her, tucking a plaid about them. She shivered and scooted closer to him.

"Do you mind?"

His heart hammered at the closeness of her, her scent of gardenia all too enticing. "Not at all."

The gig glided onto East Bay Street and Sophia kept her gaze on the gentle lapping waves as her curls whipped in the wind.

"Looking out onto the harbor always makes me think that even though everything seems hopeless now, maybe I could have a new life far away from here."

"What do you mean? Like run away?"

She pressed her lips into a firm line. "In a fashion."

Carver draped his arm about her shoulder as another shudder went through her body. "Are you not content with your life?"

"I love my siblings—Jane most of all—but they are all busy with their families. And my parents mean well in refusing me to allow me to expand my tutoring, but it does not sit well with me." At his quizzical look she added, "I used to teach my sisters, and now I volunteer at the girls' orphanage as well as with my nieces and nephews, helping them with their English studies, focusing heavily on literature and poetry. Those who care to learn, have all excelled under my watch." She smiled softly in a way that drew his attention to her lips and rosy cheeks. "Even my nephew Elton, who was set against anything poetic, but after I found a method of teaching that he not only enjoyed but understood, he graduated top of his class."

"And even with such results, your parents still refuse your request to teach?"

"Without their blessing, their friends will support them and refuse me the work. What else is there for me to do but wed a rich man who will better my family's standing in society? There is nothing deemed respectable for a woman of my social stature to do to support herself." She fiddled with her lace cuff before continuing slowly, "I am trapped. And my parents are leaving me no choice."

"Your parents wouldn't disinherit you, or throw you out from their protection. . . so, surely, you could have some say in the matter?"

She released a short, bitter laugh.

"Carver, I left to meet Jane for tea and shopping and when I returned home, I was told I was engaged to marry your stepfather. As for the birthday dinner party they were supposedly throwing in my honor, something they rarely did after it became clear I was not to be a glowing debutante with scores of suitors, was in reality an engagement party to announce our upcoming nuptials. I would hardly call that having a say in the matter."

He mulled over her sentence, anger flowing through him at her situation. "No. I can't say you did, but know this, any man would count himself fortunate to have you by his side."

Sophia wiped away at her cheeks as he turned the gig toward the park.

"Will I be able to see you tomorrow?" he asked at last, breaking the silence.

"Perhaps in the afternoon. I have a dress fitting in the morning and then Beatrice's afternoon party."

Dress fitting . . . for her wedding. Carver gripped the reins, making his horse toss his head in his desire to break free. But, like his mount, he had to rein himself back from speaking his mind and heart. Five weeks for him to squelch these feelings. She was promised to Prescott, and there was nothing the two of them could do about it. But, until then, his stepfather would expect him not to neglect her. "May I escort you to Miss Beatrice's party?"

CHAPTER 5

Carver wiped the sweat from his face as he retrieved the tennis ball from the edge of the reeds on the bank of the Ashley River during an intense game of lawn tennis doubles against Miss Beatrice and a Mr. Sydney at the lady's afternoon party. Carver handed Sophia the ball for her to serve, his fingertips grazing hers and sending a shock rippling through his arm. A cluster of women standing on the side of the court twittered behind their fans at his lingering a moment too long. He stepped back and crouched into position, cracking his neck from side to side, and waited for Sophia to launch the ball.

She threw it up in the air and slammed her racket down, sending it in an impressive arch, smacking into Miss Beatrice's nose. Her scream sent a few herons into the air from their walk along the bank several yards away.

Sophia dropped her racket and darted around the net. "Beatrice! I am so sorry. I was trying—"

"It's my *birthday*, Sophia. This is supposed to be a friendly match. Why are you playing like it's a competition?" She cried from beneath her handkerchief speckled with blood as Mr. Sydney assisted her to a set of chairs under one of the white tents dotting the lawn. "You better have not ruined my nose for the day."

"Even with a reddened nose, you would still be the loveliest lady in attendance," Mr. Sydney attempted to reassured her, but his comment only made Beatrice send Sophia another glare.

Sophia twisted her hands and apologized profusely, each apology met with another series of rebukes from Miss Beatrice and scowls from her two friends flanking her, effectively hemming out Mr. Sydney and his abysmal attempts to lift her spirits.

At her fourth apology, Carver took Sophia's hand and guided her away from the very distraught Miss Beatrice and toward the dock where a small fleet of canoes were ready for the party's use. He ignored the stares over them holding hands, but he had to get Sophia away from her so-called friends. "Are they always this unforgiving?"

"It's my fault. I should have let her win. I just get so invested in the game that sometimes I forget to play half as well as I used to with my brothers." She twisted her hands as the staff prepared the canoe for them. "They would never let me win, so I'd have to play all out for the entirety of the game, which was fine until my lungs gave out."

Carver helped her step into the swaying canoe. The last thing he needed was to allow her to fall into the river on his account. "I heard whispers of you being ill as a child, yet you didn't seem to have a hard time breathing today."

"When I turned thirteen, the breathing became less labored. But ever since, my family thinks I am still struggling." She leaned toward him. "What they don't know is that I play lawn tennis regularly with any friend willing. It is marvelous exercise, but with recovering from a cold, my lungs almost feel like the old days." She rested her hand over her chest and shuddered. "It is something I never wish to relive."

"Your secret is safe with me." He winked at her, immediately regretting the action as a canoe rounded the bend with the biggest gossip in the city perched inside, Miss Steele. He shrugged off her wide-eyed expression that melted into a smug smile as Miss Steele turned to murmur something to her escort. Carver's relationship with Sophia was innocent. Well, as innocent as it could be with his growing feelings, but as long as she did not know he harbored such feelings, it would remain innocent.

Sophia lifted her face to the sky with her eyes closed, her hand on her chapeau, as she basked in the sunlight. "So, are you ever going to tell me your dream for your future? You should know by now that I would never betray you to Prescott."

At the name, he stiffened, despite his attempts to remain neutral. "I know."

She leaned forward on her board seat, gripping the canoe on either side and meeting his gaze. "Then tell me already, Carver."

He grinned at her enthusiasm. "I want to open a department store in New Orleans."

Her mouth dropped before her expression melted into a grin. "Carver! What a brilliant idea. What kind of a department store? Home goods? Clothing?"

He drew his paddle through the water, attempting to keep them from the banks filled with fresh lily pads and thick reeds. "We shall specialize in ladieswear, haberdashery, as well as children and infants' attire and home goods. We would like the entirety of the family to be able to shop in one place."

She clasped her hands to her heart, eyes sparkling. "Oh, Carver. It sounds magical. And you should include a little tea salon where the husbands or wives of those shopping can take their refreshments and also have a wall of only the best novels to entice them to linger and order cup after cup of expensive tea!"

"That is a marvelous idea, Sophia." He patted his pockets, mumbling about needing a pencil and his small notebook to jot it down. "Where is it?"

She laughed, no doubt knowing his habit of keeping his paper and pencil on him at all times. "Never fear. I won't forget because when I come to New Orleans to see your shop, I will want to take tea and order a stack of books."

"As well as some of the dresses?"

"I shall order an entire ensemble from petticoats to gloves and parade about town to display my fine gown and bring you new clients."

He grinned, attempting to ignore the petticoat comment. He cleared his throat. "I would be honored. But it may be a few years yet before I take the leap. I've been saving almost every dollar I've earned since working with Prescott, but seeing my savings drop to almost nothing is a step that I fear in venturing out on my own."

"Well, when you do decide to act, I'll be

one of your first customers." She shifted in her seat as they glided down the Ashley River, the sounds of merriment fading into birdsong and the humming of wings from passing dragonflies. She sighed. "Thank you for getting me away. When Beatrice gets like that, nothing I say will stay her anger, and I can't seem to leave her side."

"She doesn't seem like the type of lady who you would enjoy being around."

"Carver!" She gasped, looking over their shoulders as if terrified of being overheard.

"Just an observance. She is rather a princess, while you are always ready to get your hands dirty."

She laughed, lifting up her hands that were stained with grass from her dive for the ball. "My hands aren't normally like this." She leaned forward and allowed her hands to drape into the water on either side of the canoe as he paddled them around a bend, startling a turtle into scuttling from his perch. "*I'm* not normally like this."

"Like what?"

"I feel relaxed in your presence. As if I have permission to truly be myself after years of pretending to be someone I'm not to keep my parents and society and my friends happy."

"I feel the same way about you," he whispered, fearing he had said too much as her smile froze. He forced a jovial smile. "Which I suppose is a good thing what with you being my new stepmother and all."

She scooped a handful of water and flung it into his face. He grunted at the icy water dripping down his collar and soaking him as she laughed, repeating the action with even more zest.

Carver dropped his paddle into the water and whipped a sheet of water over her, drenching her shoulders and, he swallowed as he felt his cheeks heating, her bodice.

"Carver!" She squealed and dove across the canoe to seize the paddle from him. "Not fair!"

"You can't *not* expect retaliation." He laughed, easily tugging the handle of the paddle back, but instead of letting go, she came with the paddle, landing atop him, their laughter fading as he slowly reached up and pushed a sodden curl from her cheek.

HIS CHEST WAS SOLID. Her gaze rested on his lips and for the first time, she allowed herself to wonder what it would be like to kiss him. She leaned into him, but at the sounds of laughter rounding the bend, she blinked. She could feel the flame blazing into her cheeks as she scrambled back, away from him, her breath hitching in her shock at what she had been about to do, but her hand found not the rail, but air. He lunged for her, grabbing her wrist, but instead of stopping her, he tumbled atop her, tilting the canoe and sending them plunging over the side. The water swirled up her nose as she tumbled head over heels, but she swept her arms downward and broke the surface, her skirts weighing her down. "Carver!" She reached out to him.

"I've got you." His arms wrapped protectively about her waist, drawing her up against him as she wrapped her arms about his neck. "I can touch the bottom."

Heaven help her if he didn't feel marvelous this close, his eyes bright and hair wild. Her fingers itched to run through his locks.

He glanced back to the sinking canoe and grimaced. "Let me get you the rest of the way up the bank. The riverbed is quite treacherous."

"Oh, my goodness gracious!" A woman gasped from behind them.

"Wonderful." Sophia grimaced at being caught in such a fashion, pressed against Carver's chest. *How on earth am I going to explain this one away?*

"Thank goodness, Mr. and Mrs. Rollings. Our canoe capsized. Can you send help? I'm afraid Miss Fairfield is about to faint, and I dare not release her for fear she will drown."

He squeezed her arm, and she released a moan, lolling her head back for good measure.

"Oh, my heavens! The poor dear," the

lady exclaimed as the gentleman paddled toward them. "Hurry, William!"

Sophia felt a bit guilty of acting the part of the sodden maiden, but what else was she to do with their reputations in danger? She sagged against Carver, who grunted as he hefted her into the canoe. She scowled at him.

"You cannot just become a limp deadweight and not expect me to struggle," he whispered as he climbed into the canoe and sat at her feet as Mrs. Rollings worried over Sophia.

Once the canoe docked, Carver, being a considerate gentleman, leapt from the small boat and sent one of the attendants to order his gig right away before helping her to her feet.

"Let me take care of this," Carver muttered through the side of his mouth as a crowd gathered at the end of the dock, exclaiming over their state. He lifted his arms. "Please, give the lady some room. She had quite the fright. I need to escort her home post haste."

Ignoring the calls from her friends,

Sophia leaned heavily on his arm, acting as best as she might as a damsel with her platonic hero. But, with his arm bracing her, along with his shielding her from prying eyes, truly, it was getting harder and harder not to think of him as more than what she should. Heaven save her from her traitorous heart.

CHAPTER 6

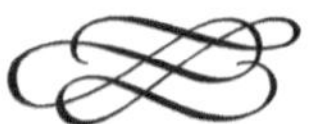

With shaking hands, Sophia tamed her bangs back into place to disguise the fact that she had been napping before her fitting, but even sleep could not help her escape from the fact that today was her *final* fitting for her wedding gown. She pressed her fingers to her swollen eyes and drew a deep breath, attempting to calm herself before heading to her mother's parlor.

After weeks at Carver's side, the idea of marrying his stepfather was not only repulsive but unnatural. And yet, despite her pleading with her parents every chance she could to break the engagement, and even bringing Jane to her defense, Father would not be moved, and she was running out of time to act. But she supposed in her heart of hearts that she was reluctant to take her meager savings and leave because she wished to see if Carver felt the same about her. *But what's the use? For even if he did return my affections, what could come of them?* Even she, the romantic, could see their future . . . which was no future at all. No one would accept that Carver's future stepmother wished to marry him.

With a sigh, she took the winding stairs down to the second floor where her mother was standing chatting with a woman in a stylish gray walking gown with scissors dangling at her waist attached to a delicate chain around her neck.

"Here comes the blushing bride. You are just in time to see the wedding gown." Mother opened the lid of the massive dress box and reverently pulled back the tissue paper with a moan. "What do you think?"

Sophia's arms hung limply at her sides as she stared at the creamy sleeves, the fine silk, and shimmering clusters of pearls sewn in the lace.

"Isn't it divine?" Mother draped the sheer veil over Sophia's shoulders and secured the comb, sighing with admiration. She unfurled the dress. "Hold the gown up so you can see for yourself in the looking glass."

Sophia did as she was told and turned, her breath catching as she beheld the magnificent creation. The high pouf sleeves would show off her slender, pale arms nicely, and the modest neckline would curve gracefully about her shoulders. The seamstress had woven a trail of pearls within roses, shamrock, and thistles on a silver ribbon that flowed from one sleeve to the other to meet in a cluster on the creamy bodice, which began again at her waist and traveled down the sides of her gown. "It looks like a version of the Princess Mary's dress when she wed Prince George," Sophia commented numbly.

"Yes." The seamstress smiled proudly at the ensemble, adjusting Sophia's veil so that it hung over her shoulder. "Your fiancé was quite adamant that it resemble the royal family's attire, but in today's fashion."

"Of course he did," Sophia murmured. *He never forgets anything . . . except to ask me to marry him.*

"You have always been such a good daughter. And your father, though he may not show it, is very proud of the woman you have become and the choices you have made, no matter how reluctant you are to trust him." Mother rested her hand on Sophia's arm. "And I must say, after these past weeks with Carver, you have taken a rather bridal glow—you look nice."

"Good." Sophia removed the veil and handed it to her mother. "I am going for a stroll."

Mother stood before Sophia, unmoving with the veil draped in her arms. "B-but you still need to be fitted for your trousseau. There are at least a dozen dresses to—"

"The dresses can wait. It is a much warmer day and I need to get a breath of fresh air to clear my head." Despite her mother's protests, Sophia slipped into her gloves, snatched the first hat and cloak within reach in the hall, and slammed the door. She hurried down the sidewalk, fighting to keep her tears in place when she realized she had left her reticule. With a grunt of frustration, Sophia tiptoed into the house to fetch her purse in her upstairs drawer when voices drifting from her mother's room halted her on her way back down.

"But do you think they will make each other happy, Ernest?" Mother's muffled question had Sophia stepping closer to the door to hear his reply.

"It doesn't matter whether or not she will be happy," Father responded, his tone betraying his agitation. "Prescott is a good match."

"A good match for whom?"

Sophia gasped at Mother's challenge. Was there still hope for her being released from this façade of an engagement?

After a long pause, Father answered. "For all parties involved. Sophia will be safe and taken care of for all her days, but more importantly, the business will be secured."

"Ernest!" Mother's voice resonated her

shock. "What are you saying? Are we in danger?"

"Prescott is getting ideas about not investing any more time into the company. And we desperately need his ideas. He is content with his share and wishes to venture out into new investments with others, but there is another customer that I am pursuing, and I need Prescott's financial backing, good name, and business sense in order to secure that client's massive order and earn their future business. And beyond all reason, Prescott has taken a shine to our homely girl. He says she reminds him of his first wife. If he marries our daughter, our legacy is secure for our sons. Do you want to see Elton, Thomas, *and* Robert out on the street, unable to support their wives and our grandchildren? Sophia's minor sacrifice is hardly a sacrifice when it comes to the financial security of this family. Her future will be secured by this marriage and in turn, our future will be secured as well."

"Do you think she will go through with it? I mean, you've heard her lackluster responses to all things regarding the wedding."

Not to mention my begging Father to release me at every breakfast.

"She must." Father's voice rumbled with finality. "Even if I have to hire a man to follow her every footstep."

At those heartless words, Sophia stumbled down the stairs and out onto the front steps, gasping for air, refusing to cry. Nothing would change by crying except make her appear as weak as she felt. Before she let her emotions get the better of her, she strode toward the shops on Meeting Street and gazed into each window without interest until a birdcage with a tiny gold finch caught her eye. She paused at the window display, her fingers splaying against the cool glass. "I know how you feel," she whispered to the golden bird as it flitted about the cage as if looking for an escape. "I long to fly, but I am caught in a cage forged by society and propriety. I am only good for singing my despondent songs of things lost and only exist to entertain all that look upon me . . . never meant to be free." She reached up, wiped her cheeks, and out of the corner of her eye, she spotted an advertisement adhered to the glass.

> *Young women, 18 to 30 years of age, of good moral character, attractive, and intelligent to waitress in Harvey Eating Houses on the Santa Fe in the West. Wages, $17.50 per month with room and board. Liberal tips customary. Experience not necessary. Write Fred Harvey, Union Depot, Kansas City, Missouri.*

Sophia's heart swelled with hope. What if she could leave all this behind? She traced the message with her fingertips, memorizing the address and flew to the telegraph office. Before she could think to stop herself, Sophia sent a telegram to Fred Harvey. Her heart pounding with hope at every tap of the wire as she took a seat on the hard wooden bench, waiting for the reply that could transform her life.

CARVER TOOK a second glance at the lady in burgundy sitting in the telegraph office and walked backward two paces when he saw her exiting. "Sophia?"

She jumped, nearly scattering the papers she had been clutching to her chest. She rolled and stuffed them into her coin purse, a guilty expression stamped upon her face. "Hello."

"Hello? I stopped by your house and your mother was beside herself wondering where you disappeared to for the past *four* hours. I've been checking your favorite haunts for the better part of an hour." He nodded to the office. "Were you in there the entire time?"

She lowered her reticule to her side. "Yes, but I would prefer not to talk about it."

Carver smirked. "I'm sure you wouldn't, but as I had to create a monstrous fabrication to keep your mother from summoning the authorities, I think I have earned the right to know. Don't you?"

She shook her head. "This is one thing I must keep to myself, so please do not press me, Carver. I cannot handle being told what to do from one more person, especially not you." Her voice broke and her tears pooled over.

"Sophia." He gently reached for her arm, longing to pull her close—to comfort her. "I'm so sorry." He slipped his handkerchief from his pocket, handing it to her. "I shouldn't have pried. Anyone could have figured out you were sending messages to your intended."

She snorted. "He hasn't even written."

"I know. I am simply creating an excuse if someone sees you here." He glanced about and as no one was near, he scowled. "It's insulting that he hasn't written. If I were to marry you—I mean, if I were to have the honor of being in Prescott's position, I would have written to you every hour of every day, Sophia." The words he had been avoiding could not be contained any longer. He traced her wrist with his finger, "I wish . . ."

At his touch, her eyes flitted up to meet his. They were filled with such intense longing, his heart clenched and in a matter of seconds, the weeks of burying his growing feelings for Sophia rose up within him. *Why couldn't I have met you first? Why did Prescott have to get in our way?* As if reading what was in his heart, she slowly pulled her hand from his. He hadn't even realized he had taken it and pressed it against his hammering heart.

"Carver, we can't . . . not now. I'm so grateful for your friendship," she choked out and lifted her face to him.

He cleared his throat and nodded. "I treasure our friendship and I would never wish to put it in jeopardy." He reached into his coat pocket and retrieved a brown paper package. "I wanted to give you this before I left."

Her color paled as she clutched the window frame for support. "You are leaving? Where are you going?"

"Tomorrow after Prescott's welcoming home dinner, I'm heading back home." He shifted the parcel from hand to hand. Why did he have to play his stepfather's messenger boy? "Apparently, the men moved up the wedding date."

"What? And yet, you are leaving before the ceremony?" Her voice trembled.

Carver's chest tightened. The telegram had been so unexpected—had wrecked everything. But that was Prescott's way. "I cannot. Not when I—" He cut himself off.

Sophia swallowed, even as a tear traced down her cheek. "I understand. What's in the package?"

"It's a farewell gift from one friend to another." He handed it to her, capturing her free hand in his as he did so. "I know I've told you this before, but I want to remind you that my stepfather is blessed to have a woman such as yourself for his bride." He removed his planter's hat, running his fingers around the brim, fighting back at the wrenching in his gut. "What I wouldn't give for a lady like you to be mine."

She wiped her nose with his handkerchief. *She kept it?*

"I hope you weren't wanting this back. Because I'd be ashamed to give it back to you so abused." She laughed even as tears fell from her eyes.

"Please don't cry. I can't bear to see you

unhappy." He reached out to take her face between his hands but stopped short. He pulled back, clenching his fists. "Sophia, tell me what I can do. Please. You know I would do anything for you."

She shook her head as if afraid to speak.

He tucked a strand of her golden hair behind her ear. "Tell me."

"I'm not sad. I'm desperate, and after trying on that fool dress for the last time this morning, it makes me ill at the very thought of marrying a man who only wishes to wed me for *business* and what he refers to as my youthful zest for life." Her cheeks brightened at the phrase, and she waved the handkerchief on the way to her nose again. "And as my family thinks my youth is quickly fading, they will not hesitate to do whatever Prescott wishes apparently—even if it destroys the hours Mother has spent planning this ridiculous wedding."

If only I had the courage to tell you how I really feel, and if only I had the audacity to do something about it . . . maybe then, I could save you from a loveless marriage. He took her chin gently in his hand and lifted her face "So you are not going to marry Prescott?"

Sophia jerked back from his touch, sniffing back her tears. "How can you ask me that?"

"Because I must know once and for all if we can have a chance together."

"Carver," she murmured, shaking her head, and stepping back, but he grasped both her hands in his, guiding her back to him. "It doesn't matter what I feel."

He leaned his forehead to hers. "Sophia. Please don't give me the polite or correct answer. Be honest with me and tell me if you wish to marry my stepfather, yes or no?"

She lifted her long lashes and stared directly into his eyes. "No."

Carver closed his eyes with his heart's ache for her, but not wishing to miss being close to her, he met her gaze once more. "And tell me, do you feel anything for me?"

"God help me." She whispered, as he found her gaze fixating on his lips. "I do."

His arms encircled her waist and closed the distance between them. His lips found hers—soft and tender, at first, but grew into a fervor as she matched his longing. Her fingers wove into his hair, drawing him closer and deeper into her kiss. When he grew aware of a couple passing by on the sidewalk, staring with disapproval, he slowly pulled away, scrubbing a hand over the back of his neck and groaning. *Oh God, what have I done? What have I done?* "Sophia, forgive me. I am so sorry."

Her smile faded at his words. "Sorry? For kissing me?"

"That's not what I meant. Sophia, you know I care for you, but you are still promised to my stepfather. There is an order I should have followed before kissing you. I need to speak with my stepfather and yours, but—"

She nodded, stepping away from him. "I well understand order. And it has never done me any favors. Goodbye, Carver. Safe travels to New Orleans."

"Sophia!" He called after her. "Sophia, wait!"

She glanced over her shoulder at him,

her hurt etched in her features. "There is no time left to wait."

CHAPTER 7

Prescott will be home tomorrow. She sank onto her bed and unfolded the telegram once more.

> *Honored to have you as an employee of the Harvey Eating House in Las Vegas, New Mexico. Waitresses needed in Hotel Castañeda immediately to train on site. Enclosed is rail pass for your earliest convenience. Looking forward to meeting you.*
>
> *Sincerely, Violet Trent, Housemother.*

Sophia glanced at the clock. The time for waiting for her future to change was over. There was nothing holding her in

Charleston anymore—not even Carver. Certainly, he cared for her. She held her fingers to her lips, still feeling the press of his lips. But there had been no declaration of love, no promise of the future. Was he even now laughing at her admission that she cared for him? Had he only been having a bit of a lark with her at her expense? *Why else would he be interested in a plain wallflower such as you?* It would be easier to leave if he didn't care.

Sophia grunted in pain at the wrenching idea that Carver could betray her so and swiped at her damp cheeks with her sleeve, ignoring the whisper in her heart that she knew his true character and that he would never abuse her thus.

"Miss, I brought you a bite to eat." Belle slipped into her room, her eyes widening at Sophia's swollen eyes. She set aside the tray and joined her. "Sophia! Whatever happened?"

In a few moments, Sophia had dislodged the painful story from her heart, including the offer of work, but leaving off the location at Belle's insistence.

Belle shook her head. "From what I've seen of Mr. Ashton, I don't think he could be capable of such a horrible act—but there have been men in the past that I thought would never mean me harm, who only wanted to trifle with me to satisfy their need for the hunt."

Sophia shivered from Belle's confession. "I am so sorry."

"I am as well, but it taught me how to discern good men from the ill-intentioned, and I don't believe Mr. Ashton to be the latter. However, Mr. Prescott seems to be hiding something, and I don't like him for you." Belle wrapped her arm about Sophia as the clock on the mantle chimed seven of the clock. Belle rose, taking Sophia's hands in hers.

"If we hurry, you can make the last train out."

"You really think I should go?"

Belle smiled. "The Lord saw fit to lead you to that advertisement. I think it is a sign of His blessing. It is a way out of marriage to a gentleman we both know is not fit to marry you."

"You'd help me? But if they find out—"

"No one need know. Everyone is helping at the neighbor's ball down the street, even the cook."

"But why aren't you there?"

She grinned. "Besides my excuse of staying to see you? It is one of the lovely things about being the least popular servant downstairs. I get left behind all the time. Now, we only have an hour to get you packed and to the station. We must hurry. You start and I'll retrieve the wicker trunk you use for the beach from your closet, along with your medium leather trunk. I wish we had time to retrieve your larger trunk out of storage, but between these two, we can pack a good amount of clothes."

The ladies quietly moved about the room and Sophia nearly stumbled over the corner of the rug in her haste to pack an extra set of underthings into her light wicker trunk. In the corner, she shoved the entirety of her pin money before dressing in her navy traveling suit and plainest chapeau with Belle's assistance. Belle grasped the trunk and did not complain of its weight as she strode from the room.

Sophia hefted her wicker basket onto her hip and stared back at the room that she had shared with her younger sister Jane, where she had grown up, and where she had dreamed of her future that never quite happened as she had hoped. Her gaze rested on the package from Carver resting on her nightstand. With a sigh, she opened her wicker trunk and buried it within. She quietly closed the door behind her and followed Belle down the servants' staircase, praying for speed and courage.

They paused at the bottom level, waiting for the telltale footfall or chattering of the staff, but as Sophia had hoped, all was silent and not a single light flickered besides the fire in the servants' hall that was but embers now as all had left for dinner at the Mosby's, her parents included. Thank goodness she avoided attending tonight due to a headache.

Belle turned the lock and they ducked out into the night. They rounded the corner of the house and Belle at once threw herself into the shadows of the mansion and swaying palmettos, Sophia following suit at the sight of Prescott hopping down from a carriage in front of the Mosby's. *Whatever is he doing here?* Her heart hammered in her ears, but they waited until he had disappeared into the house before bolting down to Meeting Street. The wicker trunk made her arms shake with the effort from holding it, but in the distance she could see a few of the houses alight from a party, which meant that there was surely a hired carriage nearby where she could relieve herself of the burden.

"How's your load?" Sophia whispered even as her arms threatened to give way.

"Have you never considered how much your breakfast tray weighs, Sophia?" Belle giggled.

Sophia's mouth slackened. In all her years of taking trays in her room, never had she considered the weight to and from the dumbwaiter. "I'm so sorry."

She shrugged. "It is a good job, but we best keep moving lest someone recognize you and send word to your parents."

Staying in the shadows of the sidewalk, she hefted the wicker trunk with a grunt as Belle hired the first cab she approached.

Throwing herself inside, she exhaled as she leaned back in the carriage, clutching her trunk on her lap as Belle directed the driver to Union Station and joined her. *God, let me have made the right decision.* She swayed back and forth over the cobble-stones, questioning herself and her escape, but each time she thought of what was ex-pected of her if she went through with the wedding, her resolve strengthened. She was not going to be silent any longer. Some-times actions were the best way to be heard.

"If you need to send a message, Sophia, you can direct it to me as my friend, cre-ating a fake name with your initials. I'll know it is from you and I'll do my best to help."

She squeezed her friend's hand. "Bless you, and if you need to reach me, my em-ployer will be—"

"No! Please don't give me any clue of your occupation or of your whereabouts. If questioned I can honestly say I have no idea where you are."

The carriage rolled to a stop at the train station. Not waiting for the driver's assistance, Belle hopped down and paid the man. Glancing at Sophia's rail pass, Belle expertly found their way to the correct platform. A sense of unease filled Sophia. She had never traveled alone, much less found her own way before.

"Here you are, Sophia. I cannot go any further for even knowing the platform you are departing from is too much information." Belle set the trunk down beside Sophia's wicker one.

Sophia glanced at the rail pass again and saw Belle had taken her to one of the second-class rail cars. The train's piercing whistle sent her heart racing as she whipped back to face her friend. "Belle, I'm afraid. I don't—"

"You can do this, Sophia." Belle pulled her into a quick embrace. "You are stronger than your family thinks."

"You could come with me?" Sophia

grasped her hands, the whistle blowing another warning.

Belle slowly shook her head. "Maybe one day I'll join you when you are safe from Prescott—should I have as much courage as you to venture into the unknown for a chance at love."

"Brave as me?" Sophia released a shaking laugh. "Kind of you to say when I am about to toss my accounts on the station platform!"

"Then you best get into your seat." Belle gently nudged her toward the car and hefted the trunk onto the train's platform, quickly followed by the wicker trunk.

With a final wave to Belle as the whistle blew, steam flowed from the wheels, and the train jerked to life, chugging out of the station. Sophia hefted the wicker trunk onto her hip while dragging the leather trunk inside behind her. She breathed a sigh of relief that the train was not crowded, and she had her choice of seats, so she decided something in the middle and by the window would be best, not too near the lavatory.

Placing her wicker trunk on the vacant

bench facing her own, she retrieved her leather trunk from the aisle and set it beside her before sinking into the hardback seat. It was devoid of the burgundy cushions in the first-class car, but the discomfort aided her in keeping a wary eye on the window, half fearing to see someone rushing up to impede her escape and half aching that Carver would rush to her and beg her to marry him. *But what if he did? Surely, the scandal of my loving the future stepson and he loving the potential stepmother would destroy his dream business before he's even opened the store.* She clenched and unclenched her fists, digging her fingernails into her palms. *No turning back. If that means never seeing Carver again . . . so be it.*

Her pulse thrummed faster with each turn of the wheel. She pressed her fingers to the cool glass, watching as the city she loved sped by until Charleston was nothing more than a speck in the distance. She closed her eyes, willing herself to sleep, but Carver's comforting brown eyes kept breaking through the barrier she was desperately trying to construct once more. *I should have shielded my heart better. But I never expected love to find me so swiftly.* She muffled her tears with her handkerchief, struggling to inhale against the smoke creeping in through the open windows.

She pressed her hand against her corset, the constriction making it all the worse. *It hurts to even take a breath in a world that he and I cannot be together. Lord, I love him. I shouldn't love him, but I do, and I can't help it.* She leaned her forehead against the window, her grandmother's words from years ago reverberating through her heart. *You will never be alone when He is by your side, remember the second book of Timothy, child.*

She closed her eyes again and pulled the verse from her deepest of memories. "'For God hath not given us a spirit of fear; but of power, and of love, and of a sound mind.'" She bowed her head. "Lord, give me strength. With this new life, make me a new woman—a woman who walks not in fear, but in power."

CARVER PUSHED his breakfast about his plate, Cook's quiche failing to entice him for the first time since his arrival. How could he have allowed Sophia to return home without explaining that he *meant* to take action, but in the right manner and time. He picked at his fruit dish, waiting for his stepfather to appear. Informing his stepfather of his feelings for Sophia the day before his marriage was not ideal, but he couldn't rightly *not* speak to Prescott of his intentions now that he knew Sophia's desires mirrored his own.

The strident ring of the doorbell made him slosh his coffee. He glanced out the front window to see the Fairfield's family crest on the carriage. *Sophia!* He trotted for the door and opened it to have Mr. Ernest Fairfield storm inside.

"Is she here?" Mr. Fairfield roared, his cane gripped in his hand like a club.

"She?"

"Sophia! Who else would I be speaking of?" Mr. Fairfield brushed past him to the parlor, flinging open the double doors so hard they banged against the silk wallcoverings as he searched the room for his daughter. "She is nowhere to be found. I thought she might be here with Prescott." He returned from his examination of the parlor curtains to stand at the foot of the stairs. "Prescott!"

Prescott leaned over the rail of the second floor, shirt sleeves rolled up, a small pot of shaving cream in one hand and razor in the other. "Ernest? What is going on?" He wiped the shaving cream at his collar with his hand towel as he trotted down the stairs.

Ernest swallowed, his scowl deepening. "Judging from the state of you, Sophia has not been here, has she?"

"No." Prescott answered, a dangerous glint in his eyes. "Where is she? It's our wedding tomorrow."

"She is missing? For how long?" Carver rested his hand on Mr. Fairfield's shoulder.

Mr. Fairfield shrugged him off. "Since this morning—perhaps last night even. When her maid went to wake her at ten of the clock, her room was empty, the bed untouched."

Prescott gave Ernest a glassy stare. "I

proposed as a favor to you only because she is young and reminds me of my first wife and you are giving me majority shares to take her off your hands." He slammed his fists on the rail, bellowing, "That daughter of yours will *not* make a fool out of me."

Carver's fists tightened. She was so much more than a pretty face, more than a bargaining chip.

Mr. Fairfield's forehead beaded as he lifted his hands as if to ward off Prescott's ire. "Have no fear. I will find her, and she will be your wife whether she is willing or not. You must forgive her. She is only a foolish woman and knows nothing of the matters of business."

Carver stepped forward. "Prescott, this is not a transaction. This is a marriage and it's for life. This is a woman's future that you are talking about."

"Don't be naïve, son. Ernest wishes for assurances that we won't dissolve our relationship with the company, which is why he is handing over the majority only on the condition of my marriage into his family. We are on the brink of being beat out by our competitors and without my continued investments and ideas for moving our company forward, our future with the Fairfields will not be as wealthy as our past. And when I threatened to end our association, Ernest made this offer as my exit would have many of our customers leaving for our competitors because they are only here out of the respectability of the Payne family name."

Carver turned to Mr. Fairfield. "Surely, your daughter's happiness means more to you than a few thousand dollars a year?"

Mr. Fairfield shook his head with a snort. "Thousands? Try *millions,* boy. I can't afford to allow her to choose to marry for love. We will lose the vision of four generations if we concede to the whims of my vacillating girl. She must marry Prescott Payne and that's all there is to it." Mr. Fairfield shoved his planter's hat in place. "It's time to go to the authorities. Prescott, meet me at my home in one hour to discuss our next steps."

Carver climbed the stairs two at a time to his room that had not felt like his in years as it had long been divested of his childhood trinkets. He sank onto the window seat and bowed his head. *Lord, what do I do? I have been an utter fool, and now she is gone.*

She had every right to require a promise from him—something to believe in and what had he done? Given her nothing but a promise of "when." With a grunt of frustration, he charged across the room, threw open the armoire and began packing. One thing was certain. She would not have stayed in Charleston and there was nothing left for him here.

CHAPTER 8

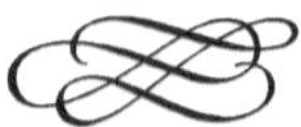

"Las Vegas! Next stop Las Vegas, New Mexico!" The conductor announced, striding through the railcar checking tickets.

Sophia's head snapped up as she awoke from her unsatisfactory nap to realize that the man sitting across from her was observing her. Her cheeks flushed at the thought of him freely taking in her body while she slept. She pursed her lips into a deep scowl worthy of her mother, and narrowed her eyes at him, hoping to shame him into looking away. He averted his gaze, but not fast enough for her liking.

She brushed at the dust from days of

travel from her navy suit, but it was coated in sooty film that she wasn't even sure a good washing could cure. Pulling her handkerchief from her beaded reticule, she wiped at her clammy forehead and cheeks, grimacing at the soot staining the once creamy cloth. She ran her fingers over the sides of her hair that her hat did not protect, directing her curls to frame her face once more.

The car shuddered to a grinding halt and her book of Tennyson's poetry on the bench seat next to her almost slipped to the floor, but she slapped her hand against it in time. Sophia tucked it safely inside her wicker trunk and made quick work of gathering her things, hefting the small, albeit cumbersome, trunks on each hip, and with a final scowl at the staring man, hobbled down the aisle, her navy skirts trailing behind her. She paused at the steps to catch her breath and looked out onto the little, dusty town of Las Vegas, a tumbleweed bouncing slowly past—a far cry from the Charleston Harbor with its lush gardens, fresh sea breezes, and seagulls cawing. *I'm about as far from Charleston as a socialite can get.*

She cautiously stepped down onto the brick walkway that served as the platform and at once released her burdens with a suppressed grunt. She lifted her hand to block the brightness of the sunset as she found the platform led directly to a massive red brick building in a Mission Revival style with two wings jutting forward on the north and south sides of the main building with a slate roof over adjoining arches leading to a covered porch. Between the wings there was a lovely courtyard with a massive live oak in the center and behind it, in the building adjoining the north and south sides, there rose a bell tower with a large sign, its painted letters reading, *Hotel Castañeda, 1898.*

Sophia inhaled the air free of soot and coughed at the scent of manure clinging to it. She pulled her last fresh lace-trimmed handkerchief out from her sleeve and held it against her nose and inhaled the lingering bit of perfume until she had noticed every male eye in the vicinity had turned in her direction. The women bent their heads together and tittered, pointing to her dress. Sophia's cheeks flamed as she dropped her handkerchief and with a sigh directed to her trunks, hefted them up once more when a gong sounded behind her, making her fumble for the handles as they slipped. Scowling, she lifted her trunks again and turned to find the culprit—a man in a dark suit standing on the train platform with a gong and mallet.

He hit the gong once more. "This way folks! Follow me to the Harvey House where your orders await!"

Her stomach rumbled to life as she thought of the meal awaiting her that she had wired ahead after days of being at the mercy of the luncheon car. She had hoped to taste the famous Harvey House cuisine along the route, but the only Harvey House they encountered during working hours was closed for remodeling after a fire.

Keeping her trunks close in the swarm of passengers, she joined the others in the march into the Harvey House. First, she would eat her fill at long last and then, her new life would begin.

A man with a close beard and piercing blue eyes dressed in a neat suit of black held the door open for her as another young man at once relieved her of her trunks. "Welcome to the Harvey House, Miss." He motioned to her belongings. "Will you be staying with us, Miss?"

"In a way," she smiled and dug the travel-worn telegram from her reticule and handed it to him. "I'm Miss Trent's new Harvey Girl."

His smile grew. "Well, then! You must have the best seat in the house for the full experience for your meal in the first track-side Harvey House. Take a seat at the table nearest the side wall to have a view of the courtyard and town. And *then* we will get to work." He motioned to the bellhop. "We can set this behind the desk in the lobby until we can get you over to the dormitory, Miss—?"

"Bird." She smiled through the slight fabrication, but she knew if she used her surname, she might as well send a telegram letting her family know where she was hidden. As the man directed the bellhop, she took in the impressive lobby with its stained hardwood floors and carved front desk.

"Lovely name for a lovely new Harvey Girl. Enjoy your meal!" He motioned her into the dining room.

Satisfied that her belongings were safe, Sophia stepped through the threshold and was met with the delicious smells of food and smiles and greetings from all of the nearby Harvey Girls. The room felt homey with a lovely crimson and white tile floor and tall windows that boasted of a view of the New Mexico meadow and foothills in the distance. Her jaw slackened at the majesty of the land. Guests surging past her to take their seats jostled her from the scenery enough to wake her to the humming dining room once more. The tables were set with flawless white linen, silver utensils, and fine china, which added a refreshing touch of elegance after days of dusty travel. The bustling waitresses were all dressed the same in severe, nun-like black uniforms with modest high collars, giant white aprons and white hair bows that softened their attire just a tad to match their smiling, youthful faces.

Before she could find a table on her own, a tall, slender girl with ebony locks approached and curtsied, flashing a wide smile that revealed a gap in her front teeth. "Welcome to the Harvey House, Miss." Her warm accent permeated her words with friendliness, as if Sophia was the only guest out of the forty people flowing into the establishment. "My name is Nora Ray. How may I serve you today?"

Sophia returned the girl's smile. "Lovely to meet you, Miss Ray. I'm Miss Trent's latest recruit, Sophia Bird."

"A new member of the family!" She embraced Sophia with a quick pat. "I will introduce you to Miss Trent and the rest of the girls after the train is fed." She grasped Sophia's arm and guided her to one of the smaller tables facing the foothills and distant mountain range. "After you eat, of course, as I know you are probably starved, but keep watch to see how things are done while you enjoy the hospitality of Fred Harvey."

At the sight of dishes leaving what she guessed was the kitchen, Sophia's stomach growled. She pressed her hand against the bone stays in her corset, trying to suppress the anger of her stomach. "Forgive me. I must be hungrier than I had thought."

"Well, then, I best hurry you to your seat and fetch your order. You did wire ahead with your order, yes?"

Sophia nodded as she sank into the wooden seat, grateful for the leather cushion instead of the hard bench seats of the train. She spread her crisp dinner napkin over her lap and nearly sighed from the luxury of such fine, clean linen after days of feeling filthy. *At least the dining experience won't be quite so different from Charleston.*

"Perfect. Would you like coffee, tea, or milk to go with your meal?"

"I never thought I'd give up having a cup of coffee right away, but tea would be lovely. I haven't had a decent cup in a while."

She smiled up to Nora who nodded with understanding.

Nora flipped the teacup upside down in the saucer. "Did you have soup, or salad? And did you have the roast, or the duckling?" She inquired, her pencil poised above her notepad.

"Soup and the duckling."

"And for dessert? The fruit tartlet, or the chocolate cake?" Nora asked.

"While the tartlet sounds amazing, I will always choose the chocolate option," Sophia answered, slowly pulling off her kid gloves. They were too filthy to set on the table, so she tucked them under her napkin to keep them hidden.

Nora sent Sophia a wink and moved to take the next table's drink order. Another girl came up on Sophia's right, flipped over the cup and poured a steaming cup of tea without even asking what Sophia had ordered before moving onto the next guest, ignoring the cups that were right side up. Another girl with a pot of coffee filled the upright ones. *Ooh, the cup placement is a code for what the drink order is.* She watched the well-orchestrated dance of service as the soups and salads began to find their places in front of each guest.

Sophia dipped her spoon into her steaming bowl of creamy tomato soup and lifted it to her lips, closing her eyes in pleasure. *Who would have thought such elegance could be found in the untamed West?* The moment she finished her last spoonful of soup, her plate of duckling and side of steaming vegetables appeared before her.

Sophia dropped her fork against the plate as a gong sounded again. She turned and saw the same man from the platform in a white apron standing on the dining room threshold with his brass gong and mallet.

"Ladies and Gentlemen, no need to rush at all, this is your twenty-minute warning. I will come again at ten minutes, five minutes, and departure time. Enjoy your meal and have no fear of missing the train." The man bowed and stepped out of view into the lobby.

Sophia devoured her meal and before she knew it, dessert had come and gone. A final gong had guests scurrying out to the train as she lingered over a cup of coffee.

When the last guest had departed, Nora wove her way to Sophia's table. "I hope you enjoyed your first meal with your new Harvey House?"

Sophia nodded, standing. "The food was most impressive and the service impeccable. I can only hope I can learn the dance as effectively and efficiently as you and the other ladies."

Nora beamed. "Our two chefs are both from Europe and have been taught in only the finest of culinary schools in Paris. As for the service, I am certain you will get the hang of it in no time." She gestured for Sophia to follow her. "I will show you to our rooms and you can meet the housemother. Her office is in our dormitory quarters across the street, but as it is about to be evening, she is most likely in the dormitory's downstairs parlor."

Sophia lifted her skirts and followed Nora across the dusty street to a brick two-story building with three sets of rustic French doors lining the first level. Entering through the middle set, Nora led her down the hall to the very first open door where she paused and lightly knocked on the frame.

"Yes?" answered the plump woman in her late forties, her rich red hair sprinkled in silver was devoid of the stark white bow the rest of the women wore.

"Miss Trent? A new Harvey Girl has arrived."

The lady stood and extended her hands to Sophia, grasping her. "Yes! Welcome to the Hotel Castañeda. Thank you, Miss Ray. I'll take it from here." She patted Nora's arm, dismissing her, and motioning for Sophia to take a seat on the divan across from the settee where Miss Trent returned. "I am, as you now know, Violet Trent, the housemother. I am here to see after you ladies' health, your needs, and most importantly, your *reputations*. You may call me, Miss Trent. It is a pleasure to meet you and to have you on our team, Miss Fairfield."

Sophia felt her stomach loosen as the kindness in Miss Trent's voice and demeanor enveloped her. "I cannot say how grateful I am to be given this opportunity, especially with my lack of experience." Sophia smoothed her travelworn skirts, hating how disheveled she appeared in front of her new employer.

"Yes, well, we will have you trained soon enough. Though, you should know we made an exception in your case with having you *not* train in Kansas first. There was a bit of a mix up with our new crop of trainees and there were only a handful of girls available to help with the opening of this new hotel, leaving us in quite a spot."

"I assure you I wish to succeed in this endeavor and will give it my all to learn what is expected of a Harvey Girl." Sophia hoped she didn't appear overeager as her father always mentioned when a gentleman overplayed his hand and revealed that he was desperate for a deal, he would agree to lesser terms.

"Good, good. Now, Miss Fairfield, I dislike to be all business right away, but time is of the essence, and I must begin on the rules straight away and then I shall introduce you to the head waitress and the rest of the staff."

Sophia cleared her throat. "Before I am introduced to the other girls, I have a rather strange request. Would it be acceptable to use a different surname?"

"Not call you Miss Fairfield? Whatever for?" Miss Trent asked, confusion in her tone. "You know we only accept girls with the highest moral behavior. If there is something you need to disclose, I suggest you do it now."

"Oh, it's nothing of that nature, I can assure you!" Sophia dipped her head. "I wish to go by my middle name because I do not wish my father to find me. You see, he wishes me to marry a man I do not love."

Miss Trent shifted in her chair, pulling a plain cotton handkerchief from her sleeve. "Oh, my goodness gracious. I understand your worry, but I am not certain if Mr. Harvey would agree to such a deception."

Sophia massaged her palm. When she had sent that telegram, she was too distressed to think clearly, but at least this kind woman would know the truth about her situation. "It makes me uneasy as well, but not as uneasy as everyone knowing my surname. Perhaps you could use my middle name, Bird? It was my mother's maiden name."

Miss Trent slowly nodded. "I suppose that wouldn't be too much of a falsehood if it was your mother's maiden name and is your legal name as well."

Sophia sighed with relief. "Thank you so much for understanding. I only mean to establish myself and give my father enough time to reconcile with the fact that I am never returning home."

"Your secret is safe with me, Miss *Bird*. Now, let's go over some rules while you follow me to your new quarters upstairs." She held open the door and motioned Sophia up the stairs. At the landing, she directed them to the left wing, Miss Trent nodding to any Harvey Girl in passing who was off duty. "There are fourteen rooms to one bathroom, so you will need to reserve your slot for bath night."

At the last door on the left, Miss Trent opened the door to reveal a cozy room with a braided rug and a window dressed in simple blue curtains with crocheted lace trim. On each side of the window were two small beds, and in the far corner of the room stood a wooden rocking chair with a lace doily draped across the top.

"This is the room you'll share with Miss Ray, the young lady you just met." She waved her hand over the quilted bed to the right of the window with Sophia's trunks tucked at its feet. "This is your bed, and I am certain you and Miss Ray will discuss how you will share the closet and such. Just keep your room clean and we won't have a problem." She looked Sophia up and down. "Yes, we should have just the right size uniform for you. I'll have a few dresses sent up for you to try. You will keep two dresses along with four white aprons and some white hair ribbons. If you get even a speck of soil on your apron or dress, you are to excuse yourself and change immediately, which goes for the table linen as well. Mr. Harvey will have nothing but perfection in his restaurant and in his Harvey Girls, but you will go over all that tomorrow with Miss Harriet Lane. She will be training you as she is the head Harvey Girl here."

Sophia's head was already spinning with the information, and as she had never had much talent for remembering names, she murmured Miss Lane's name under her breath for good measure. She could not insult the head waitress with her weak memory.

"The girls may be taken aback by your direct route to the hotel as it is *highly* irregular. Normally, you would have trained for six weeks in Kansas. All that to say, you will be *in training* for six weeks and will stay close to Miss Lane to learn the Fred Harvey system. We had an unusual week where one girl was fired for her consistent incompetence and then two girls broke contract and ran off to marry ranchers. We can manage with two girls leaving, but three? If we had known that two girls were running off in the same week, we may not have been so quick to fire Miss Pearson, but she would've been fired the minute her replacement was ready."

A tall blonde with a striking hourglass

figure stepped into the room. "Miss Trent, I hear I am to train a new recruit?"

"Yes, this is Miss Fai—Bird," she stumbled over Sophia's last name. "Sorry, my dear, I shall master your name in no time. New recruits' names sometimes elude me," she added, disguising her blunder.

"No offense taken, of course." Sophia smiled to the tall blonde. "It is a pleasure to meet you, Miss Lane."

"Good to have you, Miss Bird."

"I best be off. I have some errands to run, but I'll return tonight to announce curfew and for the head count," Miss Trent moved to the door. "Miss Lane, if you could, please be certain to inform Miss Bird on our standards of serving and decorum as well as the rules of the dormitory. I'm sure she will be a perfect fit for our little Harvey family." She smiled softly to Sophia and shut the door behind her.

Harriet turned to Sophia. "While I am ever so grateful you are here, Miss Bird, you will need to pull your weight around here even if you haven't been trained. We just fired an insolent girl who would not follow the rules, nor respect the chain of command. She thought herself above such things. But as I'm the head waitress, you will answer to me. Understand?"

"Yes, Miss Lane," Sophia murmured.

Harriet chuckled. "First off, the girls never call each other by our last names. It is too formal. Miss Trent is the only one we shall address so formally. I'm Harriet and I shall call you?"

"Sophia."

"Sophia. In front of guests, however, we shall add *Miss.* We start preparing for each train thirty minutes before it is scheduled to arrive, so I suggest you wake an hour and a half before the first train to dress and eat a quick bite. I must warn you *not* to be late for breakfast, or you will go without a meal until your lunch break. I have suffered one too many empty stomachs, and believe me, it is difficult to work under such conditions. After you have learned how to run both the counter and the dining room, you will then take your turn on the night shifts." She paused in her rapid recitation and nodded toward Sophia's soiled gown. "I've assigned you to have a turn with the bath tonight."

"Thank you. I haven't felt clean since I left my home."

Harriet smiled. "I figured you would. Get unpacked and I will see you in the morning to begin."

Sophia sighed as she sank beside her bed and knelt by her trunks. Lifting the lids, she shook the wrinkles out of each dress and laid it on the bed before pulling out her lace trimmed, beribboned underdrawers and a brown package fell to the floor. Carver's gift. She slipped the little note out from under the string and read:

To tell you what is in my heart... if only one could change what is to what could be.

Yours, C. Ashton

She pulled the string, unwrapped the paper and read the spine. *John Keats.* Her fingers lingered over the author's name. She opened the book and was surprised to find wear on the pages. She flipped to the inside cover and found Carver's name printed. *This is his own copy!* She ran her fingers over his signature and hugged the book to her chest. *God, wherever he is please bless him. Help me endure missing him.* She set the treasured book upright on her nightstand beside her Bible and heard a metallic *clink*.

She lifted the book to find a small gold locket that must have been inside the pages. Her fingers trembled as she opened it to find Carver's dear face, his strong jawline, Grecian nose and dimples twisted her heart with loneliness—his kind eyes reminding her of what she could never possess. On the opposite half, were a few faded pressed petals. She gasped in recognition. *That day in the square. He kept the flowers from my hair.* She closed the piece and fastened it about her neck, already feeling bolstered in a place all too unknown. If he had given her such a gift, he would never betray her location to Prescott.

She removed a sheet of stationary from the writing desk, having thought on the train long and hard what she would write

Carver, if she had the courage. But the book of Keats and locket with the petals had crumbled her inhibitions. She paused in her thanks, wishing she could write what was on her heart. She glanced to Keats and decided to be bold once more, since she would likely never write him again.

Dearest Carver, thank you for the lovely gifts. Even without them, I would never forget our time together. I am safe and I think I will be happy in my new position. Please, do not tell anyone of this letter, or I will regret my moment of weakness to tell you that my heart echoes yours in wishing we had met in another fashion.

Before she could change her mind, Sophia finished with a poem from Tennyson, folded the letter, slipped it into an envelope, and directed it to his New Orleans office. She should be embarrassed for having memorized his New Orleans addresses from Father's ledger in order to look them up on the map, but she could only be thankful now that she had.

A gentle knock sounded on the door and Nora slipped inside. "Normally, I won't be knocking as this is my room as well, but I figured, since you're new, I'd knock at first so as to give you a chance to make yourself decent if needed."

Sophia smiled, the note weighing heavily in her hands. "Thank you for the consideration."

Nora waved her forward to the hallway. "The girls have just finished cleaning up from the last shift and the night shift is about to leave the dormitory, so you, of course, should meet everyone as they come and go."

Sophia joined her new roommate in the hallway at the foot of the stairs as the gaggle of girls passed to and from their shifts, each introducing themselves to Sophia. At the front of the line was the head waitress Harriet with a thin, pretty red-haired girl at her side who nodded to Sophia.

"I'm Dolly Matthews." She looked Sophia up and down. "Though, with your comely features, I doubt you will need to remember my name for you will not be with us long."

"No longer than you, Dolly! If you weren't so picky, you could have been engaged at least twenty times in the past month," Nora giggled.

"Twenty-three times, actually," Dolly replied with a wink.

Sophia gasped. "Surely you are jesting?"

"If anything, she has forgotten a time or two a cowpoke has asked for her hand." A girl about Sophia's height with brown curly hair and bright green eyes stuck her hand out. "I'm Fannie Traverse. If you are looking for the best place to be picky about a future spouse, you are in for a treat. There are oodles of men falling at your feet daily."

"Not every girl is desperate to be swept off her feet like you and Dolly." Harriet teased, rolling her eyes with a laugh.

"And you aren't? We see the way you

make eyes at Sheriff Kane—" Fannie fired back.

Harriet sent her a blazing scowl. Fannie's cheeks heated as she snapped her mouth closed. Thinking it was best to ignore that little transaction, Sophia continued down the line exchanging pleasantries.

A curvaceous woman with blonde hair and sparkling blue eyes pulled Sophia into a quick embrace. "Now, don't be embarrassed if you have to ask for our names more than a few times because there are nine of us ladies . . . well, now that you are here, ten young ladies working in this fine establishment and hopefully more on the way."

Sophia took her hand. "A pleasure to meet you, Miss—?"

"Just like me to leave off that part! I'm Jenny Stuart from Chicago."

Harriet clapped her hands. "So sorry ladies, but we must see to the coming train. I am certain you will all have ample time to converse with Sophia, but you won't have enough sleep if you don't get into your beds and those who are on night shift need to get downstairs *now.*" Her gaze fell on Sophia's gold locket. "Also, we aren't allowed to wear any jewelry."

Sophia's hand at once enclosed about the dear piece. The locket was the only part of Carver she had left besides the book of poems. "Could I wear it under my uniform?"

Harriet's brows lifted. "Challenging the rules already?"

"No. I want to be sure I don't break any."

To that reply, Harriet nodded. "Wear it under your uniform, but if I ever see a hint of the gold while you are on duty, I'm afraid that you will have to be penalized. If it happens a second time, you will be dismissed. Now, you should take your bath and ready yourself for bed for you have an early morning tomorrow."

Sophia followed most of the girls upstairs, while two others sought their rooms on the first floor.

Nora grasped Jenny's arm at the second-floor landing. "Before you go to your room, I have that book you lent me," she whispered and pushed open the bedroom door.

"You both enjoy reading?" Hope kindled

in Sophia's belly that maybe she would have some kindred spirits.

"Well, Jenny does, but I could barely make it through the first chapter of the *great classic* she insisted on lending me." She reached under her feather pillow and retrieved a copy of *Emma* and plopped it into Jenny's hands.

Jenny groaned. "Such injustice to Miss Austen. Every girl needs to read at least one of her books. But, speaking of books, what do I spy on your nightstand, Sophia?" Jenny's gaze landed on Sophia's crimson book beside Carver's worn copy.

Sophia moved to show her the titles but tripped over an object at the foot of the bed, sending her scrambling to grab the short iron bedpost to keep from falling. She searched for what had tripped her, frowning at the sight of the posts of the bed standing in . . . bowls of water? She glanced to Nora's bed and found it the same. How had she not noticed them straightaway? "What in the world?"

Nora shivered, unable to disguise her

grimace. "You will find out soon enough as we all do."

"Judging from your faces, I think I'd rather not know, but now I find I must know, or my imaginings may be worse." Sophia looked to Jenny.

Jenny sighed. "And this is the part where I fear we might lose any new Harvey Girl. The bowls of water deter scorpions from climbing into our beds."

Sophia's jaw dropped. "Excuse me?"

"Scorpions." Nora demonstrated the size of the creature between her finger and thumb. "They are these tiny little leviathans—"

Sophia pressed her hands to her stomach. The truth was far worse than her imaginings. "I've read about them, but I didn't think they existed in the *middle* of a town. I thought I might see one out in the desert, but in my bedroom? Never." She shivered. *What have I gotten myself into?*

"Well, when the town exists in New Mexico, you better believe we have to deal with them. The bowls of water are only one of our precautionary measures." Nora opened the closet door and from the corner, removed a rug beater. "When you select your dress in the morning, or any article of clothing for that matter, you *must* beat it." She removed a dress and whacked it vigorously, a small scorpion falling to the floor, curling up in death.

The girls squealed and leapt atop Nora's bed, Sophia smacking her head against the wall in her haste.

Sophia pressed her fingers to her temples, drawing deep breaths. "Please tell me this is some sort of elaborate induction jest?"

"Honestly, I have yet to see one actually fall out of a dress before." Nora pressed a hand to her chest. "But why would we all have a rug beater in our closet if we were teasing you? Oh, and you are going to want to flip over your shoes and give them a good sound shake before slipping them on. You might get an unpleasant surprise if you don't."

Sophia clutched the bedframe, feeling faint.

"Speaking of shoes," Nora skirted the

dead scorpion and looked over the two pairs Sophia had already unpacked and selected a black pair in the plainest style and lowest heel. "These will do quite well for your uniform. However, they are still a bit high, but I think you must be used to wearing shoes with heels." Nora smiled and handed the pair to Sophia. "Also, judging from the quality of your wardrobe, you aren't accustomed to hard labor, are you?"

Sophia's cheeks heated. She had selected her simplest attire for the journey and yet, Nora saw straight through her attempt to blend into the group. "No, but I am willing to learn, and I'm not afraid to give it my best." *I only hope that my best will be enough.*

Fannie poked her curly head through the cracked door. "Hurry, ladies! Miss Trent is making her way across the street for the evening roll call. Best don your nightgowns or you will be dressing in the dark!"

"Well, I wish I could share a room with you two, but I've got to get back to Whiny Wailing Dismal Dolly's room." Jenny sighed and stood. "Let me tell you. It would try the patience of Job to listen to Dolly moan about her wanting a *rich* husband to come rescue her and why don't the rich young gentlemen ever propose to her over the lunch counter like the dirty, dusty old ranchers?" She lifted her face toward the ceiling. "I can only pray that our shifts will split, and we will only have to see one another in passing."

"The ranchers really do propose to her that much?" Sophia's lips parted again before she could stop herself. She snapped it shut.

Nora laughed. "Yes, but don't worry. Fannie is right about men falling at your feet. You won't be left out. I guarantee you will have ten proposals before the week is out!"

CHAPTER 9

Carver braced himself as the train halted in the station in New Orleans. It had been four excruciatingly long days since she disappeared and with each passing day, his feelings over how he had left things with Sophia worsened. He wished he could protest Prescott's order against Carver's searching for Sophia, but what could he say? He had delayed returning to New Orleans by two days in his attempts to convince Prescott, but what claim did he have over Sophia to insist that he be allowed to investigate into her disappearance?

He could kick himself for not confessing

the depth of his growing affection for her. Perhaps he could have convinced her to stay. He raked his hand through his hair, but to confess feelings of love after only a few weeks together? How was that any better than Prescott's proposing marriage after only paying court to her a few times?

Carver hopped off the train in New Orleans, his heart skipping when he spied a young lady who held herself in the same manner as Sophia. Leaving his belongings on the platform, he bolted after her. "Sophia? Sophia!" He darted around the crowded station and snatched her wrist, turning her to him and was met with a scream and a slap.

Carver released the lady who was certainly *not* Sophia, apologizing profusely for the confusion and made himself scarce before the police could be called. Snatching up his satchel and directing a luggage cart where to take his trunks, Carver wove through the streets of New Orleans toward his office on the dock. He didn't know how he was going to concentrate with Sophia having disappeared, but he knew that if he did not keep busy, he'd lose his mind to worry. If only she had let him know where she was going. He sighed, knowing that if she had, he would have taken the first train out to wherever she was hiding and return her to safety.

He greeted the dockworkers he knew in passing, who probably hadn't noticed he was out of office with Jimmy, his assistant, running things in Carver's absence. Reaching the shipping office of *Payne & Fairfield,* which was little more than a glorified shack on the docks, he swung open the pine plank door, inhaling the scent of coffee that permeated the plain wooden building with its constantly being brewed. But the thought of coffee reminded him of the lady who unabashedly admitted that she drank two cups each day. Sighing, he poured himself a cup and sank into the wooden chair behind his modest desk that was piled high with sorted, opened missives, listening to Jimmy list all the happenings since Carver's departure to Charleston.

The door burst open and the young errand boy they employed waved a stack of letters overhead. "Telegram for Mr. Ashton and the post."

He snatched up the telegram, thinking it might hold information about Sophia, but tossed it aside as it was merely Prescott telling him of another inbound shipment. The man was always meddling, and Carver was growing weary of never truly having a say. In this, he and Sophia were the same. He shook his head. He couldn't do anything without thinking of her fair face.

Riffling through the post and its many advertisements, his gaze fell upon a letter in a feminine hand. His fingers shook as he lifted it. He didn't dare hope, but who else could it be from but Sophia? He broke the seal, his heart stumbling at her thanks, hoping for more as he read her final lines.

I wish things could have been different. I do not know if we will see each other again, but I will treasure the memories of our time together for as Tennyson wrote, "What is there in the great sphere of the earth, and range of evil between death and birth, that I should fear—if I were loved by thee?" If our worlds had collided in any other fashion, I would have been yours forever. However, it was not meant to be, and I believe I shall be quite content in my new position.

Fondly, Sophia.

He sank back into his chair, wishing he had offered her more than a vague declaration. He should have offered her his hand. He should have assured her his love was stronger than any gossip. He flipped over the envelope, searching for an address, but only found the postmark, the city's name smudged so much that he could only make out the *Las* part, but the state was there in plain ink. *New Mexico.* He ran his finger over the marking and stuffed the envelop into his pocket. If he knew anything about Prescott, he would have his Pinkerton agents searching everywhere for any clue.

He looked about the cramped office for new faces and saw only the weary men he had been working with for years. Sophia had taken her future into her hands. Maybe he should finally do the same. With his life's savings, he had the means to purchase a small store and eventually, with the profits brought in by the first year, he could gradually build his kingdom and have something to offer Sophia—have a place of their own far away from any Charleston scandal that might follow upon the news of a stepson marrying his stepfather's intended.

But first, I have to find her and convince her that I was not trifling with her. He shot to his feet and snatched his hat off the coat rack with the letter burning in his pocket. He could not trust anyone he hired to keep her location secret, not with his stepfather's deep pockets. But as Carver's bags were still packed, they would stay that way until he had visited every stop in New Mexico that began with the name Las.

SOPHIA SPREAD another fresh linen over one of Harriet's tables and proceeded to place the dishes, glasses, coffee cups, napkins, and silverware in their proper places as she had been doing for the past half hour.

"The meals rotate every four days," Harriet continued her monotone lecture, dropping the menu onto the tablecloth in front of Sophia. "Memorize the menu before the first train arrives in thirty minutes. Meals cost seventy-five cents in the dining room, but only *twenty-five* cents at the lunch counter and any money left at your station will be considered your tip, but for now, any tips left at the station will be shared between you and I." She paused as if waiting for Sophia to disagree with her.

Sophia nodded to dissuade any argument. "That's a fair arrangement until I am fully trained."

Harriet's pursed lips relaxed into almost a smile with this concession. "Your first train will be arriving soon, so it is imperative you keep the rules in the forefront of your mind. And remember, in front of the guests, you are to address me as *Miss* Harriet. We are less formal in our addresses toward one another because we wish to appear friendly to our guests, but not familiar so as to encourage any vulgar behavior. Speaking of which. . ." She leaned forward and inspected Sophia's face. "Are you wearing rouge?"

"What? No!" Sophia gasped, thinking of her mother's reaction if she ever did so.

"You are excessively flushed then. Just so you are aware, we're not permitted to wear any makeup. Men will think you mean to offer more than just your waitressing services if you try to enhance your appearance in any form with cosmetics. Any deviance from this rule and—"

"I'll be dismissed?" Sophia guessed.

Harriet shrugged and moved to the counter, pouring them each a glass of water. "I know it sounds harsh, but Mr. Harvey's rules are meant to protect us."

Even though Sophia had enough money

hidden away to support herself for a year if she budgeted and some jewels she could sell for even more funds, she well recognized the value of having the protective arm of Fred Harvey and the housemother sheltering her reputation. She had always bent to her father's will.

The only difference was that now, she was getting paid and could leave whenever she wished, but she was now a working girl with a good, honorable position and she would do what it took to keep it. She finished her glass and began memorizing the menu as Harriet finished setting up for their guests.

"I should have allowed the girls from the night shift to set up the station last night like they usually do, but Miss Trent wanted me to give you more experience," Harriet explained, turning on her heel for the linen closet.

Nora finished up her table and joined Sophia in the placing of the cups, whispering, "You'll get used to her rather militant ways."

"Militant? She is only explaining how

things are done."

Nora laughed softly. "Wait until the first train comes into the station. Harriet treats feeding passengers like it's life and death and if you make a mistake, Lord help you. But as you said yesterday, the Harvey system is like a dance, so once you get the hang of it, you'll perform it beautifully."

"Unfortunately, it is a dance you have yet to learn, Sophia." Harriet interjected, setting her armful of fresh table linens atop an empty table. "As you know, the guests wire ahead what they will have, but we still have to take down their order so we know which guest ordered what meal. Stand directly behind me at all times, taking down the orders. We cannot have the guests complaining of a less than perfect dining experience." She turned to Nora. "Could you help us finish setting the rest of the tables? I am afraid we won't finish in time. I got too caught up in my instruction, I'm afraid."

"Of course." Nora flew into action alongside Sophia arranging chairs, correcting positions of silverware and cups as the gong sounded.

"Blast. Is it time already?" Harriet ran her fingers over the final table linen, aligned a knife, and straightened her apron. "At your stations, girls!"

Sophia stood stiffly beside Harriet, hands clutched in front of her skirts. Her feet were already aching, and she hadn't even served a single guest. *How does Belle accomplish all her chores with three sets of stairs?* "Where are the guests?"

"The first gong is to let us know that the train has arrived at the station and for us to finish the last bits of preparations and get to our positions. The gong is then taken to the station by the general manager, Mr. Carlton, and you, being a guest recently, know the rest with the timing of the four warnings."

"So many times?" Sophia murmured, only remembering two out the four gongs yesterday at mealtime. *I was famished and not anxiously awaiting to reboard the train though.*

"Fred Harvey wants his guests to enjoy their meals, but not so much as to let time slip away from them and then they miss their trains," Harriet whispered as the front doors swung open and in stepped the broad-shouldered Mr. Carlton with a troupe of ravenous passengers following closely behind.

Sophia's pulse pounded in her ears. This was it. Her next step toward her future. She could not fail.

The dusty guests piled through the doors, all with hungry, expectant expressions. Harriet leaned toward Sophia and whispered, "You remember the cup system from last night's dinner, yes? Usually, three girls wait on three stations at a time, and we split the tasks to serve the guests faster."

Sophia nodded. *That's one thing that I managed to remember. Cup up is coffee, or is it cup down?* She bit her lip. *Oh no.*

"Good. Then, I'll let you take the drink orders and Jenny will come behind you and fill the drinks while I see which guest ordered which meal."

Sophia nodded numbly, the responsibility that rested with the cup code pressing upon her shoulders as her head spun with the information Harriet had doused upon her.

"Smile and greet the guests," Harriet hissed through a gritted teeth smile.

Attempting to disguise her stress, Sophia smiled her greeting to each of the guests as they took their seats. She stepped toward the guest seated at the nearest corner. "Good morning, sir. May I take your drink order?"

"Coffee." He grunted, his fingertips thrumming against the clean linen.

Sophia looked at the cup in the saucer. *Cup up? Oh, or is it cup down?* She felt Harriet's eyes burning into the back of her neck and she decided to chance it. Leaving the cup upright, she moved on to the next guest. Harriet did not say a word. *Guessed right!* "Beverage, ma'am?"

"Tea, please. The train had the most vial, unnatural tasting tea that if I don't wash it down with *real* tea, I might perish." The woman shuddered, dabbing her handkerchief to her forehead, her graying curls trembling about her face.

Sophia smiled. "Having recently experienced the tea on the train ride here, I completely understand. Our tea will not disappoint." She flipped the cup upside down in its saucer. She moved around the table to each guest as Jenny came directly behind her and poured the correct beverages. Finished with the beverage orders, Sophia stood behind Harriet.

"Excellent work, Miss Sophia," she whispered and stepped forward, deftly jotting down each order.

Sophia felt rather ridiculous writing down the same order on her own notepad, but she didn't dare question the Harvey House methods.

"My stomach has decided that it would benefit more from soup than salad," an elderly woman informed Harriet. "Please adjust my original order to your tomato soup. Is that possible?"

"Of course, no problem at all." Harriet handed the list to Sophia as they headed to the kitchen. "Help me take the trays and distribute the food," she called to Sophia over the clamoring of pots, pans, and dishes being filled and placed on trays. She paused beside a station laden with prepared food.

"Six salads and twelve soups." Her voice rang out above the noise.

The chef nodded and his assistants rapidly filled two trays with the order as Harriet continued her instructions to Sophia as the next Harvey Girl placed her order.

Harriet nudged Sophia with her hip and nodded to the station where Sophia's order pad lay. "Do *not* misplace your list because it has the seating arrangement as well as their main course orders." She picked up the soup tray. "Thank you, Pierre!"

"Thank you, sir!" Sophia added, picking up her note pad and the salad tray, following the head waitress out of the busy kitchen, holding her breath intermittently, lest she drop the heavy tray as she maneuvered through the swinging doors. She set her salad tray on the serving counter next to Harriet's in the dining hall and exhaled. She retrieved the list from her apron pocket, and they studied it together.

"I'll get this half and you get the others," Harriet stated, picking up two dishes, a salad and a soup.

Sophia carefully balanced two soups and placed them in front of the appropriate guests and then, taking a second glance at the list, she grabbed a salad and a soup from the trays and placed them where she thought they were supposed to go.

"I *just* finished asking for a soup instead of a salad! She said it wouldn't be a problem." The lady gasped, looking around for Harriet. "You there!"

Harriet's cheeks flamed as she acquired a bowl of soup from the tray on the counter and swapped it out with the salad. "I'm so sorry, ma'am. This is her first day."

"I don't care if she is new, she is trying to spoil my stomach's delicate constitution and I will write Fred Harvey to tell him that his staff are incompetent!" She proclaimed, banging her fist on the table and making the china clatter.

"Please accept my apologies on behalf of Fred Harvey and enjoy this meal free of charge for your trouble, ma'am," Harriet replied.

She sniffed and dipped her spoon into

her soup. "*Humph*. Do I get an extra piece of pie?"

"Absolutely. In fact, I'll have the chef make up a box for you for a whole pie to take on your travels."

"I suppose, in that case, I will *not* write Mr. Harvey." She nodded to Harriet, setting her sparkling ear drops swinging. "Thank you for remedying the situation. You might want to train that one a little more." She pointed to Sophia with her full spoon, the soup dripping into her cup of tea.

Was this how Sophia's family treated their servants? Like they were disposable and lacking wit?

"Absolutely, ma'am. At the Harvey House, satisfaction is guaranteed. We won't stop until we reach perfection." Harriet turned from the table long enough to give Sophia a wink as Sophia straightened her shoulders and swapped out the lady's tea without a word, lest the woman accuse her of telling a falsehood over the quality of the tea.

The rest of the afternoon went along without a hitch, but the tension in Harriet's shoulders didn't seem to lessen until the last guest had departed.

Harriet pressed her hands to her lower back and stretched. "I'm so sorry about that Sophia, but Fred Harvey does not put up with incompetence and our guests know it. Only last week, I fired a girl who failed to execute the cup system correctly on multiple occasions. Since you are new and haven't even been trained, we will, of course, be more understanding, but you'll have to be reprimanded for your mistake with the salad earlier." Harriet motioned toward the tables. "Clean every dish at our station and dress the tables."

Sophia blinked at the pile of dessert dishes, used cups, and cutlery atop the soiled linen. "But isn't there a boy just for the dish washing?" She had seen him in the kitchen herself, working away at the mountains of dishes. *What was his name? William?*

"We do, but today you are going to wash your own dishes." Harriet folded her hands before her pristine apron. "I think it is better than me marking you up without giving you a chance to remedy the situation. Don't you agree?"

"If she is left alone to do all those chores, she will barely get a moment to take lunch before the next train," Jenny called on her way through to the kitchen.

"Well, then, I guess it's a good thing that *you* will be helping her," Miss Trent interjected from the dining room threshold, narrowing her eyes.

"Good thing," Jenny sighed.

"I am so sorry you got pulled into this," Sophia whispered to Jenny as Harriet explained the situation to the dish boy, who sent Sophia a sympathetic smile.

"I should have known better than to contradict Harriet when Miss Trent might be nearby. She's kind, but will stand no argument as to whom is the commander of the dining room," Jenny muttered as they headed to the dish washing station.

As there was room at the station for four workers, William silently continued his mountain of dishes at the furthest end. Closing her eyes, Sophia plunged her hands into the hot water, scrubbing the dishes and attempting to ignore the sting of the harsh soap and focus on conquering the mountain on the counter. "What happens if I break a piece of china while cleaning?"

"Most of the time, the Harvey Houses will list that as a company expense, Miss." William interjected from his station, his ears reddening as if embarrassed that he spoke up.

Something horrid flowed through her fingers as bits of food bobbed in the water. Sophia grimaced, thinking of the rancher who sneezed into his food four times. *The food he sneezed on is probably floating around in these suds.* She refrained from drawing her hands from the water and giving them a scrub in the fresh scalding hot water. *Don't think, just wash.*

A strangled laugh made her glance toward William, who must have seen her grimace.

She had finished scrubbing the fourth mound when Harriet barged through the kitchen doors. "The train will be here soon, and your tables aren't even set! Leave the dishes to soak for the dish boy and hop to it!" She grimaced at the sight of Sophia's apron and hurried out the door. "Change first, ladies."

"Sorry, William. Looks like the rest are all yours." Jenny moaned as she straightened her back and fumbled with her apron strings.

"It's my job, Miss." The shy boy grinned at them both and ducked his head, setting to scrubbing with even more vigor than before, no doubt aware of the dishes about to fill his station once more.

Jenny linked her arm through Sophia's. "At least we don't have to do any more dishes. Do me a favor and fetch me an apron from the dormitory as well, will you?"

Sophia nodded and smiled back at her new friend before hurrying upstairs. She snatched a fresh apron out of her side of the closet and hurried into Jenny's room down the hall. She could easily tell which was Jenny's side of the room as there was a small shelf, bursting with titles. Suppressing the need to read through them, she snagged a clean apron, taking the stairs as fast as she could without slipping, shaking the aprons out for scorpions as she raced. She slowed only when she reached the kitchen, keeping an eye out for Pierre and his assistants' hot pots and pans. Sophia passed Jenny's apron to her, tying her own as they hurried out into the already filling dining room, but at a glance at the tables revealed that Harriet and Jenny had successfully reset the tables without her.

Harriet rustled to Sophia's side and whispered, "Millie is supposed to be working the lunch counter with Fannie, but she has a stomachache and can't even stand at the moment, so I'm going to need you to support Fannie. Can you handle that?"

I surely hope so. "Of course." Sophia hoped she sounded more confident than she felt, but as Harriet turned away, she must have believed her. She darted behind the lunch counter, smiling at Fannie.

"Thank the good Lord. Reinforcements." Fannie gave Sophia's hand a quick squeeze. "As it is the cheapest option, the lunch counter is almost never empty. Instead of having the luxury of having the food prepared ahead of time, the men will order from the menu as they take a seat, but most of the men already know what they want as they are regulars. When you get their order, you just need to poke your head through the kitchen door and shout out the order." She pointed to the main kitchen door directly to the right of the counter.

"I don't need a ticket?"

She shook her head. "The staff will be listening for your orders. Also, the men here go through an unbelievable amount of coffee. I have no idea how they could ever drink so much coffee and not set their teeth to chattering out of their heads, but you need to fill the coffee urn pitcher by pitcher whenever you catch a moment's breath." Fannie patted her hair and took a deep breath. "Even though the lunch counter is the worst shift, you must never appear frazzled. A Harvey Girl is to always be fresh-faced and smiling but be careful not to smile *too* much. Be friendly, but not familiar," she instructed quietly. "I hope that's not too much information all at once?"

Sophia giggled. "Harriet gave me quite

the introduction this morning, so she has well prepared me."

"She does tend to be quite thorough." She laughed and patted Sophia's arm, handing her a notepad. "I'm sure you will do marvelously. Just don't accept the first proposal you hear." She winked at her and then folded her hands in front of her skirt with her own notepad in hand as the first batch of men clamored into their seats at the counter.

"Mr. Harris, would you like your usual?" Fannie smiled her greeting to the scruffy old man.

He nodded. "Miss Fannie, you know I always want my steak and potatoes."

She tilted her head to Sophia. "Place an order for one medium rare steak and mashed potatoes with a slice of apple pie for dessert." She poured Mr. Harris a cup of coffee and moved on to the next guest.

Sophia poked her head through the kitchen door, the heat from the ovens greeting her as the staff manned the stoves, chopped vegetables, and filled orders. "One, um, rare steak, mashed potatoes, and apple pie!" She called out, almost embarrassed to raise her voice so high.

"What? Speak up girl!" The chef bellowed.

Sophia cleared her throat and repeated her order as loud as she dared.

"Got it!" One of the assistants called back and Sophia ducked out of the kitchen and back to the counter, nearly avoiding crashing into Harriet.

"Watch where you are going!" She scowled. "Good thing I am only coming in with an order ticket and not a tray full of messy soup bowls. They'd be all over the floor and you'd be out of a job."

"Sorry!" Sophia called over her shoulder, too much in a rush to stop to listen to her lecture. *I'll probably get in trouble for that later too.*

"There you are." Fannie gave her a strained smile. "I need you to take care of the gentlemen on the right side of the counter. I haven't been able to get their orders yet."

Sophia grabbed her notepad and pencil from her apron pocket and paused before the giant cowboy perched on the lunch stool. "May I take your order, sir?"

The man's wide, yellow grin displayed a missing front tooth. "Are you on the menu?"

Sophia blushed to the roots of her hair, and overhearing his comment, Fannie stepped in front of her, the silver-plated coffee pot in hand.

"Mr. Gessler, I know you are not new to our establishment, so allow me to remind you that we Harvey Girls are ladies and shall be treated as such. If you do not conduct yourself in a manner worthy of a gentleman, you'll be requested to depart by the general manager, Mr. Carlton, a former blacksmith. I'm certain you do not wish to cross him." Fannie narrowed her gaze at the fellow, her fist on her hip and the steaming coffee pot hovering beyond his cup to his lap.

"No, Miss. Sorry, Miss," Mr. Gessler mumbled, turning his attention back to his empty cup.

"Good. Consider this your warning." She filled his cup and turned to Sophia. "Do you want me to finish the order?"

"I can do it. If I need help, I'll ask Mr. Carlton. Thank you."

Fannie nodded and returned to refilling the men's coffee.

"Do you know what you would like, sir?"

He rambled off his order. "Ham sandwich with the candied potatoes and chocolate pudding for dessert and coffee."

Sophia didn't even bother jotting it down and poked her head into the kitchen and shouted the order, feeling a bit wild allowing her voice such a range. *Mother would have a fit.* She couldn't help but grin at the thought.

After that first encounter, the rest of the men were quite nice, albeit a bit flirty, but the day passed in a blur, time only slowing as her feet continued to swell in her fine leather shoes that were never meant for more than a brief stroll.

"Well, your first shift is over," Harriet announced at six of the clock. "Fannie, thank you for taking over in teaching Sophia how to work the counter. Sophia, I was keeping an eye on you today and I must say, while I do see potential in you, you need to become faster." She handed her a piece of paper from her note pad. "I made a few notes on ways you could become more efficient that I think you will find very beneficial."

"Thank you." Sophia's feet burned. She shifted from foot to foot to keep the pain at bay, but nothing she could do would dull it. *I've got to take these shoes off or the only way they are coming off my swollen feet is if they are cut off.*

"But as it has been a long day and I want dinner and my bath, the lengthy explanation of the tips must wait until tomorrow." Harriet pulled her apron strings with a groan.

Sophia sagged against the counter, using it as a crutch along with each chair back to the kitchen for dinner. Hard work was much harder than she had thought it would be.

CHAPTER 10

Who knew there were so many towns starting with *Las* in New Mexico? Carver ran his finger over the photograph of Sophia that he had asked Belle to procure for him from the family's carte de visite album before he left Charleston. He smiled at the bangs carefully combed over her forehead. By the end of their weeks together, she had been wearing them brushed and braided to the side in long curls in the fashion he told her he admired.

The conductor announced the stop and with a sigh, Carver collected his satchel from the storage rack and resumed his seat, staring out the window of the small town just coming in to view and not daring to hope that perhaps this was the last town he'd have to search for her.

He snatched up his journal from the tufted seat and tucked it into his satchel. He had taken to writing his thoughts to her in his notebook that he'd originally kept for department store ideas, storing instead, his thoughts for her in the hope that she would someday read them and understand the depths of his admiration and love for her. He told her of the funny things he witnessed, of people, odd occurrences, and pretty names that could possibly be used for their children, along with a question of how many did she wish for? Three sounded just right to him.

Carver also confessed his fear of failing in opening his store and that he had an eye on a small one that was rumored to be on the brink of sale and because of Sophia's encouragement and belief in him, he had already written the owner with an offer.

The train halted and at the conductor's final call, Carver rose with his things in hand. It was time to begin his search anew, beginning with the town's hotel. *Lord, keep her safe. And please, let me find her before Prescott or his hired men.*

"I CANNOT BELIEVE Miss Trent gave us the same day off this week," Nora exclaimed as she fastened the back of her blue cotton dress.

"How are you dressed already?" Sophia slowly sat up in her bed and stretched her aching body, yawning. *I don't think I have ever worked as hard in a whole year as I have this one week.* She groaned as she stood and stretched her back again. "After working six twelve-hour shifts, one would think you would be wanting to sleep in a little."

"With all that moaning and groaning, one would think that you never had to work a day in your life." Nora laughed as she fluffed the bit of lace at her cuff.

Sophia laughed softly and reluctantly drew her feet from the bed. *Yes, you would think that . . . and sadly, it's true.* "I am rather pathetic sounding, aren't I?"

"You sound like a dying cat." Nora tossed her feather pillow at Sophia, who dodged it. "You best get yourself up and dressed because today is your only chance for the next week to see Las Vegas besides during our walk to church tomorrow morning, but that doesn't really count." Nora nodded to the water basin. "I put in fresh water for you. We are leaving in twenty minutes."

After a quick sponge bath, Sophia opened the chifforobe and selected a rather simple pale pink cotton walking suit with venetian point lace, giving it the customary three *thwacks* with the rug beater before laying it atop the bed to arrange her hair into a simple coiffure, enjoying the softening effect of the curls framing her face while keeping her bangs braided back. She slipped out of her cream nightgown and into her walking suit, sighing at the soft fabric against her skin. Her one splurge was bringing an extra hat that had taken up far too much room in her leather trunk. She lifted the lid of the hatbox, smiling at her lovely matching chapeau with pale pink ribbons, roses, and white ostrich feathers. She looked into the chifforobe's small mirror and pinned on her chapeau. *It's been too long since I have worn anything pretty. I'm so tired of wearing nothing but black dresses and white bows.*

Nora laughed. "We aren't going to a wedding. We are only walking down to the general store. With all that primping, every man within a hundred miles will hear of your beauty and come begging for your tiny hand in marriage."

Sophia's cheeks heated as she took in Nora's pretty but worn blue dress and the small pink bonnet she held tenderly as she fluffed the grosgrain ribbons. "It's all that I have in the ways of a walking gown."

"All that you have? You didn't bring anything more practical than that frippery?" She smiled, reaching to touch Sophia's lace. "Beautiful frippery, I must admit."

"I left in such a hurry that I didn't have time to buy anything plainer," Sophia tried to explain, but realized that she was only sounding more and more spoilt.

"So, you come from a wealthy family then, I am assuming. And with that lilting accent, you aren't from New York City." She nodded toward Sophia's hands, chapped from washing the dishes so many times in a week for messing up orders. "Your hands betray that you haven't used them for much labor."

Sophia kept silent, which Nora took as an affirmative as she peered into Sophia's open chifforobe, her jaw dropping as she spied delicate muslin, rich silk, and layers of lace donning the cotton.

"I didn't see you unpack. With this quality of fabric, where is the rest of your wardrobe?" She snorted. "Ladies who own gowns such as these always own more than necessary."

Sophia slipped on her gloves over her chapped hands. *I wish I had my hand cream.* "I only brought what I could tuck in my two trunks. I didn't want to unpack them in front of you when some of the girls had already commented on my traveling dress . . . I felt foolish."

"You have *more* gowns at home?" She stroked a silk sleeve. "I'd be so proud of all my fine things that I'm afraid I'd flaunt them every day!" She turned to Sophia. "I just don't understand why on earth would you want to leave all of your beautiful things and come work as a waitress when you are obviously a fine lady and could sit back and let your father take care of you? Just wait until I tell the girls."

Sophia felt the heat reach the roots of her hair. Thank goodness she had only brought a handful of dresses. Sophia stepped forward, her heart in her throat. "You mustn't tell them. Promise me you won't, Nora?"

"Why ever not? Don't you want to see Dolly turn pea green? The bossy thing is out for Harriet's job and is constantly bragging about her wealthy family and all the nice things she had growing up. Whenever she has her days off, she flaunts a new gown, parasol, or bonnet that her aunt has sent her." She rolled her eyes and held one of Sophia's favorite gowns up to herself. "It is disgusting, but she doesn't possess any gown as finely designed as yours."

"I don't want the girls to start talking about me being wealthy because I don't want anyone to catch wind of it." Sophia fiddled with the lace on her sleeve. "I don't wish to be found."

"Your parents don't know where you are?" Nora's eyes widened in disbelief as she sank onto her bed, the pretty gown forgotten for a moment.

"And I'd like to keep it that way." *And not have Father come storming in and forcing me to marry someone I don't even love.*

Nora nodded, returning the gown to the closet. "That explains a lot. I couldn't think of how you got your parents to consent to you working in the Wild West." She pinned on her hat. "I shall keep your background safe, but," she laughed, "the girls will gradually find out. Every day you have off and wear one of those stunning dresses, they'll talk and wonder about where you get your money, so I'd suggest that you try re-wearing gowns before bringing out new ones."

"Good idea." Sophia replied, following Nora out and down the stairs. Passing the Harvey Girls' personal parlor, Sophia spied Jenny sitting by the window with the book of poetry Sophia had lent her.

"Jenny! Grab a bonnet and join us. We're heading to the shops." Sophia waved her new friend over. "The outing will do us all a world of good."

"The shops? More like shop. Jones' General Store is the only good place in town." Jenny shook her head, lifting up her book. "Thank you, but it's much too hot today and I'm always hot, so I'd rather sit in this cozy chair by the window, catching any stray breeze before my shift starts tonight. Besides, I have to read more of this Keats that you are always talking about, so we can have a good long discourse about it when you join me on a night shift this week."

"The night shift? Already?" Sophia laughed nervously. "I was told I had to master the day shift before I was allowed to help run the night shift, so I must be doing something right."

Nora seized Sophia's arm and dragged her to the door. "Come on. You can't get to know the town if you stay here with your head stuck in a book on your *one* day off. You can read later. *After* you catch yourself a decent husband."

"Have fun husband hunting." Jenny laughed, turning back to her book.

"We aren't hunting," Sophia called back.

"Just a bit of window shopping," Nora giggled.

The sun beat down on Sophia as she stepped out onto the dusty main road for the first time since her arrival in New Mexico. The small town was bustling with ranchers riding into town for their Saturday shopping, wagons rolling by with children hanging over the backboard in their excitement to be away from the homestead, couples strolling about shopping, and a few young ladies in clusters standing before shop windows, gazing longingly at a new gown or bonnet.

Nora waved to a couple across the street.

"I know it may seem small to your big city, but you should know that the town of Las Vegas is actually a pretty good size as compared to most places in Texas."

"Were you raised in Texas?" Sophia asked as she read the signs for each establishment they passed.

"Born and raised. I didn't live quite so near to town, though, and only made it to town for church on Sundays and an occasional Saturday for visiting the general store." Nora slipped her arm through Sophia's. "Just don't go comparing it to your city, but you should be very impressed that a boardwalk just got put up, so our skirts won't drag the ground. And besides the church and Jones' General Store, we have a second general store, a stable, post office, sheriff's office, lawyer's office, and a bank, everything of which I will show you, but you should never use the boardwalk across from the sheriff's office." She sucked in a breath through her teeth. "That wretched saloon is there, and you do not want to be caught anywhere in that vicinity in case some cowboy stumbles from the building and into you."

The ladies gathered their skirts and darted across the street to the general store before a wagon could stir up dust. Stepping onto the boardwalk, the door to the Sheriff's station on their left swung open and a man about six foot four inches strode out and placed his Stetson over his blond curly hair. When his hazel eyes met Sophia's, he at once whipped off his hat and bowed to them. "Good morning, ladies."

Nora's cheeks turned a pretty pink, her voice turning coquettish. "Why, Sheriff Kane, so lovely to see you. You haven't been by the Harvey House in over a week. I hope you haven't starved for lack of good food?"

"Miss Ray, you are a sight for sore eyes. Unfortunately, I've been pursuing some bandits and they managed to elude me." He sighed, crossing his arms over his broad chest.

"Well, I am certain you've frightened them away from our good town and they won't be returning," Nora fairly purred, releasing her fan with a snap, wafting it slowly and raising the ebony tendrils framing her face. "And to celebrate, you should return to my table at the Harvey House for some good cooking."

"Let's hope they stay far away, so I may do just that." He turned his bright smile to Sophia. "And whom do I have the pleasure in meeting today? A new Harvey Girl, perhaps?"

"This is Miss Bird. She's just joined us at the Harvey House all the way from—well I don't actually know, but it's a big city judging by this young lady's extensive wardrobe."

Sophia delivered a swift elbow to Nora's side.

The sheriff looked expectantly to Sophia to supply the name of her hometown, but at her silence on the matter, he continued, "Well, wherever it is, it must be a little less bright with the absence of their most beautiful star." His deep voice was smooth as he bowed to Sophia and kissed her gloved hand.

Sophia gave the sheriff a small smile. "You are too kind, sir." *Why is everyone sud-*

denly calling me beautiful? Not that she would complain, but after years of being called homely by all but Jane and Belle, she couldn't help but wonder. Out of the corner of her eye, she could see Nora's smile falter, her gaze flitting to Sophia and her stylish walking suit. *I should've worn a different dress . . . maybe I can remove some of the lace to make it plainer.*

"If Miss Ray is showing you our little town, perhaps I can come along as well for an official escort?" Sheriff Kane offered each of the ladies his arm. "It's not much, but we call it home."

Sophia blushed at his forwardness but accepted his left arm. Nora glowed as she hung onto his right as he continued down the boardwalk.

Nora stopped them in front of Jones' General Store. "This is my favorite of the two general stores, Sophia. They import some darling items from the East and even from Europe for their feminine clientele, so you may find some items which remind you of your fancy city stores. Although, I doubt you have need of any of their stock, but you might enjoy perusing the store all the same."

"Sophia. What a lovely name," Sheriff Kane looked down into her eyes. "It suits you."

Sophia ducked her head, breaking the connection. "Thank you."

"You know, Sheriff, I've known you for almost a year now, and for all that time I've spent serving you at the lunch counter, I still don't know your given name." Nora batted her dark eyelashes again.

"That's because I am not fond of my given name as it is a bit too gentrified for my occupation." He chuckled. "But if you must know, it is Marion."

"Marion?" Nora blinked but recovered quickly with a smile. "Quite an elegant name for these parts, I must say. Is it a family name?"

"You see? No one out here can take a sheriff seriously with a fancy first name like that, so you best not tell anyone, or they might think I'm soft. And yes, I am named after my maternal grandfather." Kane opened the store's door, the copper bell ringing overhead.

Sophia released his arm to explore the store, squinting in the dim lighting as the floorboards creaked underfoot while she wandered about. Her gaze fell on a tin of lady's hand cream. Sophia glanced behind her and found Nora still had her arm threaded through the sheriff's and had his attention as she pointed to some ivory fabric. Sophia seized the hand cream off the shelf, sorely tempted to purchase it even if it was bordering on scandalous behavior to do so.

Mother would always send the servants to get it for the girls, saying people would think her daughters loose if they ever bought it themselves, but Sophia's hands felt horribly chapped even inside her softest gloves. *I must suffer through it. Out of my desperation for smooth hands, I shouldn't stoop to buying my own hand cream and damaging my reputation, which is silly because Mother and I both wear hand cream, and we are both perfectly respectable. Come to think of it . . . every other girl I've ever known has used hand cream.* She sighed. *But if society dictates it is improper for a lady to purchase, then I best obey even though it seems absolutely absurd.* She straightened at the thought. It *was* absurd. Why should she suffer because of a silly rule?

Before she could change her mind, she tucked the cream in arm and strolled by the last shelf in the store, stopping at the sight of a pink silk parasol with a carved wooden handle. She lightly touched the ruffled lace edge. *The quality isn't too bad, but this sun will burn my nose off if I don't cover myself.* Without looking at the price, she brought it to the counter and paid the storeowner for the items, the owner wrapping the cream in brown paper.

"Would you like to use your parasol, or should I wrap it, Miss Sophia?" The storeowner handed her the change for her purchase.

She started, surprised that he knew her name, but she supposed most of the townspeople ate at the Harvey House at some point and all would eventually know her name. Sophia slowly shook her head. "I'll use it. Thank you, sir." Her cheeks were tempted to heat that he now knew she bought hand cream, but she refused to feel ashamed. She accepted her items with a nod, feeling a bit dizzy with her small victory.

Nora grasped Sophia's arm. "I can't believe you just paid that price! He overcharged you by two whole dollars. Why, you could have ordered it from the catalogue for far cheaper if you were only willing to wait."

Sophia gritted her teeth at yet another mistake. "I suppose there is supply and demand to factor into the cost."

Kane chuckled. "Listen to you, Miss Bird. With phrases like 'supply and demand' and 'factor into the cost,' one would think you knew a thing or two about business."

"My father and brothers would always discuss business matters in front of my mother and myself," Sophia replied, secretly proud she had the ability to converse about numbers as well as any businessman. *It's only a shame they don't respect me enough to listen to my opinion.*

"But it is obvious that she *doesn't* know that much about good business, or she wouldn't have overpaid for such frivolousness." Nora rolled her eyes as if she were miffed at the attention Kane was showering Sophia. "You should've at least tried to haggle with him on the price a little."

Why does she care what I spend? It's my money. "Maybe I happen to think the investment is worth it as it will keep my skin from burning and peeling like your nose," she mumbled under her breath.

Nora stiffened and, seizing Kane's arm, turned them back in the direction of the Harvey House with Sophia trailing behind, their perfect day spoilt by Sophia's careless retort over a parasol, even if it did offer relief from the ever-oppressive sun.

Leaving the pair of them in the front of the dormitory, Sophia tromped upstairs and tossed the offending parasol on her bed and removed the hatpin from her honey blonde hair as Nora slowly followed her inside, scowling at Sophia.

"Knock. Knock." Dolly Matthews poked her head into their room and immediately squealed. "Why, is that the parasol you have been saving for months to buy, Nora? I can't believe you finally bought it! The sheriff is going to melt when he sees your raven locks under such a dainty parasol."

Sophia's lips parted in surprise as she met Nora's gaze. "You didn't—"

Nora shook her head, pasting on a false smile. "I decided I didn't want it and let Sophia buy it instead. Her complexion is much more in danger of burning than mine."

No wonder she was so upset. This was the prettiest of the parasols.

Dolly's eyes widened. "Really? You've been talking about it for so long." Dolly lifted the parasol from Sophia's bed and opened it, twirling it, and making the lace ruffles dance.

She rested her hand on Nora's arm. "I'm sorry for what I said. I didn't mean—"

"It is forgotten already." Nora gave her a quick embrace, and Sophia knew she had a true friend in her.

"You must let me borrow it when I go out with my beau on my next day off," Dolly continued her promenade about the room, admiring the craftsmanship.

Sophia smiled to Dolly. "Of course. The only days that I will ever be needing it is on my one day off and Sunday morning."

Dolly squealed and pulled Sophia into a swift embrace. "Thank you, dear. I will bring it back without a mark. My beau is going to be knocked off his feet. I might even get another marriage proposal under my bonnet."

CHAPTER 11

"Let me close with this Word of encouragement from Isaiah sixty-one, verse one. 'The spirit of the Lord God is upon me,'" the preacher cried out, nearly making Sophia jump in the hardback pew as he captured her full attention with his commanding voice. "'He hath sent me to bind up the brokenhearted, to proclaim liberty to the captives, and the opening of the prison to them that are bound.' Some of you are in a prison that was forged of something strong. Sin. Maybe it is made of addiction? Or lust?"

He peered down into the congregation and while Sophia couldn't say for certain, she felt as if he was looking straight at her . . . as if he knew she was so exhausted from her shift that she could hardly keep her eyes open.

"Or perhaps it is a cage of *fear,* but listen to the Word of the Lord. You are not without hope. He has the key, and He is willing to set you free. All you need to do is trust in Jesus as your Lord and Savior, and He will release you from your prison. Trust in Him, and you will be free. Let us pray." He bowed his head and lifted his hands heavenward.

The preacher's ending words and prayer brought forth Carver's words from that night that seemed so long ago. *Lord, have I put myself in this cage of fear? I had thought it was society that placed me in that prison, but they don't have power over my mind unless I allow them.*

Sophia descended the chapel's steps with the rest of the congregation, feeling renewed as she looked out over the field of wildflowers before the pretty pale blue church. *Lord, thank You for revealing this to me today. Remove this fear from my heart and allow me to live in the freedom You have given me. The freedom of a life in Christ Jesus.* The hot breeze caressed her cheek, reminding her to open her infamous parasol and shield her nose from the sun.

"Sophia, you coming for lunch?" Jenny grasped Sophia by the elbow, steering her to the edge of the crowd. "Pierre has made a new dessert he wants to test on us before attempting to add it to the specialty list, and I know that if anyone has a refined palate, it's you."

"Oh! That sounds splendid." She glanced toward the grove of scrawny trees behind the church. "But it's been almost five weeks since I've left Charleston—"

Nora slipped beside them, grinning. "Finally! After all this time, you've finally let it slip where you are from. Good work, Jenny! I suppose I owe you a dollar."

Sophia lifted her brow in question. "A dollar?"

"We had a wager going as to who would get you to slip first." Jenny laughed, glancing behind her at the preacher standing at the church porch bidding his congregants farewell. "But we best not proclaim such a thing after Sunday service."

Suppressing her laughter, Sophia shook her head. "I'll be a little late to luncheon. I just need to be under the trees, so I am going to give those cedars a chance to impress me with their unique beauty. I also heard from the girls that there's a small river nearby, so I may be about twenty minutes before I join you."

"Don't be too long, or I will get worried about you. Watch out for snakes and remember, the next train should be here in under two hours, so be sure you only stay away for thirty minutes as you need time to eat, change, and prepare any little details for your table."

"I will!" Sophia waved to her friends and glided away from the churchgoers and into the shade of the cedar trees. She drank in the fresh air, absent of the stench of horse manure and sweat, and in the serene shade, she lost track of time as she walked in the direction of the river.

She lifted her face heavenward. "Lord, in only a matter of five weeks, this is the second time that Isaiah sixty-one has been brought to my attention. I feel You're trying to teach me something about Carver. Now that I have recognized I have allowed my fear to govern me, are You telling me it is right to allow myself to love and be loved by Carver, despite how we met?"

A twig snapped behind her and whirling about, her heart caught in her throat at the sight of the lewd giant from the luncheon counter, Mr. Gessler.

"I thought I saw you slip away after the service." He grinned at her, his eyes roving over her body as he stroked his graying beard.

She sneered at him, offering no Harvey Girl welcome. "Do you even attend Church?"

"On holidays." He shrugged, strolling toward her, swiping his hat off as if that would put her at ease. "I saw you from the saloon window. Nothing prettier than findin' a young lady in the woods praying to the Lord."

"I must be on my way. The ladies are expecting me for Sunday lunch." She refrained from worrying her bottom lip as she marched around him, giving him wide berth as she tried to pass.

"Hold on there, little lady. I didn't follow you all the way out here for you to turn around and leave." Mr. Gessler grunted, closing the gap between them even as he kept one hand in his pocket and the other clutching his worn hat. "You don't think I caught your hints at the lunch counter for the past three days?"

Sophia stared at him blankly. "That is a load of nonsense. I served you like I serve everyone else." *And if anything, Fannie and I were quite firm with you.*

"Yeah, but you didn't get everyone else a free apple pie for dessert like you did me on that second day." He grinned, revealing his all too familiar yellow and brown-splotched teeth.

"That is because I didn't spill hot coffee on anyone else," Sophia retorted as she closed her parasol and gripped it like a sword.

"Exactly. I was the *only* one, making me special."

Is he serious? She would have laughed if she wasn't so anxious to be away from him. "I really must be going."

He snatched her right wrist. "And I said I wanted to talk with you."

"Let me go!" Sophia slapped him across the face with her left hand, raking her nails into his cheek.

Mr. Gessler grunted in pain but held her fast, laughing as he pulled her toward him. "I like my women to have a bit of fight in them. Makes sparkin' and courtin' a little more fun."

"How dare you?" Sophia stomped down on his shin with her ice pick heeled boot. Mr. Gessler cussed and loosened his grip for a second, which was just enough time for Sophia to jerk her wrist away and ram him in the stomach with her parasol's wooden handle. Hiking up her skirts, she bolted through the grove, weaving around brush and fallen limbs.

"You honestly think you can get away from me?" He cackled after her, his boots crunching the parched grass and cedar twigs as he ran. "Ain't no use, little lady!"

God, help me! You are my protector, and I will not fear. She prayed as she leapt over a fallen tree. A branch snagged her skirt, ripping the delicate lace, and she tumbled headlong into the arms of Sheriff Kane. "Kane!" She cried out, her chest heaving.

The sheriff tucked her behind him, drew his gun, and shot at Mr. Gessler' feet. "Move one step closer and you're a dead man," Kane fairly growled.

Mr. Gessler raised his hands above his head. "Aw, come on, Sheriff. We was just havin' us a little fun playin' tag."

Without a moment's hesitation, Kane strode forward and brought the butt of his revolver down across Mr. Gessler' head, knocking him out. Kane squatted down and withdrew two lengths of rope from his belt, wrapping it about Mr. Gessler's hands and feet, and secured him with his back to a cedar.

Kane jogged back to her, took her hands, and flipped them over to inspect them for scratches. "Did he hurt you?"

Sophia pulled out of his grasp, her decorum returning. "Apart from a slightly bruised wrist, I am well," she assured him, but seeing his eyes rest on her trembling hands, she tucked them behind her. "I am well," she repeated, moving to retrieve her parasol, and stumbled over her skirts.

"You are far from well, Sophia." He scooped her up in his muscular arms. "I'll take you back."

"Please, I don't want to make a scene," Sophia's voice grew tight as she felt the raw power in his arms, remembering how it felt to be in Carver's arms months ago when she had slipped while skating and then again in the Ashley River. A dull ache filled her as she pressed her hands against his navy plaid shirt, pushing herself away from him. "Please, set me down. I can walk just fine on my own."

"At least let me carry you to the edge of the grove. You are worn out and I need to get you back and I don't want to risk you fainting." Kane's arms tightened about her.

Sophia shook her head. "If you allow me to lean on your arm, I am certain I can manage fine on my own."

His face expressed his concern, but he

honored her request and gently set her on the ground, leaving his arm securely wrapped around her petite waist. "I didn't realize how delicate you were until you were in my arms."

Sophia tucked a stray curl behind her ear and re-pinned her hat before noticing the smear of dirt marring her lovely parasol, inwardly moaning. "I may seem to be on the delicate side, but I can assure you, Sheriff Kane, I can manage to walk home." She cleared her throat. "But I'm quite glad you appeared when you did. What in the world brought you out this far away from town?"

He grasped her hand and guided her around a fallen branch. "I asked Miss Ray if you had attended service because I didn't see you afterwards, and she said you had gone for a walk . . . which is not a good idea to do alone in these parts."

"So, you came after me?" Her cheeks heated for having wandered too far away from the path and needing to be rescued.

"And I am glad I did." He held out his elbow to her at the churchyard. "May I see you home?"

Thinking of Nora's reaction to the parasol, she had no desire to repeat the quarrel over the man of Nora's affections. "I'll be fine on my own. Thank you again."

He lifted his Stetson to her. "Any time, Miss Bird."

Checking her watch pin, her heart faltered that she had not only missed luncheon, but she had precious little time to change for the train. In a flurry of petticoats, Sophia dashed to her room and changed, tying her apron strings as she hurried into the Castañeda, her heels clicking against the red and white tiles.

"Heard you had a nice walk with Sheriff Kane." Dolly stood at her station with her arms crossed, and before Sophia could explain what happened, she continued. "He has been flirting with me for the past six months and has been courting me off and on, so I would suggest that you would be respectful of his attentions to me and not throw yourself at him, like Nora."

"Excuse me?" Sophia asked. "I am certainly *not* throwing myself at him. I was merely walking by myself when he joined me. I never once sought him out."

"It's all over town how you come from money, so now he's just interested in you for your wealth." Dolly unfurled the linen over the table, smoothing it out with such vigor that she could wear a hole in it. "If you have *any* self-respect you will drop his suit."

"What do you mean all over town?" *Surely, Nora hasn't been telling tales?* "I have done nothing—"

"Oh, come off it," Dolly thumped down each piece of silverware. "You are flaunting your wealth to everyone with your fine dresses bedecked with lace and well, everything." Dolly examined the tablecloth and rubbed out any wrinkle, real or imaginary. "You lost any pretense of attempting to hide your wealth when you bought that parasol Nora has been wanting for over three months now. She has told every single one of the girls how much she has been saving and how eager she is to get that parasol and you up and buy it the minute you have a day off."

"We resolved that issue at once. Obviously, I didn't know! Otherwise, I would have never bought the fool thing," Sophia retorted, her pulse teeming. "Besides, you were quick enough at asking to borrow it."

Dolly lifted her nose at that remark. "You are her roommate, so how could you *not* know?" She fired back. "You aren't the only girl with money. Kane just thinks you have more, but you are probably a girl whose family has fallen from wealth, which is why you must work for a living. Once the fashions change, the secret will be out because you probably can't afford to keep up appearances like I can." Dolly scowled as she inspected the glasses for any spots.

"If you're so wealthy, why don't you quit your job, play the lady, and lure Sheriff Kane with your own money?" Sophia scraped a chair into alignment.

"Because I enjoy earning my own keep. I am dependent on no one, and I can decide my future for myself," Dolly snapped as she put the finishing touches on the table. "I'm not here out of necessity, but rather out of choice, and that is why I am next in line to be head Harvey Girl because

I have the *passion* it takes to make this place run and not the desperation of a girl who has nowhere else to go and is only here because she is out of options." She glared at Sophia. "I don't have time for all this nonsense. Just mind you stay away from the sheriff. I'm not like Nora. I won't let you have *my* 'parasol' without a fight. The sheriff is mine." She stood back and took in the tables. "Jenny, Sophia is to serve tables with you from now on. You are both to help Fannie fill her drink orders. Oh, and I've decided to split your shift."

"And what gives you such authority?" Jenny interjected.

Dolly raised a single brow. "When Harriet is off, I am on call and in charge." She turned on her heel, calling over her shoulder, "Sophia, you will work until six o'clock and then take a break. Tonight, you are needed at the lunch counter from eleven o'clock to five o'clock in the morning. Now, get to work and pull your weight or I will recommend to have you fired faster than you can blink if you don't quit on your own before then. The night shift can be a bit challenging."

Sophia's nails dug into her palms at Dolly's outburst, jumping at Jenny's touch on her shoulder.

"Didn't you hear the gong? The train has arrived."

Sophia scurried over to her tables and stood with her hands delicately folded in front of her, determined to put the ugly business with Mr. Gessler out of her mind. She greeted the guests as Harriet had instructed her to do as each one took their seat and began to claim their orders of soup or salad. *A Harvey Girl is to always look friendly and fresh and never flustered and flushed,* she recited in her head as she continued to smile and take orders from each guest. *Who cares what Dolly thinks is going on with Sheriff Kane and me? I have never encouraged the man and do not intend on doing so.*

Sophia smiled as she asked a guest at her table, "Coffee or tea, ma'am?"

"My dear, I would love some tea," the elderly lady sighed. "Finally, a place that is civilized enough to offer a beverage besides water or whiskey!"

Sophia flipped the china cup upside down in the saucer. "We aim to please at the Harvey House, ma'am." She moved down the table for the rest of the orders as Jenny followed behind her with a pot of tea and coffee in each hand.

When Sophia reached the other end of the table, she realized that Jenny was no longer behind her, so she hurried over to the counter and grasped a coffee pot and tea pot and began to fill her tables' orders as well as the orders at Jenny's table. She leaned over the left shoulder of the last guest at the table to pour coffee when someone from behind bumped her elbow. The pot slipped in her grip and the spout poured directly onto the man's lap.

"What the—" He scrambled back, knocking the wooden chair over in his haste to rise.

Sophia gasped, mortified. "I am so very sorry, sir!" She dabbed his shirt with her apron. *Even his shirt is burning hot! Oh, I hope I didn't hurt him.*

"Sophia?" He breathed, his voice sending his chest under her hand vibrating.

She jerked back, gasping as she found his dear face. "Carver?"

"Sophia, I can't believe I actually found you!" He took in her appearance, his grin spreading. "Never would I have guessed you decided to become a Harvey Girl. You look lovely in black and white."

She smoothed out her coffee drenched apron, her cheeks flushing at her appearance and at being found out by the man she loved. "What are you doing here?"

"Searching for you, but I was only following the trail you left behind and never thought I'd actually find you this quickly," Carver explained, his face betraying his shock in seeing her and his concern for her wellbeing. "I feel like my chest may explode. Are you well? After I discovered your disappearance and received your letter in New Orleans, I've been searching New Mexico. I only got this far because of the postmark."

She ached for him to confess his love for her—to be wrapped in his arms, but she glanced about and found every eye in the hall on them. Now was certainly not the time for such declarations.

Dolly bustled out from the kitchen, followed by Fannie. "Miss Sophia, what has happened here?" she whispered as she reached the table, grasping Sophia by her arm and drawing her to her side. "Sir, I am so sorry about all of this. Normally Miss Sophia is supervised, but I thought she could handle herself. Apparently, she cannot. The meal will, of course, be on the house, and we'll give you a few future dinner tickets for your trouble."

"Miss Bird." Miss Trent joined them with her hands folded so tightly that her knuckles were turning white. Keeping her smile plastered on her face to disguise her ire, she hissed, "Your apron is unsightly. Go change immediately and finish your tête-à-tête with this gentleman *after* you have seen to the rest of our guests and finish serving dinner."

"Of course, Miss Trent," Sophia curtsied, her gaze darting hungrily back to Carver.

He gave her a small bow, his eyes locking on hers. "Miss *Bird*, I look forward to finishing our conversation and catching up on a few things."

Sophia could hardly contain her smile, her cheeks warming under his gaze. "Indeed, Mr. Ashton. Please excuse me while I make myself presentable." She wove through the guests and dashed across the street to her room. Closing her bedroom door, she leaned against it with an elated, yet heavy, sigh. *God, please don't let it be too late for us. Please don't let me have ruined my chances with Carver because of my fear.*

CHAPTER 12

"Please, have a seat, Mr. Ashton." Sophia sounded stiff as a Miss Trent showed them into a private parlor downstairs where she said the girls were allowed to receive gentlemen company.

He glanced at Sophia and assumed the seat beside her. Did she consider him gentleman company, or a nuisance? But memory of their last moments together and the letter in his pocket said otherwise.

"I'll send one of the girls with some tea and scones." Miss Trent strode through the doorway, leaving the door ajar, adding with a smile, "I'll be in the dining area if you need me. Miss Bird, you may have two hours, but

I expect you to be back at your station at the end of that period until morning. You have a long shift ahead of you."

"Thank you, Miss Trent." Sophia ran her fingers over the arm of the settee as the housemother departed, the creak of the hallway floorboards confirming her return to the dining room.

Carver cleared his throat and tried to keep his heart from hammering out of his chest. He had actually found her. Her cheeks were fuller and had more color now, brightening her blue eyes and nearly chasing away the dark circles under her eyes. He had considered her a beauty before, but this newfound confidence he spied in Sophia made her all the more irresistible. "I like the way you are wearing your hair now with the bangs braided back and curls framing your face. It's quite becoming."

She lifted her fingers to her curls. "I've never liked wearing a fringe and well, I knew you liked it brushed back."

"I do." *Lord, give me the words.* "We were all very worried about you."

Sophia nodded slowly. "I imagined my family would be."

Just your family? "How could you do that to them? To me?" He rested his elbows on his thighs and grasped her hands in his, looking up at her. "I thought we were . . . good enough friends that you would confide in me."

"How could I? I was leaving your stepfather practically at the altar. It would have been highly inappropriate. And besides, given our last conversation, why would you worry about me? You always said that I could take care of myself, and I believed you." She motioned to her gown. "The work is hard, but it's good to work hard and earn my own way."

"I know you can take care of yourself, but how could you think that I wouldn't be anxious when I found out that you ran away? I've been searching for you since you left." Carver encompassed her petite hand in his.

Her lips parted in surprise. "You have?"

"Your friendship means so much to me." Sorrow etched her face, his stomach twisting. He was doing this all wrong. *Why am I still speaking of friendship?*

"You know I never intended to hurt you. I only had to get away, and the answer for my escape wasn't clear until—" She pressed her lips firmly together.

He well knew the moment she spoke of and he had regretted it every day since. "I sometimes have a difficult time explaining myself when it comes to matters of the heart." Carver ran a hand over the back of his neck. "If only you would've allowed me to help you voice your concerns to my stepfather and your father, maybe you wouldn't be in hiding from him or your family."

At her silence, he glanced about the charming, but plain, parlor in comparison to her parlor at home. Its braided rug added some much-needed color against the stark hardwood floors, white walls and plain furnishings, but the mantel was softened by a lace runner with a porcelain figurine and a vase of wildflowers atop it. "You have found quite a haven for yourself in Las Vegas. I only wish you didn't feel forced to run away, not when I could have spared you from the ordeal by speaking sooner."

"At the time, I thought I was running away from Prescott, but now I realize I was running away from my fear. It was more than a marriage to Prescott. I was afraid of being trapped in something I never wanted. My entire life, I have never been allowed to make any decisions for myself except for what I would like to wear each day, but even then, I was subjected to sweet Mother's opinions about how I dressed my hair."

She tucked a loose strand of silky golden hair back behind her ear and sighed. "I was always afraid of doing or saying something my father would dislike or society would deem improper, so I followed the rules and kept *mostly* quiet, but in my heart, I knew I didn't want my husband to be picked out for me like everything else in my life. I was afraid of being tied down to a stranger and afraid of being tucked away on a shelf as a trophy, only to be admired on special occasions and never sought after for input. I was afraid I would never be able to choose anything for myself."

He leaned toward her, their foreheads nearly touching, her sweet gardenia perfume drawing him. "And are you still afraid?"

"Out here, I didn't have anyone but my Harvey sisters and Christ to rely on, and because He is my protector, I'm not afraid, or alone." She laughed. "Can you believe it? I'm not afraid even out here in the Wild West because at last I know I am under the protection of the Lord. I know Jesus loves me for me and not because of who my family is, or how much money I can bring to a marriage."

Carver traced her wrist with his finger, admiring her newfound certainty. "I have always seen your confidence, Sophia. Even if everyone else tells you that you're weak, you're the strongest woman I know."

Sophia's throat caught as she bit her lip, blinking as if to keep tears at bay. "Working here, I have found I am much stronger than I thought."

"So, you like the working life?" He turned over her hands, and at the sight of newly formed callouses, he ran his thumb over them, pride filling his being. "You seem happy."

Sophia smiled and did not pull her hand from his. "I am quite content."

"I'm glad to hear that, but I know the amount you're paid for the extent of work you do must shock you?" He grinned, remembering his first days on the job as a lad, earning what the others did for the summer after his mother married his stepfather. Prescott was hard, but everything he did, he did with a purpose in mind.

Sophia laughed. "Yes! It's appalling how much money I used to spend. What I make here in a month, I would spend in a day at home." She shook her head, sighing. "Some of the girls come from families who depend on their pay. My family has so much . . . I don't know why my father would risk my marriage, my life, for the sake of gaining an extra million or two each year. It makes me even more confident in my decision of calling off the wedding." She met Carver's eyes. "There are girls here whose fathers would do anything to make them happy. Their fathers would sacrifice *anything* for their daughters, but my father didn't even take the time to listen to my concerns, and it makes me wonder if he really even loves me."

Carver squeezed her hand. "You are his daughter, but even though his idea of what makes you happy and your idea of what makes you happy do not match, please don't ever think that you aren't loved by your parents."

Her eyes welled. "Oh, Carver. It's so good to see you again."

His gaze rested on her lips, remembering their softness. "I've missed you with every breath." He leaned toward her and paused a breath away from her lips, silently begging her to kiss him. "Did you miss me?"

"Knock, knock," A woman in a pale green gown called from the doorway with a tea tray in hand.

Sophia jerked away from him and folded her hands in her lap, clearing her throat. "Mr. Ashton, this is Miss Harriet Lane, the head Harvey Girl, who is supposed to be enjoying her evening off."

Carver rose and bowed. "It is a pleasure."

"The pleasure is mine, Mr. Ashton." Miss Lane smiled at the two of them, setting the tea tray on the small side table by Sophia. "I just returned, and when I heard you had a caller, I didn't wish to miss the chance to meet him."

"So, you supervise Miss Bird?" Carver's eyes twinkled with mirth. "Was she quite clumsy at first?"

"Let's just say that spilling coffee in a customer's lap is the least of her transgressions."

Sophia blushed but laughed at herself as she poured two cups of tea. "It's true."

Carver chuckled. "But I am certain that she is quite proficient now."

"Under my training, she has taken to her role as a Harvey Girl quite well." She looked back and forth between Carver and Sophia. "Well, I'll let you two be, but let me know if you need anything. Miss Trent has me posted in the chair just outside the door. We'll be seeing you at the dance, yes?"

"Dance?" Carver turned to Sophia.

"The Harvey House is hosting a dance tomorrow evening to raise money for the church. The tickets are only twenty-five cents," Miss Lane interjected, "but, of course, you will have a ticket free of charge because of the mishap earlier."

"I would love to attend." He caught Sophia's gaze. "If that is agreeable?"

"I was going to ask you if you'd like to go," Sophia replied as she smoothed her austere black skirt.

Carver nodded to Miss Lane. "Then consider me in attendance. I wouldn't dream of missing a Harvey House dance when my favorite lady is in attendance."

Miss Lane smiled her approval. "I wish I could stay and get better acquainted, but I know Sophia wishes to catch up and I have a new novel I am wishing to read."

At Miss Lane's departure, Sophia handed a steaming cup for Carver, their fingers brushing and sending a charge through his arm. He cleared his throat. "I know that last we spoke, I confessed my reservations, but I didn't explain my intentions as clearly as I would have liked."

At the slamming of the front door, Sophia nearly leapt from the settee, Carver slowly following suit, gritting his teeth at yet another interruption.

Sophia flung open the door. "What's going on?"

A Harvey Girl stood in the hallway, flushed and breathing hard. "Forgive me for interrupting." She nodded to the three of them. "But there are at least twenty more passengers in the dining room than we were anticipating for this train, and we are quite understaffed. We need Miss Harriet and Miss Sophia at their stations at once."

"I'll be down as soon as I change." Miss Lane hurried into a room down the hall as the two ladies stepped outside.

Not certain of what else he could do, he followed Sophia outside and onto the boardwalk, disappointment weighing his chest that he had not been able to speak his heart.

Sophia patted her hairbow, checking it

was in place as they crossed the courtyard, pausing under the live oak in the center. "Are you staying in the Castañeda? I can show you to the front desk."

"Please. It would give me the excuse to be by your side for a few moments more. Can you send someone to tell me when your shift is over? How late will you be working?"

"Until five o'clock in the morning." She sighed.

He shook his head in disbelief. "I thought Miss Trent might be exaggerating. I can't believe you have to serve all hours of the night."

Sophia shrugged. "Usually, night shifts are scheduled all week for two girls before the next rotation, but my night shift is just for this one evening as I am needed to cover one girl's shift, but I won't have to start working again until lunchtime tomorrow, so I can rest somewhat."

He halted at the front door of the hotel. "I suppose this is where I will leave you."

"It was wonderful seeing you today,"

Sophia tilted her head back to gaze into his eyes. "I wish I could visit more, but . . ."

"I understand. You're a workingwoman now," Carver finished as the doorman reached for the doorknob and they stepped into the bustling lobby. "I'll head up to my room, but I'll enjoy seeing you at the dance tomorrow evening. Perhaps, you can spare an hour before your shift tomorrow?"

"Miss Bird! What a pleasure to see you in the lobby." A man in a plaid shirt and worn leather vest with a sheriff's badge displayed on his chest scraped back his chair as he stood from a small round table lining the lobby to greet her. His eyes fell on Carver, running over him, measuring him. "Howdy. I'm Sheriff Kane."

Carver nodded his greeting, trying out the word. "Howdy."

"Sheriff Kane, I'd like you to meet Carver Ashton."

Kane's eyes lit up at the sound of his last name. "Ashton, huh? Any relation to Prescott Payne? He married an Ashton."

Carver felt Sophia stiffen beside him. If he

was a friend of Prescott's, he could wire Prescott and all would be lost. "Prescott Payne is my stepfather. Are you a friend of his?"

"I don't know about friend. But he's my mother's brother."

Carver's jaw dropped before he snapped it shut. "Well, I'll be . . . not a day goes by that my stepfather doesn't surprise me. Nice to meet you, Sheriff."

At the sound of the dinner gong, Sophia quietly excused herself and darted away to her station as Kane sank into his chair.

Kane motioned to the walnut spindle back chair across from him. "I don't know which is more astonishing, that an Ashton is in Las Vegas, or that you've had the pleasure of making Miss Bird's acquaintance in Charleston. How do you two know each other?"

"My stepfather and hers are business partners."

"So, of course, your families know each other well." He laughed. "Maybe if things had been different, I would have been the one to court the lovely Miss Bird."

Carver's gaze followed Kane's to the

lovely form of Sophia already at work in the dining room. "So, um, Sheriff Kane, how did your mother come to move so far from Charleston?" *And why is it that I have never heard of you?*

Kane shrugged. "She was cast out. My ma was only seventeen when she first met my father. He told me the instant his eyes fell onto her red curls and green eyes, he fell deeply, madly in love with her and after a fair amount of wooing, he bedded her." His eyes once more found Sophia's figure, the hunger in his expression making Carver wish to deck him.

Carver clutched his fist under the table and slowly released it. "As she was cast out, I'm guessing someone discovered their indiscretion?"

"Her father did not approve of his only daughter, Cordelia, wanting to wed a poor store clerk, but when Mr. Payne discovered he had ruined her, he tossed her out of the house without a penny to her name. But my pa was never interested in her money. Pa married her that day and took his bride West where no one knew them. Here, in Las

Vegas, he was just a man, and she was just his beautiful wife to be respected, and they made a good life together despite their beginning."

"So, Cordelia inherited nothing?"

"Her father gave the entirety of the fortune to Prescott." Kane released a bitter laugh. "What did your stepfather invest my mother's half in? Entrapping a rich wife?"

"Or two." Carver's jaw clenched at the admission. "Yes, my mother had wealth, but it was her kindness, gentleness of spirit, and beauty that captured my stepfather's attention and heart."

Carver resisted the urge to press his cousin into a promise not to contact Prescott after their chance meeting, but perhaps his embittered state against his family would keep him far from the telegraph's office, giving Carver enough time to convince Sophia of his affections.

"Better watch them sentiments. Out here, a man could be run out of town for being such a weakling."

Seeing no need to defend his character to a stranger, Carver reached into his vest pocket for his pocket watch. "I best be making my way upstairs. It's been a long day. Sheriff Kane, I wish you a pleasant evening."

"And you as well, *cousin*." He nodded, his gaze returning to Sophia as he took a long draft of his coffee.

CHAPTER 13

The counter slowed down around one in the morning, so to keep busy, Jenny and Sophia began scrubbing the counters, shelves, and floor.

"So, this young man that you spilt coffee on . . . who is he? The girls were quite curious as to how you two met." Jenny's eyes sparkled mischievously at Sophia as she returned stacks of glasses to the freshly dusted shelf.

Sophia felt the heat creep into her cheeks, but she continued vigorously scrubbing the counter even as she angled away from Jenny. "We met because he is the son of my former fiancé, but his stepfather and I are no longer engaged."

Jenny gasped and fumbled with her armful of glasses. "What? He was to be your *stepson*? Out of all the things you could have said, *that* I never would have imagined."

Sophia grimaced and dipped her rag back into the suds-filled bucket and set to work on a stubborn spot of hardened syrup under the lip of the counter. "I know. It is not exactly the ideal way to meet, but my engagement was arranged by my father. I tried for months to find an honorable means of refusing my father's request, but in the end, I couldn't, and I ran."

"You seemed to be pretty close to the son, though." Jenny placed the last glass on the shelf and began to remove the coffee cups from underneath the counter to wipe the shelf. "Dare I ask how that occurred?"

"He looked out for me while his stepfather was on an extended business trip, and we became close."

"So, you do like him. Perhaps even love him?" Jenny smiled playfully.

Sophia shrugged and tossed the rag in the dirty bin, wiping her hands on a clean rag. She reached for the mountain of freshly ironed napkins and set to folding. "He's nice."

"Nice? He's the most handsome man I've ever seen!" Jenny giggled. "If you don't want him, please let me know and I'll gladly attempt to win his heart. You'd put in a good word for me, wouldn't you?"

Sophia rolled her eyes, smiling, but even though she knew Jenny was jesting, she couldn't help the twist in her gut at the thought of Carver with another.

Jenny yawned. "I am never going to make it until morning." She slumped against the counter. "Need . . . sleep."

"I suppose that it's the excitement of my first night shift, but I feel quite awake."

"At least that makes one of us." Jenny rubbed her eyes with her fist. "I don't know how I'm going to manage. Maybe I should have some more of that fresh coffee the night chef just brewed?"

"I think I can handle the crowd," Sophia laughed, nodding to the empty lunch counter, "if you want to slip into the staff dining room and rest."

"Fifteen minutes? That's all I need to feel alive again." She paused with her hand on the kitchen door, strangling another yawn. "But only if you are sure?"

Sophia shooed her through the door. "In the unlikely event that it starts raining guests, I'll fetch you."

Jenny gave Sophia's hand a squeeze. "Bless you," she whispered, swinging open the kitchen door, most likely tiptoeing past the sleeping night shift chef, Harold.

With Jenny gone, the stillness of the night enveloped Sophia. She folded and folded, thinking all the while of Carver, wishing she could assure him of her feelings. *I need to wait and see if he still has feelings for me, or if his feelings have changed at all in the weeks since we've seen each other . . . I know it hasn't even been two months, but he must've thought that I'd run away for good. Beatrice was probably thrilled to have the Payne and Ashton men back on the market. How she would laugh if she could see me now.* Sophia arched her aching back. She didn't have to imagine very hard everything that Beatrice would have to say about this to her friends.

The front door banged, and Sophia jumped, dropping her partially folded napkin onto the floor. She grunted as she picked it up, hesitating only a second before tossing it into the dirty bin. *Fred Harvey would have a cow if we ever used a napkin that fell on the floor.* She straightened and relief flooded her at the sight of the customer.

"Miss Bird? What a pleasant surprise to find you working the night shift." Sheriff Kane grinned and swiped off his Stetson, his spurs jingling with every thud of his boots on the tiles as he meandered to the counter, setting his hat on the stool beside him.

"What can I get for you, Sheriff?" She returned his smile. Having the friendly sheriff at her counter would help the time pass.

"I'd love a cup of your strong coffee. It has been a long night." Sheriff Kane sank atop the stool and sighed, rubbing his face in both hands, and giving his cheeks a little slap. "I need to wake up."

"I'll get that right away." She whisked into the kitchen and fetched the pot of coffee on the stove, vigilant to move as silently as possible around Harold as he had a reputation of being extremely irritable when he was awakened for any reason other than cooking. "Here you are, Sheriff." She removed a china cup and saucer from under the counter and poured the steaming liquid. "Whatever are you doing out so late?"

"I saw a couple of suspicious strangers get off the last train and head straight to the saloon. I wanted to be sure they weren't here to rob the town blind while I slept. They've been gambling and are now being entertained by the—well, they are being looked after." He lifted the cup, gulping the piping hot coffee.

Sophia's eyes widened at his action, even as his words brought forth a blush. "Won't you burn your throat?"

He drew another mouthful of coffee, finishing off the cup. "Nah, I've been drinking it this way since I was a kid. Ain't nothing that's too hot for me to eat." His large hand enveloped the coffee cup as he raised it for Sophia to pour him a second. "So, I found out from Nora that you love poetry. What's it about young men writing frilling little nothings on a page that gets you so enthralled?"

Sophia refilled his cup. "Nora told you I was 'enthralled?'"

He chuckled, taking the time to stir in a spoonful of sugar. "She mentioned you and Miss Jenny have started a book group between the two of you and spend your time off discussing poetry up and down until you are blue in the face. She thinks y'all are a mite strange, and I have to say that it doesn't make much sense to me either to be spending what precious time you have off in a book instead of enjoying the great outdoors." He lifted his hand to stave off a retort, adding, "It's not that I don't respect your enjoyment of reading that stuff, because I do. I just don't understand you women's obsession with their frilly writings."

She returned to folding the linens. "To begin, I could argue that Tennyson's and Keats's work are anything but nothings for there's always something more to find every time I read it. There are meanings within meanings and lines between the lines. Their poetry is so much deeper than it lets on and it's the joy of interpreting that Jenny and I enjoy—some are letters of love and others despair. It's quite beautiful, really, how these men express their love and dreams on the page."

"Well, there's something about a man who writes his feelings and quite another about a man who has the courage enough to look a beautiful woman in the eye and tell her how he feels." He slowly set down his coffee cup and met her startled gaze.

She fumbled with her napkins, her heart flipping nervously.

He fiddled with the rim of his cup as he continued staring into her eyes. "Sophia, I know we haven't known each other too long, but I was hoping—"

"Thank you so much for letting me rest a moment," Jenny called as she shuffled through the door, stretching. She froze in the middle of her stretch as she realized they had a customer. Dropping her arms, she smiled her greeting to Kane. "Nice to see you, Sheriff."

"And you as well, Miss Jenny." He smiled to the ladies. "Well, I guess I better get back out there. No one else is going to apprehend anyone but me." He tugged on his Stetson and leaned down to Sophia, his scent of woodsmoke and sweet tobacco filling her senses. "Do me a favor?"

"What is it?" Sophia took a step back, still a little flustered at his comment.

"Watch out for Gessler. Since nothing happened that day in the woods, I couldn't detain him, but I told him if he comes within fifty yards of you, I'll see he regrets it. If he does bother you, let me know immediately."

"I will," she nodded firmly. "Thank you."

"Your company over this fine cup of coffee is thanks enough." He pulled out a few coins from his pocket and set them on the counter. With a lift of his hat, he disappeared into the night.

Jenny scowled. "Mr. Carson will throw Mr. Gessler from the house if he tries to step foot in here after his behavior toward you. Don't you worry about that. Now, what is next on our list of cleaning?"

After the sheriff's visit, one or two linemen arrived for an early breakfast before their shift and when dawn's light burst through windows facing the valley of wildflowers that melted into the foothills, Sophia paused in her cleaning to bask in the beauty of the new day.

"Good morning." Nora tied on her apron, her face still swollen from sleep and the early hour, followed by three other girls. "Anything exciting happen on your first night shift, Sophia?"

Covering an enormous yawn, Sophia shook her head as Nora came behind the counter, pouring herself a cup of freshly brewed coffee. "After midnight, it was so quiet. It made me almost long for the hurriedness of the day in the silence and monotony of the night. The only interesting thing that happened was Sheriff Kane stopped by while he was taking a patrol of the area."

"A patrol?" Nora's voice squeaked, sloshing coffee into her saucer and, with a hiss, dropped the cup on the counter, flicking her hand to rid it of the burn of coffee. "What did you two discuss? I know we aren't really supposed to engage in conversation with the customer during the day, or even very much at night either, but obviously he came in to talk with you, right?"

Nora's cheeks appeared unnaturally flushed, but as she held the sheriff in great affection, Sophia dismissed it and reached for the rag to wipe up the cup and saucer, sliding the coffee toward Nora before wiping down the counter. "I think he only wished for a cup of coffee." *Well, at least it started that way.* She bit her lip. "He only stayed for about fifteen minutes."

"For *one* cup of coffee?" Nora crossed her arms, unconvinced. "He gulps his coffee in under a minute."

Sophia smiled. "Yes, yes he does. He downed four cups in the matter of ten minutes. He was slapping his cheeks to stay alert, so it must have been important."

"Mmhmm," Nora murmured, off in her own thoughts. "I'll bet it was important. He didn't say anything else? Anything about me?"

"No, I'm sorry. He seemed a little preoccupied with the men in the saloon." Sophia freed herself from her apron. "I'm going to grab a bite from the kitchen and sleep until lunch."

Nora nodded to Dolly who joined them and went straight for the coffee as well. "You do that, and if the Sheriff stops by asking for you, should I be surprised?"

Too tired to retort, Sophia grabbed a blueberry muffin from the kitchen and trudged across the street, falling into her bed without even bothering taking off her shoes, her half-eaten muffin tumbling from her nightstand onto the braided rug.

CHAPTER 14

"And there'll be a picnic outside the church and all manner of games to celebrate!" Fannie pinned on her chapeau, twirling in the mottled looking glass, Sophia's parasol in hand. "I can hardly believe my half day off fell on the night of the church social, giving me a *full* day!"

"Oh, why don't you just rub it in a little more," Dolly mumbled as the girls groaned with jealously.

"While it is a holiday, it's not for the Harvey House. There are trains to be fed. But you'll *all* have a holiday this evening at the dance as we are closing the dining room," Miss Trent informed the group and, for once, Dolly seemed to be in disagreement with the housemother as she sighed with the rest of the girls.

"Enjoy your day off, Fannie," Sophia called as the gong sounded. "Just be sure to tell us all that happens."

"You're one to talk," Nora snipped. "You got to sleep a bit and didn't join us until lunch."

Sophia tilted her head. "Are you well? You aren't normally so, um . . ."

"Irritable?" Nora placed a hand on her abdomen and sighed. "You're right. I'm sorry for my sharp tongue. I feel wretched. I think I caught something from one of the passengers. There was a small boy I served two days ago who sneezed on my face when I bent down to pour his milk."

Sophia's jaw dropped in disgust. "No. What did you do?"

Nora grimaced. "Only what Mr. Harvey would have approved. I wiped my face with my apron and pretended nothing happened."

Sophia suppressed a shiver. "I would've had to excuse myself to bathe my face, but if you aren't feeling well, I'm sure Harriet will understand." Sophia placed a comforting hand on Nora's arm.

"She would understand all right but would insist that if I wasn't fit to serve during the day, I wouldn't be fit to dance tonight!" She pressed her lips into a tight line. "And I must dance with the sheriff tonight."

"Oh?"

Nora ran her handkerchief over her forehead that was beading in sweat. "How else am I to get him to at last propose marriage?"

"So, you've decided for certain he is the gentleman you want?"

Nora straightened her shoulders. "I am more than certain, as well he should be, after his string of empty promises."

"What—?"

She shook her head at Sophia's forthcoming question as the gong sounded again. "We'd best hurry."

The girls' black skirts swished as they rushed to their stations. Harriet planted a warm smile on her face, but her eyes betrayed not ire at their tardiness, rather disappointment in Miss Trent's decision.

"I can clear the tables alone after the guests leave if you want to catch the end of the day festivities," Sophia whispered.

"No, Miss Trent was right. I have to see to it that the dining room is decorated for tonight, so I can't possibly leave." Harriet sighed, her expression softening for a moment. "But thank you for the kind offer."

The ladies danced their way through dinner, and after the last guest had been well wished on the rest of their journey, the girls began the transformation of the dining room into a ballroom as the Harvey House men cleared away the middle tables to make room for dancing, keeping the small tables for refreshments at the corners, and lining the walls with the chairs.

The girls took pink, white, and blue ribbons and decorated the columns and hung the flowers over the doorframe while wildflowers of complementing colors were placed in vases and sprinkled throughout the room to add to the festive air.

"Time to dress!" Harriet called out after

the floors were swept and everything was in its place, ushering them out of the Castañeda. "We've only an hour before the guests will begin to arrive, and we must make ourselves as pretty as we may. Remember," she added as the girls bustled toward their rooms, giggling and laughing, "we are part of the decorations, so try to incorporate any of the colors into your garb."

Nora hurried into the room before Sophia, gasping at the spray of tiny cream roses on the nightstand with Sophia's name on the card. "What a darling little nosegay!" She buried her nose into the blooms. "Whoever sent it to you? Or do you already know the blooms are from that handsome Mr. Ashton I've heard so much about from the others?"

Ever since Carver's arrival, Nora, though kind as ever, was subject to such drastic changes in mood that Sophia was never certain where she stood each day. But, for the moment, Nora seemed genuinely pleased for Sophia. She reached for the nosegay, smiling. "You think he is smitten with me, Nora?"

"I've seen the way you two look at each other. The *pair* of you are besotted!" Nora giggled, twirling back to the small looking glass hanging by their door to arrange her shining ebony locks. "Do read the card to me." Adding under her breath, "As it seems *I* will not be receiving one of my own."

Sophia kept silent on Nora's comment and opened the card. "'For the brightest star in . . .'" she paused, disappointment clawing up her throat.

"Is it so romantic that you cannot even read it to me?" Nora giggled, and with her hair caught in one hand with her hairbrush still gripped in it, swiped the card out of Sophia's hand. "'For the brightest star in Charleston. Las Vegas is all the brighter by your presence. M.K.'" She lowered the card, frowning. "Who is M.K?"

Sophia gritted her teeth, awaiting Nora's tears and certain anger.

"Marion Kane. The flowers are from Sheriff Kane." Nora's brush clattered on the floor, her hair tumbling to her waist.

"Clumsy me," Nora murmured, bending to retrieve her brush. "He is quite handsome a suitor as well, but my vote is for Mr. Ashton, but if you won't have him, maybe I will join Jenny in line for his hand."

"You know my affections do not rest with the sheriff, yes?"

"Of course." She smiled weakly as she wound her hair again, affixing a blue ribbon to it. "I'm going to fetch the hot tong from the fireplace downstairs."

With a sigh, Sophia slipped out of her uniform and wrapped herself in her lilac silk dressing robe. She reached for her silver brush, running it through her locks before braiding it loosely and arranging it into a delicate bun on the base of her neck with a few loose strands about her face.

Nora closed the door, hot tong in hand, setting to curling the hair framing her face, but her hands were shaking so badly that Sophia gently removed the tong from her and dressed Nora's hair, finishing it with her own ivory comb atop the coiffure, along with a cluster of the cream roses.

"An ivory comb?" Nora's fingers traced the floral etching. "It's stunning."

Sophia smiled at the effect of the comb and flowers in Nora's high coiffure. "It suits you. Your dark locks will seem even darker with the ivory against it."

Nora smiled at herself in the mirror, a bit of color returning to her pale cheeks. "Thank you."

A knock sounded on the door, and it creaked open. "Miss Bird, aren't you the popular young lady tonight? Another nosegay has arrived for you!" Miss Trent smiled, handing Sophia a sprig of bluebonnets.

"Oh, how lovely. I haven't seen bluebonnets in years." Sophia took the small bouquet and inhaled the delicate scent of the cobalt wildflowers. "No wonder these were my grandmother's favorite."

"Another nosegay?" Nora's voice lifted. "Are they from Mr. Ashton?"

Miss Trent shrugged. "A gentleman left these with Dolly at the front of the dormitory and she said he didn't leave a card, so I don't know. I must finish getting ready, so you two will have to solve the mystery without me."

Sophia placed the bluebonnets on the dresser next to the remainder of the sheriff's nosegay and went to the closet and selected the one evening gown she managed to pack, a blush silk masterpiece. She grimaced as she reached for the rug beater. The gown had been so badly wrinkled in her journey to New Mexico that it had taken all her efforts to return it to its former glory. After a few good *whacks* to the gown, she slipped on her silk stockings and matching evening slippers before stepping into her gown, loving the silk caressing her skin as she moved the ruffled sleeves into place.

Without a word, Nora worked the silk buttons down Sophia's back into place. Sophia sucked in as Nora pulled her corset strings tighter to button the middle row. The good food at the Harvey House had added a bit more padding to her hips while the hard work had given her strength that made her once delicate frame heartier. Would her father even recognize her with her sun kissed cheeks, and newfound strength?

"What gown are you wearing tonight, Nora?"

"I didn't want to show anyone because I wanted to surprise the girls." Nora fastened the final button before twirling over to her side of the closet and digging through the back, removing a crimson silk brocade gown with a gold lace trim. "Isn't it elegant?"

Sophia gasped. "The workmanship on this gown must have cost a small fortune! Where on earth—"

"I made it," she answered, beaming as she held it up against herself. "I spent the money I was saving on that um, well, the parasol and bought the materials for a new dress with this dance in mind. I've been staying up late every night for the past few weeks sewing." She shrugged. "Which may be why I feel so under the weather."

"How did I never see you sewing?" Sophia ran her fingers over the length of the sleeves, examining the perfect stitches.

Nora rolled her eyes. "You are an outlandishly heavy sleeper. I dropped my scissors on the ground, and it was loud enough to wake Miss Trent downstairs, but you slept right through it."

"Well, it's stunning. Why would you work as a waitress when you could make a significant living as a seamstress in one of the big cities? Like Charleston or New York?" Sophia lifted the hem, admiring the gold embroidery. "I know twenty girls who would love to own a dress like this, including my five sisters."

"I don't really feel like moving away from all I've ever known, and no one around here really has need for the latest fashions. They like the practical, standard dresses that are easy to alter with the changing styles, but I say that you can't wear a practical dress every day."

"How did you learn to do this?" Sophia helped Nora into her magnificent creation, moving behind to fasten it.

"I taught myself. I saw pictures in catalogs and newspapers, and I tried to copy them."

"It is unbelievable the mastery that you

have by only looking at pictures!" Sophia grasped Nora's hands. "You are stunning. You're going to have to bring a broom to keep all the young men away tonight, including the sheriff, whom I have no intentions toward, not now and not ever."

Nora slowly nodded. "I know that, I really do, but I'm so terrified of losing him."

"If he doesn't wish to be caught, you know there are ten more men behind him more than willing to offer you their hearts and home."

"I don't want any others—not when Kane has promised me his heart." Nora turned in the chifforobe mirror, admiring the contours of her body in the dress as she pulled on her elbow length gloves. "He only needs to be reminded how much he admires me and help him overcome this fear of marriage."

"Then I have just the item to complete your ensemble." Sophia dug through her trunk and pulled out an ostrich fan along with a painted silk fan. She flicked open the gold dyed fan and handed it to her. "This will tie in the gold trim, and you can send him secret messages by the art of the fan." She doubted the sheriff had any idea there was a language of the fan movements, but a lady could prove most alluring behind one.

"Oh, Sophia." Nora's eyes filled. "I don't know what to say."

"Nonsense. It is only a fan!" Sophia tugged her white kid gloves securely over her elbows before selecting Carver's locket to adorn her neck.

"To you, perhaps." Nora fluttered the fan, cooling her heated cheeks. "Shall we?"

Music floated through the open window as the piano in the dining room began to play along with the two violinists the Harvey House had hired for the evening. Arm in arm, the girls hurried across the street where flickering torches lit the courtyard path to the hotel. They gathered in the dining room as Fannie dashed about putting the last finishing touches on anyone's hair that appeared in need as Nora proudly displayed her dress to the group.

"So, how are things going with the Sheriff, Nora?" Jenny asked, fluffing the sleeves of her sapphire calico that, while modest and plain, showed off her full figure.

Nora's eyes widened, her cheeks paling. "He, uh, called things off between us a few weeks ago, but I'm hoping to capture his attention again tonight."

Sophia bit her lip at this news. *Why ever did he call it off? He clearly was fond of her that first day we met in town together.*

"I'm sorry to hear that, but every man in the room is certainly going to notice you in that stunning shade." Jenny rested her hand on Nora's arm.

Nora cleared her throat and fanned her face with the golden ostrich feather as Dolly waltzed into the hall, wearing the exact shade as Nora. The women stared at each other. Dolly's gown was trimmed in a cream lace with a scoop neck, but Nora's workmanship made her gown the superior.

"Nora, where did you get your material?"

"Obviously at the same general store as you, Dolly," she replied, disappointment marring her lovely smile from moments before.

"Well, as the next in line to be head waitress, I believe I should wear my dress. You must change at once," Dolly demanded, planting her hands on her hips. "Your neckline is positively scandalous."

"No," Sophia interjected. "Her dress looks nothing like your dress besides the obviousness that it is cut from the same fabric. Just because you're second waitress doesn't mean that you are the head. If you don't want to wear the same color, then go change, but don't expect Nora to change as well."

Dolly glared at Sophia before turning on her heel and heading toward the dormitory.

"Oh, you are going to pay for standing up against her," Harriet whispered as she joined them.

Nora gave her arm a squeeze. "But thank you nonetheless."

Sophia grinned. "If a month's worth of her cold shoulder is the cost of you capturing the Sheriff, it was worth it."

"THE LAST TIME I saw a man in a tailcoat was Charleston," Sophia commented from behind.

"It was a risk, I admit, but I do remember how much you secretly admired me in one." Carver turned and caught her hand, pressing a kiss atop. He glanced about the room and sucked a breath through his teeth. "I may be a tad overdressed."

Sophia laughed. "It will do the men good to see the latest fashions."

He grinned at the sight of his nosegay of bluebonnets pinned over her heart and a few sprinkling her coiffure where her ivory comb usually decorated. "I hoped you'd like them. I picked them myself."

"They are prettier than any hothouse flower I've ever received."

"Miss Bird, you look stunning." Kane gave her a stiff bow in a navy suit that seemed almost too small for him, his badge catching the candlelight. He gestured to Sophia's hair with one of the glasses of punch in his hands, offering her the other. "But I see you didn't care for the nosegay I sent you?"

Carver fought to disguise his ire and reached for the glass from the sheriff, handing it to Sophia and slipped her free hand around his arm.

Sophia blushed as she took a sip. "The flowers are beautiful. Thank you for thinking of me, but as my—Mr. Ashton sent me a nosegay as well, I gave your flowers to Nora to wear as they were lovely with her new gown. Though, I have to say, I was surprised to find hothouse blooms were available this far west."

"There's a lot of things about the West that would surprise you, especially with the railroad practically at our door." Kane looped his thumbs in his vest pockets. "We are incredibly civilized, or rather, we try to be. It keeps us feeling like we are not quite so far from home."

"Such as?" Carver interjected.

"Take for example, Sunday church. Many would have given up the practice long ago if it didn't give them some form of nostalgia and remind them of the comforts of home." He tossed back his punch and set the glass on the windowsill.

"And of soul," Sophia added. "Everyone needs to gather to worship."

He shrugged. "If you're into that sort of thing. I go because that's what my mother wishes, but I see it as a crutch. Out here, you have to be your own man and not rely on the charity of others."

"There's so much more to church besides just attending because that's the thing to do," Sophia replied. "And it isn't a crutch. It's the foundation—"

"Interesting concept." Kane cleared his throat. "But this is a party and as such, let us move away from such talk."

Sensing the man was about to ask Sophia to dance, Carver turned to her before Kane could make his move. "Shall we?"

Sophia nodded to the sheriff and allowed Carver to sweep her onto the dance floor for a lively polka that left them laughing and gasping for air. The waltz played next, and he pulled her close, willing time to stand still.

"In all of the chaos of yesterday, I didn't ask what I have been dying to find out," she whispered, looking up at him.

The worry in her eyes made his heart falter, but he shook his head and sighed. "About my suit? It will never be the same again."

"My parents." She swallowed as if fighting back a wince. "How are they?"

"Your father is anxious, and your mother has made herself near ill with sorrow at your departure," he replied, turning them in time with the music, the skirts of the other ladies creating a blurred kaleidoscope of color behind Sophia as he could not keep himself from staring into her beautiful eyes. He loved seeing the color in her cheeks and the confidence with which she now held herself. "Not to intrude on your privacy or your wishes, but perhaps you would allow me to telegraph them to say that I found you and you are doing well? The work and climate here seem to agree with you. Your parents would be pleased to see their daughter blossoming in New Mexico."

"I'll send them a telegram soon. I just needed enough time to pass to cool Father's temper."

He nodded. "I suppose I will have to be

content and rest in the fact that I know you are well."

"Thank you, Carver. How did you like your accommodations?"

"Very well. My only complaint is that the general manger keeps hitting that infernal gong every five minutes. Doesn't it drive you mad hearing that all day every day?"

"I've grown used to the din, but now, it just makes my heart race at the thought of all the people I have to feed and keeping them on time. Speaking of which, what did you do yesterday after I left you with the sheriff?"

"I had an interesting conversation that led to Kane bringing his mother to meet me this morning."

Sophia blinked. "Truly? How was she? He's *never* brought her to dinner at the Harvey House."

"She lives on a small horse ranch that she says is not too far from town, but one that is definitely not an easy ride for a meal —no matter how delicious." He cleared his throat. "But as for her character, she told me straight away that she doesn't blame my stepfather for her not seeing a penny of her inheritance."

Sophia gasped and missed a step, stumbling into Carver's chest. "She really said those things to you? There are few in our circle who could be so generous and forgiving."

He nodded. "She said that her marriage to Mr. Kane was a gift from the Lord and their son was the greatest inheritance she could ever hope for in life. Her love for her late husband is truly inspiring."

She lifted those wide eyes up to him and he could not wait a moment longer. He whirled her to the nearest door and led her outside on the veranda. There was only one other couple conversing in the left corner, so Carver led her toward the right, enjoying the moonlight splaying through the arches. She turned her back to the dirt road, leaning against a brick column, staring up at him.

Her lips called to him. Perhaps he could risk kissing her? Carver glanced over his shoulder to the dining room window and spied Sophia's roommate taking the sheriff's arm, looking quite stern as they whispered together, the sheriff's frown deepening. Carver leaned his forehead toward hers, all thoughts of Kane and others fleeing in her presence.

"What did the sheriff have to say about his mother's being disinherited?" Sophia questioned, interrupting his plan of kissing her.

"Kane was polite, but I felt such a burning resentment rolling off him like smoke from a fireplace with the flue shut." He shook his head. "That man hates the Ashtons."

The front door swung open, and Miss Matthews approached them with two glasses and a bright smile. "Mr. Ashton, have you tried our delightful raspberry lemonade? Mr. Harvey has fresh fruit sent to us on the trains. You should try it," she handed it to him across Sophia, her hand bumping Sophia's puffed sleeve.

Sophia gasped as the cool, dark pink liquid splashed her shoulders and seeped into the bodice, down her elbow length glove and trickled onto her dance card.

"Oh no! I am so, so sorry." Miss Matthews whipped her handkerchief out from her bodice and dabbed Sophia's collarbone.

"I'm certain you are, Dolly." Sophia brushed her off. "Excuse me while I go change, Carver."

Carver attempted not to glare at the offending Harvey Girl for interrupting their moment. "At least allow me to hold your dance card while you change." He sent her an apologetic look over the mishap as he accepted the card, reached into his pocket, and withdrew his pencil, marking his name on every line as Miss Matthews attempted to draw him into conversation.

Miss Matthews laughed and snagged his arm. "How sly of you, Mr. Ashton, but as you seem to love to dance, there is no sense in missing out while you wait for dear Sophia to change. Shall we?"

"Wait!" Harriet called out to her, following her down the steps and into the courtyard.

"I saw through the window what happened." Spying the stain by moonlight, she clapped her hand over her mouth. "Perhaps if we soak it right away in the tub, we can save it."

"Thank you," Sophia trotted up the steps with Harriet behind her, hating the tears threatening the night over a spoilt gown.

"I can't believe Dolly would stoop so low as to try and ruin your beautiful dress." Harriet closed Sophia's bedroom door and set to work unbuttoning the piece.

"I am not. Ever since Dolly discovered a rich gentleman was staying in the hotel, she has been throwing herself at Carver." Sophia peeled off her soiled gloves and threw them onto her bed. "And besides, in her mind, it is fair that I change as I made her—a dress for a dress."

"Sadly, I do not disagree when you put it like that, but I will see to it that she is severely reprimanded as we cannot rightly prove it wasn't an accident." Harriet slipped the gown off Sophia's shoulders and allowed it to fall into a billowing heap on the floor. "However, I've seen the way she treats him while he is such the perfect gentleman that he wouldn't say anything other than what is polite so as not to hurt your position here. But I cannot blame Dolly for trying."

Sophia dipped a hand towel into the water basin and patted down her sticky shoulders. "First you call him a perfect gentleman and now handsome? Do I need to be wary of you now too? You'll have to get in line behind Jenny and Nora."

Harriet gathered the dress in her arms, leaning against the doorframe as she winked at Sophia. "Undoubtedly. He is just my sort of gentleman. Besides the fact that he traveled across the country to find his love, he dances like a dream."

"He does, doesn't he?" Sophia giggled as she dried her shoulders off with a clean hand towel and retrieved an ivory blouse with lace at the throat and trimming the three-quarter length puffed sleeves along with a pink skirt. Not as lovely as her ballgown, but it would do.

"The gown is in the tub and as it is already a blush color, I think it can be saved." Harriet looped her arm through Sophia's, assuring her that she looked quite the picture.

As she stepped into the dining room, Carver at once found her. He grasped her elbow and pulled her closer. "You are breathtaking." He returned her dance card with a bow. "And I believe the other gentlemen have noticed."

Sophia flipped open the card, laughing. "Judging by the dance card, I don't think there are many dances left, but the good thing is that I see the rest are yours."

He swept her onto the floor as the music began anew. "You are all mine for the rest of the night."

For the rest of the night. She couldn't remember the last time she had been so happy. In Charleston, she had been so careful to conceal her affection for Carver, but here, it felt right to be in his arms—to have him stare adoringly in her eyes as they danced song after song, sometimes conversing and sometimes simply enjoying being together without anyone attempting to keep them apart. How had she made it this long without seeing him?

Mr. Carlton stood on the musicians' makeshift platform in the corner of the dining room and lifted his hands, announcing, "And now, gentlemen, please take your partners for our final song of the evening, 'After the Ball is Over.'"

"You are happy here, aren't you?"

"Very," she answered as Carver whirled them off the dance floor, out onto the veranda and down the steps to the courtyard under the branches of the massive oak tree. "I love this place. I feel as if I have finally found myself here."

"I can tell. You are positively glowing." He threaded her arm through his as they strolled in the moonlight down the boardwalk. "You seem surer of yourself, more confident in your decisions."

"I am. I enjoy my independence. I don't think I could ever go back to just being Miss Fairfield of the Ernest Fairfields again." She looked off into the horizon where the outline of low-lying cedars ended, and the dark sky began. She bent down and picked a wildflower and slowly threaded it through a buttonhole on his vest, her hand resting against his chest, her desire mirrored in his gaze.

"And I would never want you to." He rested his hand atop hers, keeping it over his heart. "It is so easy being with you, and I haven't felt right since we parted. But I must ask you something. Has my stepfather spoiled our chances at being happy together, Sophia?"

"I-I hope not." She pressed a kiss to his hand holding hers, sending her heart to pounding at her boldness. "You could have anyone you want in Charleston, Carver—anyone in the country really." She motioned back toward the Harvey House. "Why, there are nine women in there who would marry you at the drop of a pin. Ladies who don't have complicated pasts with your stepfather."

"I don't want another lady. I want you—complicated past and all." Carver smiled down at her, his love shining through. "You know me better than anyone else and know that I cannot lie to save my life."

She reached up and brushed a lock of his

dark hair back. "I guess I do kind of know you well."

"And that's what surprises me!" Carver laughed, flashing his darling set of dimples. "You like me even though I am not as successful as my stepfather. You don't care about Prescott's money. You don't care about how old the Ashton name is in society. You care about *me,* and you respect me for my character and not how much I can bring to your father's business. To borrow a line from Keats, 'I love you the more in that I believe you have liked me for my own sake and for nothing else.'"

Sophia shifted closer to him, lifting her head to him. "And in your own words?

He wrapped his arms around her. "Sophia, you have my heart and always will. I love you more than I knew was possible."

He pulled her to him and gently kissed her, sending a thrill through her body and her arms to wrapping about his neck, deepening the kiss until they were both breathless.

"And I love you," she whispered, leaning

her head against his chest, the rapid beating of his heart matching her own.

He sighed. "You don't know how I've longed to hear you say those words." He slowly laced his fingers through hers and kissed her hand. "You know, if we were to marry . . . we don't have to go back to Charleston if you don't want to."

"What?" She pushed back from him to see if he was jesting.

He met her startled eyes and smiled. "I know you are concerned about how our marriage would make it uncomfortable for your family and mine because we work so closely together, but I can start my new business elsewhere."

"You would do that for us?" She clutched his arm, her heart soaring with hope at his mention of marriage.

"I know the shipping business in and out and know Prescott's competitors. I have grown up hearing about little else, and I know I could do well with a department store in New Orleans," Carver answered, excitement in his voice. "I didn't want to say anything until I was sure you were happy to see me, but I have already resigned my position with my stepfather."

"I know you only spoke of possibly setting up shop elsewhere, but I didn't allow myself to hope—" She laughed, shaking her head. "And *if* I was happy to see you? I was ecstatic. But you resigned? Does that mean you are ready to begin?"

"Well, long story short, I have purchased a store from an old friend who is retiring. It's small, but it's a start, and I plan to build it into the finest department store in New Orleans."

Sophia clutched her hands to her lace jabot. "If we lived in New Orleans, there wouldn't be anything holding us back from marrying—not prior engagements, not society, and certainly not my family."

"Nothing. I can support you, Sophia, not near as well as your father had hoped right away, but I can give your father the satisfaction of having the Ashton name tied to his family, even if the money is delayed while I make it. If you'd just say the word, I will surrender all for you and start anew."

She cupped his face in her hands, aching

to kiss him senseless. "Wherever you go, all I ask is that you allow me to be by your side to love you and support you all of your days. And I don't care if we live in a mansion on St. Charles Avenue or in a flat, as long as we are together."

"Thank you, Lord, for this woman," he whispered, lifting his face to the sky. He captured her hands in his, and reaching in his pocket, he withdrew a ring with a large solitaire diamond on a thin gold band.

Sophia's breath caught. "Oh, Carver."

"Let me share forever with you, my dearest." He knelt on the parched grass. "Sophia, this was my mother's ring from my father. I have been hoping that one day I would find a woman she would have approved of, and I know from the bottom of my heart, she would have adored you. Will you do me the honor of becoming my wife and making me the happiest man alive?"

Sophia took his face in her hands once more, bent, and kissed him. "Yes." She kissed him again, deeper this time. "Yes. With all of my heart, yes."

With a cheer, he shot to his feet,

sweeping her into his arms. "I can't believe it. You are going to be my wife."

She laughed as he twirled her around, her skirts swirling. "We are going to get married!"

His eyes danced as he set her down. "And now that we are, I find I cannot delay our preparations for a future together a moment longer. I will leave in two days for New Orleans and prepare a home for my bride, and the very minute the house is ready for you I will come back and carry you away." He picked her up again and swung her around, laughing. "My sweet, darling bride."

CHAPTER 15

Sophia readied herself before the small looking glass, adjusting the ring hanging from her locket's chain to fall beneath her riding habit's neckline, holding the secret of their engagement close to her heart. After having their lives open to society and its opinions for years, they decided to enjoy their engagement privately for a day before announcing it to the girls.

But, to keep it a secret, Carver had invited her for a morning ride before her shift began in the afternoon to discuss their future away from the Harvey House and its many listening ears.

Our future. The magical word warmed

her as she pinned her green riding hat into place and draped the white tulle scarf over her face and around her neck and let it fall dramatically over her shoulder.

"Really? You brought an entire riding *ensemble*?" Nora paused in the doorway in her dressing robe, her wet hair falling past her waist, smelling of lavender from her bath.

Sophia shrugged. "Well, what else should I wear while riding? I can't wear pants and be seen by Carver or any other man who happens to cross our path."

"A *split* skirt, my dear. That's what every other woman wears out here." Nora sank onto her bed, running a comb through her hair, her cheeks pale even as she released a soft laugh. "Though, I must say, as a lady who loves fashion, my heart is struggling with envy." She paused in her laughter, slapping her hand over her mouth and leaning forward.

"Aren't you feeling any better today?"

Nora shook her head, her lips pressed into a firm line as she drew in a deep breath.

"I feel as if I shall never feel like myself again."

Sophia poured her a glass of water from the pitcher atop the dresser. "Can I get you something before I leave?"

Nora accepted the glass with a nod of thanks and gave up brushing her hair. She flopped onto her side away from Sophia, the gentle breeze from the open window fluttering the curtains. "I think I only need some rest before my shift."

Sophia quietly closed the door behind her, eager to see Carver, only to find Dolly hanging on his arm, her face falling slightly at the sight of Sophia.

"I was just telling Carver that the Las Vegas Hotel has the best tea in town and that he should be sure to enjoy some during his visit."

Sophia's brows rose. "Oh? I wouldn't let any of the Harvey staff hear you say such a thing."

She shrugged. "They all know it to be true as well, and Mr. Harvey has been alerted. He is selecting a new brand of tea and sending it at once."

Carver met Sophia's gaze, and she closed the distance between them, claiming his free arm and tugging him away from Dolly, sending Dolly her sweetest smile. "You must excuse us. We do not wish to miss any riding time."

Dolly pursed her lips. "Yes, we wouldn't want that."

Perhaps we should reveal our engagement tonight—if only to keep Dolly away from Carver. She glanced over her shoulder to see Dolly still watching them, her frown deepening.

With her riding skirt trailing behind her, the townspeople turned and stared as if she were an exotic bird that had accidentally flown into their town. By the time they entered the stable yard located on the edge of town, her cheeks were burning, but Carver hugged her hand in the crook of his arm as if to offer her reassurance.

"Has Dolly Matthews been cornering you for the entirety of your visit?" The question she had been attempting to strangle broke free.

"I didn't wish to make you feel any unease. Yes, she has, but let us not talk of anything troublesome this morning. It's been far too long since we have been riding."

"Far too long and far longer since I've gotten away from everyone for a bit of *quiet* for a change. The girls have endless topics to discuss, and I seem to have forgotten what it was like living with five sisters." She sighed, rubbing her forehead between two fingers. "I'm afraid that, at times, my quiet nature comes across as sullen or boring."

"Thoughtful, yes, but never sullen and definitely not boring. You are the most intriguing woman I have ever met. What other woman in my acquaintance would run away from a rich fiancé to work as a waitress in the Wild West?"

Sophia dipped her head as Carver ordered two horses to be saddled, her soul unused to such genuine love and tenderness bestowed without expectation tied to it. *And to think, he will be my husband.*

Sheriff Kane brought three horses around to the stable yard, all impressive mounts. "Good morning, Miss Bird."

"Sheriff? Whatever are you doing leading the horses?"

"My ma owns the stable, and now that Pa is gone, I like to pop in here every morning on my way to work." He ran his hands over the nearest horse's mane, a fine chestnut.

At the sight of the saddles, Sophia worried her bottom lip. "Sheriff, none of these saddles are sidesaddles."

"Nope." The sheriff handed Carver the reins and surveyed the back of her skirt. "But you've enough skirt to keep you more than decent, little lady. I wouldn't be too worried." Kane held the stirrup for her. "Up you go."

Before Kane could assist her, Carver moved in front of him and enveloped Sophia's waist and lifted her onto the painted horse. "You can wrap your knee around the horn of the saddle if you don't want to ride astride."

Sophia nodded and proceeded to do so.

Kane frowned. "Not to be disrespectful, Miss Bird, but that's just asking for trouble. I'm not too comfortable with you trying to ride sidesaddle on a western saddle on one of my ma's rented horses. I couldn't sleep at night if—"

"I am an accomplished horsewoman, so I'm certain I can handle this challenge." Giving the horse a friendly pat on the neck, Sophia sat straight in her saddle, determined not to show any signs of weakness to the man.

Kane shrugged. "Suit yourself, Miss Bird, but I'm sure you are aware that things can go wrong even to the best of horsemen. You aren't in Charleston anymore. This is New Mexico. Things happen."

"I'll take care of her," Carver responded as he mounted his chestnut mare.

Kane whacked the dust off his hat and tugged it on with a nod. "Let's get going then."

"Let's?" Carver and Sophia asked in unison as the sheriff mounted a dappled gray.

Kane gave a short laugh, directing his horse through the gate, Sophia's horse following his friend. "Riding here isn't anything like back east *that* I can tell you. You are safer with me."

"You've been to the East?" Carver called from the back of the line.

"Yes. Not everyone born in the West has a desire to never leave." He turned in his saddle to glare at him for a half second. "In any event, you really don't want to venture off without a gun to protect you." He patted his gun belt affectionately as he directed his horse to the left of Sophia's. "These greenhorn dudes come out here and think they are invincible and above owning a rifle."

Carver pulled along the other side of Sophia. "I didn't say I didn't own a gun."

Kane flicked up the brim of his Stetson. "A city bred boy like you? Well, owning a gun is one thing, but knowing how to shoot is entirely different."

"My father believed in teaching me ways to protect my family, with my fists as well as with weapons." Carver kept his eyes on the horizon, his retort steel. "I have been shooting under the finest instructors since I was strong enough to hold a rifle."

"That is all well and good in theory but

being able to *defensively* pull a gun is another." The sheriff shrugged. "In case you run into trouble, it never hurts to have the law escort you on your little tour."

Sophia cleared her throat. The men were getting out of hand. "You would think after being here almost two months I would've seen more of Las Vegas, but by the time my day off from the Harvey House comes around, I've been too tired to venture outside of town."

"Well, besides that once," Kane replied, his voice trailing off a little too suggestively for her liking.

Sophia ducked her head to avoid a low-lying oak branch. "Yes."

"What happened last time you ventured out?" Carver tucked low in his saddle as he followed.

Flashes of memory of Mr. Gessler chasing her sent her heart to pounding. She averted her gaze to the dusty trail, concentrating on anything other than the topic at hand to keep her voice from trembling. "I went for a stroll after church and was nearly accosted by a drunkard, but

Sheriff Kane found me in time and arrested him."

Carver's jaw clenched, his eyes alighting with fury. "And was this man dealt with, Kane?"

The sheriff reined in his horse to hold up a branch for them to pass under. "I gave him a few days of jail time, but since no crime was actually committed . . . just the threat of one, I had to let him go."

Carver snorted. "You call that justice?"

Kane released the branch, allowing it to smack Carver in the back of the head. Kane rested his palms atop the other on the saddle horn, his gaze turning dangerous. "Out here, the law is a little bit different, Mr. Ashton. I made sure he suffered in another way to serve as a warning to leave Miss Bird alone."

"Good. If that man ever comes near you again, Sophia," Carver shook his head, "Heaven help him."

Kane led them through the cedars and down to the river Sophia had tried to reach on her own that day which seemed so long ago. The horses forged through the river, the water splashing her boots. To avoid getting her hem soaked, Sophia lifted her habit, cautious not to expose her ankle.

"It hasn't rained in a good while," Kane called out above the noise of the sloshing of the horses. "You can't tell it from its height today, but when it rains hard, this river swells up and has been known to flood."

After a mile, Kane halted his horse. "Not sure what you wanted to see of our little town, but this here is about the prettiest vista you will find for miles."

Sophia inhaled the clean, sharp air and looked out onto the rolling oak and cedar covered hills that rose into mountains. *So stunning and so completely different than the beauty of Charleston.* She glanced over to Carver at her left and found him staring at her as if he too were wishing to share this moment alone with her. He reached his hand for hers and opened his lips to say something when a wolf howled, her mount skittering to the side.

She gently pulled back on the reins and spoke reassuringly to the horse, hoping to stay its fears as it pranced in place and shook its mane with a snort.

Kane leaned his head to the right and gave his neck a crack, reaching for his gun belt. "Where there is one, there is always more. Did you bring one of your guns, *dude*?" He drew out the insult with a grin, along with his gun.

Another, and even closer, howl caused her horse to jerk its head and scramble backwards. She threw her leg over the saddle in an attempt to control him astride. There was no recovering as the horse charged into a gallop. Sophia's veil, though stylish, made it difficult to see too far ahead of her, but she clenched her legs against the horse and crouched low, holding onto the horse's mane as well as the reins. The horse leapt over a mound of brush and Sophia nearly lost her place in her saddle, her skirts tangling in her stirrups.

Her heart racing, she hiked her skirt up and threw it over her legs. She could practically hear her mother swoon at her exposed stocking-covered thighs. The horse raced into a grove of cedar trees and Sophia pressed low against the horse's neck to avoid the branches scraping her face as she pulled back on the reins, speaking firmly, trying to get him to calm while letting him know that she was in charge. The horse finally slowed to a trot and then a walk until it stopped. She threw her leg back around the saddle horn and arranged her skirts to cover herself just as she caught sight of Carver and Kane racing toward her.

The men slowed their horses and carefully guided them next to hers so as not to spook her lathered mount. "Are you okay?" Carver panted as he reached for her horse's reins, winding them around his saddle horn.

Normally, she would have protested such an action, but it was a relief to have the horse anchored for a moment.

Kane swiped off his Stetson and beat it against his thigh, hooting. "That was some horsemanship! I have never, *never* seen a female ride half as well as you just did." He gestured to the reins now on Carver's saddle. "She don't need us to protect her when she can sit like that."

Sophia unwrapped her disheveled scarf,

freeing her face, and rearranged it about her neck. "It was the one active thing my parents would allow me to do besides lawn tennis. I lived for my riding lessons each week."

"You can tell!" Kane laughed. "The boys in town will never believe it when I tell them you could have put us all to shame on our Founder's Day race."

"I believe that's enough riding for one day," Sophia laughed, Kane extolling her the whole of the journey back to the stables where she had to leave Carver to settle the bill so she wouldn't be late for work.

She was halfway back to the Harvey House when she realized her head felt uncharacteristically light. *Blast. Serves me right for taking my hat off after the ride for a bit of air. Maybe if I tie any and all possessions to my body when leaving the house, I won't leave everything everywhere!* She whirled her skirts around as she fairly ran back to the stable.

"My ma married for love and look where it got her, rotting in a soddy on a dilapidated horse ranch." Kane's voice floated from the office.

She sank into the shadows of the side of the building and held her breath, listening.

"Pa had no money and no connections, but Ma thought she could survive on her love for him without her inheritance—*my* inheritance. I didn't want to be stuck here. I come from rich blood, *your* stepfather's blood, Carver. If my ma had chosen differently, how would my life look now? How would your life look? Your life of leisure working with my uncle's business would have been mine as I should have been his partner."

"There is no point in living in the past—"

"The past is still affecting me *today.* So, of course, I wish I could change things and with Miss Bird's arrival I *finally* can. You don't need Sophia's wealth, but you see, I do, and you better believe that I will use my influence to gain her hand even if it means making you look dirty. . . dirty enough to land in my jail, and who knows, maybe the telegraph lines will be down and you will have to have a trial without your fancy lawyers. You are in my town now."

Sophia peered through the small crack

in the door to see Kane lay his gun atop his desk as he casually released his gun belt's tie.

"You would dare to threaten *me*?" Carver's broad shoulders rolled back, his fists tightening.

"I'm warning you. Stay away from Sophia," He growled, spittle flying into Carver's face.

"She is my fiancée." Carver took a menacing step toward Kane as if daring him to strike first. With his training in the ring, Kane would be no match for him.

"Until there is a wedding band on her finger, she is still available." Kane retorted.

"If you feel you must flirt with her, go ahead. I am confident in where her heart lies, but if you so much as touch her without her willingness, I will end you."

Sophia sank further into the shadows as Carver charged out, slamming the office door, and charging toward the Castañeda. *This must stop. Once and for all.* She barged through the door, allowing the plank door to bang against the wall in her haste.

Kane's scowl dropped at the sight of her in the threshold. "Miss Bird?"

"Sheriff Kane, I have never encouraged your advances. In fact, I have tried to discourage them as much as possible, and judging from the conversation I just overheard, it seems I was right in doing so."

"Miss Bird, I don't know what you are talking about." Kane strode around his desk, perching on the corner, grinning at her as if confident that his good looks would see him through any unpleasant situation.

"Please. I could hear you both clear as day. I am asking you politely to cease your advances on me for they are futile."

"I suppose they are 'futile' because your heart is elsewhere, am I right?" He sneered. "Carver has been given everything on silver spoons and golden platters. Don't you want a real man?" He shoved up his sleeves and lifted his hands, displaying callouses and scars marring the skin up to his forearms. "These are badges. I have worked my whole life for everything I have and I'm proud of it, but I'm not content to just be a sheriff. I want to be more. Is that so terrible?"

"Ambition is a good thing, but the way you are going about to obtain your dream is abhorrent. You've turned your back on a perfectly sweet girl who is head over heels in love with you, and for what? Money."

"I know better than most that love isn't everything in life. Besides, my attentions are elsewhere." Kane crossed his arms, his gaze burning into her. "Where was Carver when that old cowpoke tried to take advantage of you? Where was *he* when you needed protection? Are you so enamored with his status that you're blinded to the fact that I was there when you needed me, and I am here now? Where was he? You will love me before your contract is up, Miss Bird. I guarantee it."

"I love Carver and Nora loves you. I hope to the good Lord that she sees who you really are, but if she doesn't, you better endeavor to deserve a woman like her." She turned on her heel and bolted for the shelter of the Harvey House.

CHAPTER 16

"Train after train after train," Sophia moaned, unlacing her shoes, and slipping them off her throbbing feet after a long night. She rubbed her arches and flopped back on the straw tick mattress, sighing. "Remind me again why we do this?"

"Money." Nora tossed Sophia's apron in the dirty clothes hamper to be sent on the train for cleaning before reaching into the closet for a gown.

"Well, I can definitely say that out of the many things being a Harvey Girl has taught me, the value of the dollar has been the most pathetic lesson. All these hours for only $17.50 a month." She stretched and yawned.

"I don't know what you are complaining about. We get food, lodging, uniforms, and a fair wage for doing a reasonable, honest, and honorable job." Nora laughed as she buttoned her uniform, readying for her seven o'clock morning shift. "But if I dare to guess, back home you'd probably spend a month's wages in a week."

More like a day. Sophia closed her eyes for a moment, but a fierce knocking broke her sleep, and she fought back a disgruntled comment as Nora opened the door to the offending person.

"Yes, Dolly?"

Dolly pushed past Nora and strode over to Sophia. "You left your station with a spoilt tablecloth!" She planted her hands on her hips. "Are you *trying* to get me removed from the running as head Harvey Girl? I would've thought after yesterday you would've been going over everything, scrutinizing every single detail."

Sophia struggled to sit up. "You mean after I accidentally dropped a napkin and had to return to the linen closet for a replacement as the patrons arrived?" *It was most likely only a tiny speck of coffee I missed on that tablecloth.*

"It's *Miss* Dolly to you, Miss Sophia, because you are *still* on duty," Dolly corrected her. "Now, are you going to get out of bed and fix that tablecloth, or am I going to have to report you to Miss Harriet?"

Sophia glowered. "I think Harriet would understand as I have worked a fourteen-hour shift and through the night because there was a full house, and I couldn't rest. I think one tiny speck of coffee will hardly be noticed."

"The Harvey system revolves around perfection. Now, you have two minutes to get downstairs and remedy the situation, or I shall report your negligence to not only Miss Harriet, but Miss Trent, along with your disregard for the Harvey standards, and have you on the road to dismissal." Dolly twirled on her heel and slammed the door.

"Well, then. I guess I'm not done after all." *Will she ever forgive me for standing up for*

Nora and her new gown? She leaned over, grabbed her shoes, and slipped her foot inside. The toe of her stocking caught on something small in her shoe. "What in the worl—?" Her words cut short with a scream as she felt a needle pierce her foot.

"Sophia! Oh, Sophia. Why didn't you shake out your shoes?" Nora cried as she ran to her, seized the boot, and threw it across the room.

Sophia's screams contracted into hysterical sobs as she sank to the floorboards, clutching her tingling foot, and spied a scorpion crawl out of the top of her boot across the room. In a flash of skirts, Nora squashed it with the rug beater. *I've been stung.* The room began to spin. The poison was already taking effect.

"Sophia?" Nora gently slapped Sophia's cheeks, tears streaking down her own. "I'm so sorry. I'm so, so sorry! Stay awake for me."

She grabbed for Nora's hand, but her vision blurred, and she had trouble formulating words. She blinked again and again, but her eyes grew so heavy she was forced to relinquish herself to the darkness and collapsed into Nora's arms.

She was first aware that she was no longer sprawled on the floor, but in bed when she heard the clink of glass. She dragged an eyelid open to see the lamps had been lit and a man in a black suit was mixing something in a glass vial.

"While most scorpions aren't lethal, there's always the chance," the man explained to Nora. "Since you were able to kill it, I was able to determine that it is *not* lethal. We will just have to wait and see how Miss Bird reacts to the venom as it has only been in her system for twenty minutes, but for most people, this kind of scorpion sting would only cause slight swelling and mild discomfort." He cleared his throat, further waking her.

I have been unconscious for twenty minutes?

"If it wasn't lethal, why did she scream like a banshee, Doctor?" Nora replied. "She scared me near to death!"

"It's likely that since she is from Charleston, she has heard all manner of things regarding the gravity of a scorpion's sting . . .

nearly all of which are greatly out of proportion, which has led to her fainting spell." He finished the concoction and proceeded to pack away his instruments and medicines.

Sophia chuckled. "So, I'm being a weak, city bred woman?"

"Oh, thank God," Nora cried as she sank down on the bed beside Sophia and grasped Sophia's hand. "I was so worried."

"I'm afraid I might have been a tad bit theatrical, but in all fairness," Sophia looked at the doctor, "it hurt worse than anything I have ever felt, but I have never had a high tolerance for discomfort." Sophia gingerly tested her injured foot by pressing it against the bedpost and found that, although it stung, it was far from unbearable. Apparently, every novel she had read about the subject had greatly exaggerated the power of the scorpion's sting.

"Just stay off your foot for the rest of the day and let me know if it swells any more," he replied, unamused as he lifted a spoonful of bitter medicine to her lips. "Get some rest, ladies."

At the doctor's departure, Harriet sailed into the room and crossed her arms, rolling her eyes. "Surely, you could've thought of some better scheme to not change the table linens? It's only too bad that you chose not to wait until just before your shift begins again at six o'clock this evening. I may have given you the night off."

Sophia and Nora laughed, and Harriet's fake scowl shifted into a soft smile.

"I changed the tablecloth myself and no one shall be reported to Fred Harvey." She sent Sophia a smirk. "At least, not tonight anyways for I'm sure Dolly will only watch you all the more closely. Now, shall we get you in the parlor where you can rest and read should you awaken?"

CARVER WAITED for Nora to slip outside for her morning shift to beg her to allow him inside to see Sophia. Against her better judgement, she allowed him into the parlor, looking over her shoulder at every creak of floorboards.

"I could get into some serious trouble for this, Mr. Ashton. Only the doctor is allowed in here at this hour. Will five minutes do? That's all I can spare watching in the hallway before my shift," Nora whispered.

With a nod of thanks, he slipped into the tiny parlor, crossing to where she laid on the settee in a cream shirtwaist and pink skirt with a poetry book nearly touching her nose. He tripped over the corner of the braided rug in his haste to get to her and upset the side table.

"Carver! You can't be in here!" She gasped as he righted the piece.

"I know, but I was so worried when I heard about the scorpion. The entire hotel was talking about the incident." He scooped Sophia's hands to kiss them, studying her face. She was quite pale and the dark circles had returned under her eyes.

"Well, that's embarrassing, but it probably wouldn't be the best indicator that our marriage would go well if you weren't worried." She gestured to her foot. "I was a little more dramatic than need be, but in my defense, I had no idea some scorpions are less, um, lethal, than others."

"I had a horrible time trying to secure permission to see you. We need to inform people of our engagement because I'm afraid it is the only way I would be able to convince Miss Trent. I had to sneak in with Nora's aid."

"It was fun keeping it to ourselves while we could, but I agree that it isn't the most practical of things. When do you wish to announce it?" Sophia looked up at him through her eyelashes in a way that made him want to kiss her again.

He shook his head free from the fog Sophia always seemed to bring about his usually sharp mind. "Now. I need to leave tomorrow evening to finish some deals in New Orleans to get the department store stocked and well, after a discussion with the sheriff, I think it is best the town knows."

"When will you be back?"

"In October." Just saying the words brought a pang to his gut, but he pushed forward. "It will take that long to get the store up and running and for me to find a house worthy of you living in it. And I was thinking it might be for the best that you finish out your six-month contract. I'd hate to take you to a new place and start our lives together in a hotel room when you love it here so much with your Harvey sisters."

Sophia offered him a smile. "We will just have to enjoy the time we have together between shifts."

"But first." He nodded to the necklace he knew was under her high collar.

She laughed and coaxed the gold out of her collar, slipping the ring from the chain and handing it to him.

He held it up in the morning light streaming through the parlor windows, the diamond sparkling and dancing against the walls. "It was meant for you, someone who brings light and joy everywhere they traverse."

Her cheeks turned rosy as he gently slid the ring on her finger. "I'm almost afraid of wearing it in public for fear of having it stolen!"

Carver grinned. "The ring I can replace,

but I don't want any fool to get it into his head you are up for the taking and try to run off with my future wife."

She held her hand out to examine her ring. "I think I would have a thing or two to say about that, but I suppose people will just find out one by one as the girls begin to notice my ring."

"Sophia, I brought you some tea." The parlor door creaked open, despite Nora's protesting, and Harriet entered with a tray with Nora close behind. They caught sight of Sophia's extended hand, and both released squeals that could wake the house.

"Which won't be long!" Carver laughed.

"Sophia Bird! Look at the size of that ring." Harriet poked her head into the hallway and shouted, "Jenny! You have to come see this."

"Don't shout! We'll get into trouble," Nora hissed.

"The afternoon calling time won't apply for a gentleman visiting his injured fiancée!" Harriet reassured her as heels clomped on the hardwood floor from the hallway and stairs as the girls flooded the room.

Nora grasped Sophia's hand to study the ring. "How long have you two been thinking about this?"

"We've been secretly engaged since the social," Sophia admitted.

Nora's jaw dropped as she placed her hand over her stomach, shaking her head in disbelief.

"You've had a secret that delectable for this long and you didn't share it with me?" Jenny engulfed Sophia in an embrace. "I'd be angry, if I wasn't so happy for you two!"

Sophia giggled as she untangled herself from Jenny's embrace and reached for Carver, her face wreathed in smiles. "We wanted to keep it between us for only a few days, but I'm so glad you all finally know, and I can actually wear my ring on my hand."

Nora's eyes welled as she bent and hugged Sophia. "I'm so surprised and happy for you. I only wish you could've told me sooner," she whispered, pulling away and running out of the room.

"What's this I hear about an engagement?" Miss Trent bustled into the parlor, the room erupting in squeals as the Harvey Girls rushed to explain all.

Carver glanced to Sophia. He didn't know Nora, but her reaction to their engagement was beyond odd, but as Sophia was all smiles, he didn't mention it and enjoyed his future bride's laughter.

CHAPTER 17

"I should've known better with a pretty, smart girl like you than to expect you to sign a second contract. We are fortunate you've lasted this long, really." Miss Trent embraced her, offering her congratulations before glancing at her pocket watch. "The train should be here any minute. I'd best be getting to the dining room. Keep that foot elevated as much as possible and get some rest before starting your shift. Mr. Carver, follow me. We have made enough allowances for one day regarding gentlemen callers."

With an apologetic smile to Sophia, Carver disappeared with the housemother as Nora closed the door and sank down beside Sophia.

"You need to go! The train—"

"I only had to tell you again that I am so sorry about your foot and everything that has happened to you lately." Tears filled Nora's eyes.

Sophia adjusted her pillow and leaned back. "You threw my shoe across the room and saved me from getting stung again. Or can scorpions only sting once? Like bees?"

Nora twisted her hands and looked up at the ceiling as a tear trickled down her neck as she muffled a sob with her hand.

Sophia sat up, her stack of back pillows toppling to the ground. "Whatever is the matter?" In the ensuing silence, Sophia squeezed Nora's hands. "Tell me what is going on. Perhaps I can allay your fears?"

Nora's shoulders shook from holding in her emotions. "I didn't know that you and Mr. Ashton were so serious. I went by the stable this morning and heard what Kane said to Mr. Ashton."

"Where were you? I was there too."

"I was in the office broom closet. I was

waiting for Kane and panicked when he brought in Carver."

"In the broom closet?" Sophia shook her head against pressing further on that score at the moment. "But, if you were in there, you would've heard my rebuking him."

Nora pulled a handkerchief from her cuff. "I departed directly after Carver through the backdoor. Kane wants nothing to do with me."

"I'm sorry I wasn't able to confide in you sooner, but Carver and I wished to enjoy the secret a little longer. Haven't you ever held a secret that warmed your heart, yet you couldn't wait until someone knew?"

Nora's countenance shattered as she buried her face in her hands, sobbing. "Once, but now it's my secret that is crushing me. If I had known you and Carver were planning on marrying, I never would have—"

"You never would have . . . what?"

"I am the one who's been trying to get you to break your contract and return home," Nora whispered, her voice cracking.

Her grasp on Nora's hand slipped. She

stood and limped to the window, gathering her words. "You mean to tell me everything that has been happening to me, the *scorpion,* the mysteriously soiled linens and aprons, the second load of china I broke, and who knows what else, is because you have been trying to get me to leave?" She whirled around to face her friend who nodded, tears flowing.

"And the coffee pot lid when you poured it on Carver. I bent it so that when you came to the last cup, it would spill."

"How could you? I thought we were friends?" She sank down onto the rocker beside the window, gazing through the lace at the street. "I don't understand."

"We *are* friends. But then I panicked. I didn't know what else I could do." Nora picked at her spotless apron.

"Why would you think your unrequited love justified such actions?" She frowned, anger filling her that, because of Nora, she wouldn't be able to walk without pain for days. "Do you really hate me so much that you would want to injure me?"

"The sting was an accident. I never

wanted to hurt you. I only wanted to scare you into going home." Nora smoothed out the lace trim of her soiled handkerchief as she raised her eyes to meet Sophia's. "Sheriff Kane was about to ask me to marry him before you arrived. He had made me all sorts of promises and I was about to have the fairytale life I have always dreamed about. What else was I supposed to do when I saw the only man I have ever loved throwing himself at you? It broke my heart to watch the interest he once showed me be bestowed upon another—especially a girl who has only ever had it all with no doubt scads of money."

"If he is so fickle as to drop you the moment he sees me, be *glad* I came along and saved you from such inconstancy." Sophia clenched her fists, attempting to keep her temper controlled. "If he acts like this now, what makes you think he will act any better once you are married? The man is fickle and his eyes wander."

"Yes, he is fickle, but it's a little late for that to matter." Nora pulled on a strand of her ebony hair. "When I was secure in my relationship with Kane and the thought never crossed my mind that I might lose him, I informed him in casual conversation that you came from money—a lot of money. Well, his eyes lit up and I immediately realized what a horrid mistake I had made."

Nora wiped her eyes with her fist. "I am such a fool. I *knew* he always wanted to be rich and move to a big city. I knew it, but I still told him because I believed him to be true to me. But he saw you as his ticket to wealth and his chance to redeem his mother's financial choices, but—" her voice wavered and she paused to collect herself. "Before you came to town, he made such promises to me with passion-filled kisses and love in his eyes that he convinced me to slip into bed with him."

And with those words, the anger ebbed from Sophia's bones and in its place was only pity. "Nora."

"We were only together once and I regretted it ever since, but once was all it took." She placed her hand on her abdomen and sighed as her tears kept falling. "I have never been regular, so I didn't think much of it at first, but I know for certain now."

Sophia sank down beside Nora and wrapped her arm around her waist. *That's why she was ill.* She rested her head on Nora's shoulder. "You're two months?"

She nodded, rubbing her forehead. "As soon as I begin to show, my reputation will be shattered, and I will lose my job. I've spent weeks begging him to love me for me until the social when I told him about the child. He was so angry with me."

The cad. How dare he treat her so? "There's still time to convince him otherwise."

Nora released a bitter laugh. "The man wants nothing to do with me now that you are here. Can't you see why I was so scared? The only way I could see to fix my problem was to frighten you to the point you left on the next train. I knew with you out of the picture, he would want me again. He would want our child." She took Sophia's hand and squeezed it. "Sophia, I promise I never intended to bring you harm. It was my fear, this horrible, dreadful fear, that caused me to be so wretched."

"I only wish you would've told me, and I would have been firmer much earlier with Kane that his attentions to me would result in nothing." Her eyes wandered to the window as she sighed. "I could've saved you so much pain."

"I wish I had . . . I was just so scared. Can you ever forgive me for betraying our friendship?"

"Of course." Sophia hugged her, thinking of all she had learned in her short time at the Harvey House. Sophia gently stroked her on the back, trying to calm Nora's tears. "I used to be terrified too, and fear can make us do some foolish things. But when I stepped away from my parents and came out here on my own, alone, I learned to lean on the Lord for confidence and slowly, day by day, I have released my fear and anger."

"I've asked for the Lord's forgiveness and know I have received it, but I am still frightened. I don't know how to be a mother and raise a child without a father. My child will be treated differently, and I will be seen as a fallen woman. Men will see it as an invitation to make unwanted advances. I am a good woman. I just love him so much that I-I got confused." Nora shook her head at a loss of words.

"I know you are a good woman. I'm here for you, Nora, if you will let me." She grasped her Harvey sister's hand and began to pray for the Lord to give them each direction and courage to face the storm ahead.

CHAPTER 18

The train's whistle seared him, needlessly reminding him once more of their impending parting. He looked down at Sophia, drinking in the sight of her. Even in her stern uniform, she was the loveliest woman he had ever beheld. *First, I must provide, and then she will be my wife.*

"Carver . . ." Sophia pulled him to a stop at the platform, pausing before a first-class car. "I have had something pressing on my mind since yesterday."

His heart lurched. She wasn't thinking of ending things with him after all, was she? "Oh?"

She nodded, worrying her bottom lip. "I

have a friend who is in trouble, but I think if I had access to my funds, I'd be able to fix her predicament. However, I do not think it would be wise to contact Father about my inheritance until after we are wed."

Carver stifled his sigh of relief. "If it is funds you need, you are welcome to access my bank accounts at any time. I will notify my banks and tell them to add your name on the official accounts. There is not as much as what your inheritance will be, but I have been saving whatever I've earned with Prescott, as well as monetary gifts, since I was a lad and what is mine is yours."

She pressed her hand to her heart. "Carver, you are too kind. Under any other circumstance I would use my funds, but I am rather limited at the moment." Sophia rose on her tiptoes and kissed him softly. "Thank you. I shall repay you the minute my funds are given to me."

Carver grinned. "Your kiss is payment enough, my love."

She sighed, glancing at the passengers boarding the train. "I don't wish to say farewell."

He closed the short distance between them and held her delicate form in his arms as a gentle breeze caressed them, swishing her black skirts. "It won't be long before we meet again, but at this moment, three months seems an eternity away."

The whistle blew again, and the conductor issued the final warning to board.

Carver held her face in his hands and gently returned her kiss. "To be apart when I have at last found the love of my life . . . it wounds me, even as the hope of our reunion burns within." His throat ached from withholding his need of asking her to leave all behind. *She deserves a home—one as lovely as the one she left behind in Charleston.* He sighed. "The waiting will be worth it, my love."

"I have waited years to marry, a few more months will not make a difference. I never thought I would feel so about a man, but you have changed everything for me."

"Because of me, you lost your home . . . your family and friends."

"They gave me no choice, but you came after me. You saw me as something worth more than a business transaction that you couldn't control. I know you would never attempt to change me." She wrapped her hands about his neck and pressed her forehead to his.

"Who would want to tame a lovely wildflower such as yourself?" He pulled a lock of her hair through his fingers, memorizing the silkiness. "You were a breath of fresh air in my life, and I consider myself blessed that no man recognized your unique nature for what it is—a treasure. Thank you for waiting for me, Sophia." He pressed her hands to his lips, kissing each palm, aching to kiss her fully, but the platform had grown too crowded, and he cared too much for her reputation.

"I have waited a lifetime for you, Carver, and I'd wait another if I had to in order to become your wife."

His fingers slowly released their hold from hers as he stepped backward and onto the train. She pressed her hand to her lips and sent him one last kiss that he ached to return in earnest. He waved to her as the train pulled out of the station until she was but a memory burned into his heart.

THE MORNING SUN beat down on Sophia as she hurried down the sidewalk in her uniform before her shift began. Nora had been ill all morning and with every heave, she seemed to despair further, and because of this, Sophia knew she needed to act—to be stronger than ever before and face her friend's need before it was too late.

Determination alone brought her to the sheriff's station door. She paused at the threshold and steeled herself, charging into the station. "Kane? Are you here?"

Kane poked his head in from the back room, emerging with coffee pot in hand. "I thought I recognized your voice. I didn't expect you to pay call after our last . . . *discussion*." He set the pot down on his desk, sitting on the edge and crossing his arms over his broad chest.

Sophia's gaze flitted to the two men behind bars playing chess as well as the deputy polishing a rifle in the corner. This topic would be hard enough to get through without an audience. “Can you spare ten minutes to take a stroll with me?”

“You’re not going to yell at me again, are you?” He grinned at her playfully.

She crossed her arms. “It depends on your answer.”

“My answer? I am intrigued.” He snatched his Stetson off the coat rack. “I’d love to get away from this stinking office anyhow. I burnt some grits on the stove in the back room and it’s smelling up the whole place. I’d sure hate to be the drunkard I locked up in the back cell, but that’s what you get for disturbing the peace at one o’clock in the morning.” He chuckled and followed her out the door toward the pretty blue church, the emerald field beyond it dotted with colorful bursts of wildflowers. “So, what brought about the change of heart?”

She paused beneath the cedar trees beside the chapel. “It’s not so much a change of heart as a need to address an issue on behalf of my friend.” Sophia’s voice shook, but she pressed onward. "I know what you did."

"Excuse me?" Kane's expression was blank, but his eyes sparked with alarm.

Sophia fiddled with her cuff for a second to gather her courage. She cleared her throat. "I brought you here today because I am concerned for my friend's reputation and that of your child's."

"My child's?" Kane's jaw dropped. "What lies has Nora told you?"

Her eyes narrowed. "Nora's tales are obviously not lies as you named the lady to whom I was referring."

He rolled his eyes. "What *other* lady would you be referring? Nora has been throwing herself at me ever since you arrived in an attempt to capture my attentions away from you." He took her hand in his, patting it. "I am obviously enamored with you, and she cannot stand it, so in a moment of desperation, she has told you that she is with my child. She may be with child, but it is certainly *not* mine."

"You really expect me to take your word over Nora's?" Sophia jerked her hand away.

"Don't think for a minute I haven't seen the way you flirt with her, Harriet, Dolly, or Fannie the minute you think my back is turned. Or how you have been leading Nora on, or that I have forgotten your conversation with Carver. How foolish do you think I am to be taken by such a charlatan? I have never given you any sign of encouragement and yet, you threw Nora aside in your lust for wealth. You are a man without honor."

Kane's eyes darkened and he took a step toward her as Sophia stumbled back, but he caught her by the wrist, and for the first time, Sophia was afraid of what he might do to her. *Didn't really think this one through, did you?*

"Them's powerful words from one so tiny." He growled.

She kept her spine stiff, along with her resolve. "I am prepared to offer you funds to marry her."

His expression froze, his hold on her slowly loosening as a gleam flickered through his eyes. "How much?"

"A thousand."

He snorted, casting her arm aside and

spat on the parched earth. "A pittance to what I am owed."

She folded her hands before her skirts to disguise their trembling. "Which is why I am prepared to offer you three thousand as soon as Carver and I are wed and I have access to my inheritance." *If Father decides to give it to me.*

"And I am supposed to just wed the girl and trust you to your word? Sorry, rich folk don't really bring much trust to mind." He crossed his arms and leaned against a cedar tree. "Try again."

"I will write out a contract. A thousand worth in jewels and two more upon my marriage to Carver."

He ran his hand over his jaw, tapping his finger on his cheek before straightening. "Make it the jewels now and a thousand dollars, plus *three* more to be transferred at once upon our marriage and we have a bargain."

Sophia was careful not to allow her shoulders to relax as she had been prepared to offer him six thousand, though she would have been loathed to ask Carver for such a sum. Her father would be proud of her negotiating. "But, if you breathe a word of this arrangement to Nora, the deal is off."

"Agreed." He stuck out his hand.

She shook it and dropped it at once before he could catch her unaware again. Gathering her skirts, she fled to the safety of the Harvey House, not daring to look back at the man who held her friend's reputation in his hands.

CHAPTER 19

Carver's hands shook as he accepted the keys from Mr. Mason. He had done it. He had actually finalized the purchase of a department store at the end of St. Charles Avenue at the price he wished. At the man's departure, Carver allowed himself to bask in the moment, studying every room in the store, admiring the merchandise, taking a moment to rearrange whatever he wished. The fourth floor was a storage of sorts full of old bits and bobs, but with a good cleaning, reorganizing, and slight remodeling, he would have the new men's haberdashery up and running within a few weeks.

Taking the stairs down to the first floor, as the liftman had gone home for the evening, Carver found the perfect place for Sophia's tearoom bookshop, grinning with anticipation over her reaction to their store. His bride would love this place as much as he did. It would take a few months or so to get it just as he wished, but until then, he had enough merchandise in stock, and on the way, to make a profit even in his first month.

He withdrew the photo of Sophia, running his finger over her lovely face. "I wish you were here with me now, but soon, my love, I'll show you the kingdom we will build together."

"Mr. Ashton?"

Carver jumped as he shoved the picture back into his inside coat pocket, his neck heating. "Mr. Bennett. You're here early." He released a nervous laugh at being caught speaking to a photograph.

Mr. Bennett opened his pocket watch, frowning. "I'm right on time. Now, are you ready to see those two houses on St. Charles

Avenue? They won't last long on the market."

"The sooner I purchase a home, the better." Carver motioned Mr. Bennett out the front door, a thrill running through him as he locked up his new store. The future was bright indeed.

SOPHIA DIDN'T SLEEP WELL for the next month. With Carver's departure, she felt a hollowness inside that drifted into her dreams, which led to sleepless nights as the terror of Prescott finding her and claiming her as his own before Carver returned became all too real. To distract herself from how tired she was each morning, Sophia threw herself into her work. When customers were agitated, she did everything in her power to calm them and when they were hostile, she was friendly, and when they were too friendly, she made certain to flash her diamond ring and mention her fiancé, thankful Miss Trent made an exception to the strict no jewelry rule for her engagement ring.

Two more months until my contract is up. She reassured herself as she grabbed a rag to clean up after a child who had knocked over his mother's coffee for the second time that afternoon. *It may not be as grand or glorious as my brothers' jobs, but there's value in earning your own keep,* she reminded herself as she mopped up the table linen, knowing she would, of course, change it again when the guests departed.

After the rush of guests had subsided, Harriet tossed her rag atop the counter, mopping her forehead. "Can someone *please* tell me where Nora is? I haven't seen her all morning. She missed the first train and will miss the second if she doesn't get here in a hurry. It's inexcusable to run off when the train must be fed!"

"She received a letter early this morning and then dashed out without saying a word. I only hope everything is okay." Sophia stacked her table's plates, knowing all too well that Nora had been tossing her accounts this morning. *Hopefully, the sickness will soon abate.* Judging from what she knew from her sisters' pregnancies, it should be lessening now that Nora was nearing the end of her third month. "I had thought she'd be back before breakfast, but I'm starting to get worried."

"Well, she better have a good reason for at least not leaving word of where she was headed." Harriet mumbled about blatant disregard for others and the rules that were established by Fred Harvey himself.

Sophia had just finished placing the last of the settings on the table when the gong announced the arrival of the next train. Smoothing her hair back, she stood next to Harriet at her station and folded her hands in front of her apron. Her eyes widened as guest after guest crossed through the doors. *Where is Nora?*

"It's a full house. I am going to have *words* with Nora Ray," Harriet growled through her gritted smile. She turned to Jenny. "Go to the dormitories and fetch the night shift girls. We need all the help we can get."

Every seat in the dining room and

counter was filled with hungry guests from the train and some regulars from the town and it was all Sophia could manage to match Harriet's flowing pace, smiling and taking orders and revising orders as quickly as the head waitress. She did her best to see the drinks were kept filled to the brim and to whisk away a plate as soon as the guest was finished with it. Within half an hour, every guest left satisfied and full and the staff near drained.

Sophia collapsed into a vacant chair at her station after the last guest departed and felt, for the first time in years, her lungs struggling to keep up with the rush.

"I feel the same way." Harriet sank onto a chair across from her. "You really proved yourself today. While I admit that your training got off to a slow start, you are quickly becoming one of the best girls we have, and we will be sorry to see you go."

"I have learned a great deal under you, and I will miss you all greatly."

"Except, perhaps, Dolly, eh?" Harriet winked and pushed herself to her feet with a groan. "Come on, we have an hour until the next train comes."

Nora burst through the dining room doors, beaming. "Did you miss me, ladies?"

"Where have you been?" Harriet plunked her hands on her slim hips, her lips pursing so hard a thin white ring formed about her mouth as the girls gathered to Nora, asking where she had disappeared.

Nora stuck her left hand into the group, displaying a gold band on her ring finger. "I was getting *married!*"

Sophia squealed with the rest of the girls who swarmed to embrace her as Harriet's jaw dropped before splitting into a smile. Sophia felt as flabbergasted as Harriet looked. She had gotten the sheriff to sign the contract for the one thousand and the jewels, but he had refused to marry Nora until Sophia came into her inheritance. *What made him change his mind?*

"I didn't know you and the sheriff got back together! It is the sheriff, yes?" Dolly gawked at the simple gold band that meant so much.

Nora blushed. "The sheriff and I had been talking about getting married for a long time." Her gaze shifted to Sophia for a half a second, acknowledging her half-truth. "We decided only this morning during his breakfasting at the lunch counter that we shouldn't wait a second longer to share our lives together!"

"And you just dropped everything and ran to the preacher with him?" Fannie clasped her hands to her chest. "How utterly romantical. I wish that would happen to me!"

"It was a quiet, yet beautiful ceremony. I'm elated." Nora squeezed Sophia's hand as the girls sighed in delight.

"Yes indeed, why wait?" Dolly replied, her frown softening. "I'm happy for you, Nora, but unfortunately, you will have to forfeit a month of wages and your rail pass for breaking contract."

"Don't talk contracts when she just got married," Harriet gently elbowed Dolly. "We will sort that bit out later."

"I'm glad at least you decided to inform us you are quitting before you left in your haste to the altar," Miss Trent interjected, joining the group. At Nora's shocked expression, she laughed. "I'm only teasing. Congratulations, my dear. Not every girl has the privilege of marrying for love. You should consider yourself blessed."

Nora's blush deepened. "Thank you, Miss Trent. I would've told you, but it was quite spontaneous." She giggled, staring at her ring. "I feel like this is a dream, but every time I pinch myself, I find the ring is still on my finger."

Harriet clapped her hands. "All right ladies, while we're all excited to see our own dear Nora married, we must prepare the dining hall. The train must be fed."

Nora gave Sophia a quick embrace and whispered, "Thank you."

"For what?" Sophia replied, hoping Kane hadn't told her as per the contract, but the train's arrival gong sounded before Nora could reply.

"Hurry ladies," Harriet chided and swept the linens off of Sophia's table.

Dolly rushed to set it with a fresh linen.

"Nora, congratulations, but we'll have to celebrate with you another time. Sophia, grab the tableware!"

CHAPTER 20

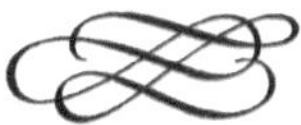

A knock sounded on his office door immediately followed by the creaking of hinges. "Mr. Ashton, sir? There is a man here to see you," the store's page called from the threshold, standing at attention.

Carver didn't look up from the catalogue he was attempting to create with a sketch artist, a project that was far more complicated than he had originally thought to obtain customers outside of the city. "Who is it, Tom?"

"A Mr. Prescott Payne."

Carter froze at the name. It had certainly taken his stepfather long enough to come to

New Orleans to take over the shipping business after Carver delegated his position to the former manager. He rose, straightening his jacket. "Send him to the tea salon."

"Already done, sir," the boy answered, pulling his shoulders back with pride.

"Well done, Tom." He clapped the boy on the shoulder. Leaving the artist to continue alone, Carver strode down the hallway, his heart hammering. Now was the time to tell Prescott of his intentions toward Sophia, if they were not becoming clear already through Prescott's chain of spies.

He smiled to the customers milling about his store, admiring the wares, as he wove through the first floor of home goods to the tea salon where every table was in use and half of the customers at the tables were enjoying a novel from Sophia's library.

He instantly sensed the man's presence. His stepfather sat in the corner round table, glaring at him as a footman delivered a triple tiered tower of tea sandwiches, scones, and chocolate dipped strawberries, along with a pot of what Carver knew would be Earl Grey.

He took a seat without waiting for Prescott to offer it to him. It was *his* department store after all.

"I see you finally found a backbone." He motioned for Carver to pour himself some tea.

Carver met Prescott's gaze. What was he referring to? Sophia or the store?

He nodded, a rare look of approval in his eyes. "You've done quite well for yourself. When my agent in New Orleans sent me the report on you and your store, I couldn't quite believe that you had actually taken such a risk, but," he flicked his wrist toward the store, "it is certainly impressive what you have accomplished on your savings."

"Thank you, sir." Carver poured himself a steaming cup. It had never been his favorite blend, but he did not wish to appear rude and not take a drink with his stepfather.

"And what is even more impressive is the fact that you seem to be under the impression that you are now engaged to *my* fiancée." His eyes turned dark, his voice nearing a growl.

Carver fought the urge to grip the sides of the table. "She is no longer *your* fiancée, Prescott, and one could argue that she never truly was yours to begin with as you arranged it all with her father."

Prescott's head reared back at his challenge. He released a slow chuckle and reached for the sandwiches. "That's not what her father's contract states, and he is too weak from his bout with pneumonia to negotiate different terms. I have come to issue you a warning."

Carver met his gaze, narrowing his brows, and daring him to try.

He took a strawberry and slowly bit it, dabbing its ruby juice from his lips as he rose. "Release Sophia from your so-called claim on her, or you will wish you had."

Carver clenched his fists but refused to take the bait. "You don't even know where she is."

"No. But it is only a matter of time until I find your future stepmother." He gripped his cane in one hand and his hat in the other as he rose from the table. "As a consolation prize, upon my marriage to Miss Fairfield, I will release your inheritance in full. However, if you persist in this unnatural pursuit, I will have no other recourse but to disinherit you."

"A LETTER FOR YOU, MISS BIRD!" Miss Trent called as Sophia passed the Harvey parlor after her shift.

"Really?" She accepted the letter, exhaustion leaving her bones in the excitement of hearing from her fiancé. She raced up the stairs to her room and hungrily read the return address again. *Carver.* She slid her finger under the envelope and carefully broke the seal, opening it as she sank atop her bed, tucking her pillow under her chest as she kept her shoes off her mattress and propped herself up on her elbows.

My dearest Sophia,

I cannot wait to bring you to New Orleans as my wife. The store is a beauty, and the customers are thrilled with the tea salon bookshop that you suggested. In fact, ladies are taking their tea there even without the excuse of waiting for shopping friends or spouses.

And now, for even more exciting news, I have secured a house for us, but it will take about a month or two for it to be dressed in a manner that I believe you will find pleasing. I am hurrying it along as quickly as possible because the sooner it is finished, the sooner I can come claim you as my bride. The outside must be painted, the floors need refinishing and the whole house needs fresh furniture as the former owner was a lady with five cats.

When you arrive, please add

your lovely touches to our home. It feels marvelous to write "our" home. I can hardly believe that the Lord has blessed me with a woman as kind, intelligent, and beautiful as you, my sweetheart. I—

"Sophia, whatever are you smiling about?" Harriet laughed from the hallway. "I'd bet a dollar Carver is sending you little notes of his undying affection." She rolled her eyes and grinned as she and Fannie plopped onto Nora's now vacant bed. "That man is smitten with you!"

Sophia flushed but didn't deny it as she rose to change. "*And I am* quite *smitten with him.*"

"I'm not surprised that you went for Mr. Ashton. I figured you would never go for one of the men around here. They're a little too rough around the edges, aren't they?" Fannie giggled. "Me now, I don't mind a little rough as long as they have plenty of gold or cash to help cushion them!"

"Fannie!" Sophia exclaimed, pulling on her silk robe over her nightgown.

"What? I ain't ashamed of admitting that I like a man with a bit of money," Fannie replied with wide, innocent eyes.

Sophia rolled her eyes and shook her head with a laugh as she let her hair loose from its tight bun and began her hundred strokes. "What about Joshua?"

Fannie shrugged. "Eh, I don't really care for him anymore. He's a little too dirty for my taste. His fingernails always have grime under them. I keep telling him that a gentleman washes and keeps his nails looking pristine, but he just laughs at me, so I am going out with Alexander tonight."

"You're rejecting Joshua because of the state of his *nails*? For Alexander the banker? He may be cleaner, but he is not half as nice as Joshua!" Harriet shook her head. "Now, I thought that you were a little vain, and you yourself admit to being vain, but this brings it to a whole new level." Harriet removed the brush from Sophia's fingertips. "Here, let me. I miss brushing my mama's hair."

Sophia gratefully surrendered the brush

and closed her eyes, enjoying being pampered.

"I gave him fair warning," Fannie said as she took the file from Sophia's dresser and shaped her nails. "I told him on multiple occasions that if he didn't change his ways, I'd be going out with Alexander tonight."

"Tonight?" Sophia asked. "It is going to be an awfully short visit because curfew is in ten minutes."

Fannie laughed, handing her the nail file. "True, but the Midnight Express leaves after curfew."

Harriet clapped her hands over her ears. "Fannie! I told you. You cannot say such things if front of me, or I will have to report you to Miss Trent."

"The what?" Sophia worked on her nails that were in a sorry state.

"Nora *never* told you about the Midnight Express?" Fannie asked, her mouth agape. "She used to take it all the time before you came along, so I suppose she didn't feel the need to tell you if she had given up on using it herself." She looked to Harriet. "Better cover your ears again."

Harriet rolled her eyes, but proceeded to do just that.

Fannie leaned toward Sophia and whispered, "The Midnight Express leaves from Jenny's bedroom window. There's a lattice we climb down and go a courting with our men."

Sophia's jaw dropped. "You *break* curfew?" *And not to mention, you are going to meet a man as well. . . which explains how Nora was coaxed.* "I find it hard to believe that you, who is so concerned with Joshua's state of nails defining his gentleman status, would go traipsing out into the night unchaperoned."

"And that's why I am sure Nora did not tell you!" Fannie laughed. "You are an old prude."

"I am not." Sophia crossed her arms.

"Then prove it. I'm not going out with him alone, of course. Come with me and Dolly tonight. We always have a grand old time. It'll be a small party with a bonfire and some special desserts."

Sophia shook her head firmly. "Not a chance."

"You need to loosen your corset strings." Fannie scowled as she threw a pillow into Sophia's face.

"I won't tell on you, but I won't lie either if you get caught missing," Sophia replied, pressing her lips into a firm line.

Fannie giggled. "You may say you aren't a prude, but your face says otherwise!"

Realizing how she must look, Sophia laughed and motioned for Harriet that it was safe to listen again.

"So, Nora and the sheriff. Anyone else think that was a bit of a surprise?" Fannie took the brush from Harriet and began stroking her own glossy hair.

Harriet shrugged. "People do irrational things when they are in love."

"Lights out!" Miss Trent called through the hallway.

Fannie giggled as she tossed the brush into Sophia's lap, pausing in the doorway after Harriet had left. "I'll be visiting Jenny's room in ten minutes. Dolly and I can't be late for our evening out, so if you want to come, be ready."

"I thought it was the *Midnight* Express,

not the Ten Past Ten Express," Sophia teased and slipped out of her robe and under her blankets.

Fannie rolled her eyes. "Well, then, it wouldn't sound nearly as romantic, now would it?"

With the girls' departure she lowered her lamp's wick and finished the letter, gasping at the postscript, reading it once more.

P.S. Write home. Your father was recently ill and is on the mend, but I think it would bring comfort to them knowing you are well.

Sophia turned down the wick completely and tried to ignore the fact that she needed to write home, but with the breeze and room devoid of Nora's snoring, Sophia quickly fell into a deep slumber.

"Sophia," a whisper broke into her dreams of Carver. "Sophia!"

"Uh, what is it?" Sophia blinked in the

dim candlelight, her body shaking from the intrusion of her slumber.

"Shh. Come with me," Jenny whispered.

"Why?" Sophia rubbed her face, trying to wake up. "Is it a full house in the middle of the night?"

"No." Jenny handed Sophia her silk robe. "Put this on, and please do be quiet."

Sophia pulled on her robe and stumbled into Jenny's bedroom. "What is going on?"

Jenny pointed outside. "It's Dolly. She's fallen on her wrist and she's too hurt to climb back inside. What do we do? Miss Trent will be forced to fire her and Fannie on the spot if she discovers them." She wrung her hands. "And I know with all of Dolly's big talk, she needs this job just as much as I do."

"She's not wealthy?"

"Her aunt is the wealthy one, and from what Dolly used to confided in me, she only sends Dolly her daughter's cast offs as her way of taking care of her orphaned niece. If Dolly loses this position, she will be forced to return to a home where she isn't wanted."

"Well, how do we get her inside unnoticed? The back door is always locked after eight o'clock and only unlocked for shift changes, both times Miss Trent is there and she would catch Dolly and Fannie for certain." Sophia snapped her fingers. "Harriet! She has a spare key in case Miss Trent loses hers."

Jenny shook her head doubtfully. "You think Harriet would be able to help without feeling that she must report it?"

Sophia sighed. "Well, she's always saying that Harvey Girls stick together, so maybe sticking together means Harriet might help her just this once."

"If you think it might work?"

"It's the only plan we have." Sophia tiptoed down the hall, tapped lightly on Harriet's door, and waited a few seconds before tapping again, praying that Miss Trent in the room next door wouldn't hear and come inspect.

Harriet tugged open the door. With her blonde hair cascading to her hourglass waist, she rubbed her eyes. "Yes? There's no train right now. What's wrong?"

"It's Dolly. She fell trying to get back up the lattice," Sophia whispered.

Alarm flickered across Harriet's features. "Is she hurt?"

"It's her wrist. The girls don't think it's broken, but it hurts too much to try to get back up the lattice, and she needs the key to the back door. I know it is against the rules, but Dolly and Fannie will get fired. Could you—?"

"While I do not condone breaking the rules, Dolly is still my friend. I'll get the key."

Harriet disappeared into her room. The sounds of rummaging in a drawer drifted out. Harriet draped her dressing robe over her shoulders, grasping the skeleton key in hand. In their bare feet, the girls crept down the stairway. Harriet quietly inserted the key and grimaced at the scraping of the turning lock. Sophia held the door open, and Harriet waved Fannie and Dolly inside.

Harriet gently took Dolly's wrist in hand as Dolly whimpered at Harriet's light prodding.

"Do you think it's just sprained, or broken?" Tears streaked down Fannie's cheeks as she stood behind, gripping Dolly's ruined hat in her hands.

Harriet shrugged. "My uncle was a doctor, but I think it is a good sign that you aren't howling in pain. If it is still hurting tomorrow as badly as it is tonight, I want you to go straight to the doctor, but for now, we need to get some ice from the icebox to help with the swelling." She turned to Sophia. "Jenny, Fannie, and I are going to get Dolly upstairs. Do you think you can manage to sneak into the kitchen without waking the night chef? I'm not so worried about the girl on shift catching us. She won't say a word, but Chef Harold—heaven help you if he wakes up." She pressed the key into Sophia's hand. "Lock up afterwards."

Clutching her dressing robe tight against her neck, Sophia darted across the moonlit road and into the Castañeda, past the sleeping desk clerk, and behind Millie who was preoccupied cleaning the lunch counter. She tiptoed into the kitchen and past the massive, sleeping chef on her way to the icebox. She grabbed a clean rag from the counter, carefully opened the wooden door, and prayed that a piece of ice was already chipped off the ice block. Under a tray of oysters was a medium chunk of ice. *If these oysters start to go bad . . .the chef is going to kill whoever took the block of ice.* Sophia carefully lifted the tray enough to slide the ice out from underneath it. She grabbed the chunk with the rag, quickly closed the door and darted out the back door and around the hotel toward the dormitory.

"Well, if it isn't the all proper Miss Bird out in her dressing robe."

His voice stopped her in the middle of the street. She slowly turned, clutching the ice with both hands, the cold seeping through the rag and numbing her fingertips. "Mr. Gessler, please excuse me."

"Oh no, not until you've paid the price for being caught in such a state." He sprang at her.

Suppressing her scream, she bolted for the dormitory, slamming the door, and locking it behind her as the drunkard pounded on the door.

Miss Trent flung open her door and, spying Sophia in her dressing robe, holding the now dripping ice, her jaw dropped. "What happened?"

Her stomach turned and she decided a version of the truth was best. "Dolly is hurt. H-Harriet gave me her key to get her ice."

Miss Trent pursed her lips. "And I'm guessing you were seen."

She nodded. "Mr. Gessler."

Miss Trent withdrew a revolver from the folds of her night gown and opened the door, pointing the barrel of her gun straight at his chest, pulling back the hammer and chambering a bullet. "Go home. You are fortunate I don't place a bullet in your sorry hide for messing with one of my girls, you cad."

Mr. Gessler's slurred mumble faded as he stumbled back, hands raised.

Miss Trent locked the door once more, turning back to Sophia, calm as could be, as if threatening an aggressive man with a gun was an everyday occurrence. "The punishment for being out of your dormitory room is usually dismissal, but as Dolly is hurt, I see your act as a compassionate one. How did Dolly get hurt?"

"She fell."

Miss Trent's lips twisted to the side. "I bet she did. But, you had best not tell me anything else, lest I be forced to act. Get on with you." She waved her up the stairs.

"Well, I certainly hope it was worth you almost breaking your neck!" Harriet scolded the two girls as Sophia slipped into the room with the ice.

Dolly scowled, cradling her hand. "Took you long enough, Sophia."

"I was detained." Sophia rested the ice on Dolly's wrist, the fishy scent filling the small room.

"Ugh, it stinks!" Dolly complained, twisting her nose away from the ice.

"That's because I risked the wrath of the chefs by taking it from under the oysters for tomorrow's lunch."

"I don't understand why you insist on your little Midnight Express adventures," Harriet set aside the ice and wrapped the rag around Dolly's wrist before reapplying the ice.

"I know it was risky to climb the lattice, but how else am I supposed to find time to be courted?"

"Oh, I don't know. Maybe in broad daylight during your lunch break or in the evening on the porch after your day shift? We have calling hours for a reason." Harriet scolded her friend. "I warned you before and now see where your heedlessness has gotten you? You can't possibly lift plates of food with that wrist. You will be half as efficient tomorrow."

Fannie sniffed back her tears. "I didn't mean for you all to take on extra work. I just wanted to make Joshua jealous of Alexander, but you were right, Jenny. Joshua was at the bonfire too tonight and he and Alexander got into a huge fight over me. Alexander made an advance toward me, and Joshua jumped on him. The fight got so bad Sheriff Kane stepped in and locked them both up for the night. I barely got away before the sheriff had a chance to recognize me."

"Good for Joshua!" Sophia exclaimed.

"I hope you are going to go back to him," Jenny added. "If he will take you after your actions."

"Whichever suitor Fannie chooses, Dolly needs to rest if she is going to serve this morning." Harriet rubbed her forehead and checked Dolly's watch pin on the nightstand and sighed. "We only have two hours before dawn, and we need to go down. Jenny, I am going to need you to run the counter by yourself this morning with Fannie, who *will* be taking an extra shift to make up for their little escapade. Can you manage it?"

Jenny laughed. "Of course. How hard could it be for two Harvey Girls?"

Dolly sent her an apologetic look. They *all* knew exactly how hard it could be to run the fifty-one-seat lunch area.

CHAPTER 21

The next morning, Sophia laid out the writing supplies she had purchased at the general store atop the parlor's shared writing desk. *It's time to put the past behind us. I'm sure when Carver and I are married and settled, my parents will forgive me for running away.* Her left hand clutched her gold locket as she slowly dipped her pen into her inkwell and, with a shaking hand, pressed her pen to paper and broke the silence.

Dearest Mother and Father,

My time in the West has taught

me many things. For years I struggled to live under the rigorous and unforgiving eye of society. It made me afraid to speak my mind for fear of being judged, but I am not fearful anymore. I discovered that as long as my conscience is clear before the Lord, it doesn't matter what society thinks of me.

With this newfound freedom, I have come to realize how happy life can be. To think that because of my fear of society, I almost missed out on the greatest gift of my life—the gift of loving the man to whom my heart belongs.

I am so happy to tell you both that I am engaged to Carver Ashton, and we plan on marrying as soon as our home in New Orleans *is prepared. We would love for you both to attend our wedding, but we realize Father's recent illness, or obligations at home, may prevent your coming for the wedding in two months, but rest in the peace of knowing that I am marrying the best man on earth and my former roommate is designing my gown for me and is now working on the finishing touches. Never fear. It will be a gown to rival any Worth confection.*

For the next few weeks, you may find me at the Harvey House where I work as a waitress at the Castañeda Hotel in Las Vegas, New Mexico. If you can't travel to New Orleans when I telegram that Carver and I are about to wed, please do not be distressed. Carver and I shall return to Charleston a few months after our marriage to visit and tie up any loose ends. I hope my letter finds you better, Father. Mother, kiss the babies for me. I miss them so!

With all of my love, Sophia.

"Sophia!" Harriet called from the door-frame, panting. "I know your shift doesn't start for another two hours, but Nora's replacement, Lucy, is working her first shift with us, and the girl is grossly unprepared, despite her training in our Topeka house. I don't know why they keep shipping us girls who aren't ready to serve. I will have to fire this one before the week is out, I'm certain."

Sophia laughed as she picked up her apron. "She can't be all that bad."

Harriet stared at her, blankly. "She has dropped not one, not two, but *three* soup bowls into the customers' laps. She must have heard how you caught a rich husband and is attempting to pull off the same feat."

"Very droll."

"Please come and I'll let you have tomorrow off."

"For a day off?" Sophia trotted out the door at once for fear Harriet would change her mind. She found Lucy flushed and scrubbing away at a stain on the hardwood floor. "Stubborn stuff, is it?" Sophia smiled as she gathered dishes from Lucy's station.

Lucy leaned back on her heels. "I thought I was prepared, but nothing trains you for not knowing a soul and this dreadful heat." She waved her hand, fanning her limp brown hair.

Sophia nodded as she stacked a tower of bowls. "Yes, the heat is dreadful. Take care to drink lots of water or else you might succumb to it."

"How's the girl I am filling in for? Nora, right?" She stretched her back and stood, revealing she was a solid foot taller than Sophia.

"Happy as can be." Sophia called over her shoulder as she brought the bowls to the kitchen and returned with fresh linens as the front door opened and Nora bustled inside in a sunny yellow dress with her basket in front of her abdomen that Sophia knew she was attempting to disguise as long as possible. "Speaking of Nora, allow me to introduce you. We were just talking about you, Nora. Lucy, this is Mrs. Nora Kane, the sheriff's wife!"

Nora smiled her greeting to Lucy. "I hope you enjoy working here. These girls are the best people in the world."

Lucy curtsied. "Nice to meet you, ma'am! I wish I could chat, but I have a lot of work I have to get to before Miss Dolly starts yelling at me again."

"I know how that is. Have a good day!" Nora called after Lucy as the girl snatched her dirty rag from the floor and hurried into the kitchen. Nora waved Sophia over to her and sighed. "Well, I knew it would happen sooner or later."

Sophia's heart clinched. "Knew what would happen?" *Kane didn't leave you, right? Please let it not be so.*

"My corset doesn't fit anymore and now

everyone will see that I am not with child from my honeymoon," she whispered, her eyes filling with tears as she moved the basket aside and let Sophia see that it was swelling with her darling baby. "I'm four months pregnant now, and unless she is very tiny when she is born, people will know."

"It will be fine." Sophia clasped her friend's hand in her own. "You will look a little plumper, but people won't know until the baby is born. People's tongues may wag for a time, but the dust will settle down by the time your second baby comes along. You will have to pray for the strength to endure it."

Nora bit her lip, sniffing back her tears. "I know, but I'm so worried for the baby." She placed a protective hand over her abdomen. "I don't want her, or him, to be treated any less than any other little girl or boy because our timing was a little off."

Sophia squeezed Nora's hands. "Parents may whisper, but the talk will die down long before you need to ever worry."

"It's my prayer." She adjusted her basket

in front of her stomach once more and cleared her throat. "I was hoping you might be able to come over tonight after you get off work? It's been forever since we had a decent, uninterrupted chat, and I've already bought some baked goods for the occasion."

"You have only been married two whole weeks, and you already want me to come over for dinner?" Sophia giggled nervously as she set out the silverware. *Considering my last conversation with Kane, this would be one awkward dinner.*

Nora caught Sophia's wrist. "It will be more of an afternoon high tea. Please? Kane will be gone until late this evening, and I desperately need someone to talk with. It is rather difficult going from a houseful of sisters to only myself and a not so talkative husband."

"I suppose if he will be gone, I could accept your invitation, but I can't stay too long." *Heaven knows what Kane might say if he catches me there.*

Nora beamed. "Thank you! I can't wait to show you what I've done with his—our little house."

Within a few hours, Sophia was dressed in her pink striped chiffon afternoon dress with a simple cream chapeau that she had purchased from the general store and crossing the street to the Kane household.

"Welcome!" Nora gave Sophia her famous Harvey House smile as she ushered her inside, drying her hands on the corner of her pristine apron.

Nora had unpacked her belongings and sprinkled a feminine touch about the house with fresh blue curtains, a doily here and there, and a red knitted throw that she had placed over a wooden rocking chair.

"How lovely, Nora."

"You can have a seat at the dining room table if you wish while I get the tea brewing," Nora called over her shoulder, making her way to the kitchen. "I wasn't sure what time you would be able to get off, so I've been keeping the water warm. It should only take a moment to get it to boil."

"Allow me to help." Sophia set her small reticule on the oak table.

"Absolutely not. You are my first guest, and besides, I know for a fact that besides serving, you are about as useless as me in the kitchen," she giggled as she set out the china teacups before rustling into the kitchen to place the tea leaves in the pot. "I've been waiting for years to buy my own china, so I am excited to share this afternoon tea with you."

Sophia sank onto the stiff oak chair and spied in the room adjacent, a bundle of rags on the floor next to the rocking chair in the process of being braided. "What are you creating now?"

"Creating?" Nora came back from the kitchen with her hand on her stomach and one behind her back to see what Sophia was referring to. "Oh! I am making a braided rug. I have already made a smaller one for the bedroom, but I thought the front room could use a little brightening up and nearly all of Kane's shirts and blankets had holes in them, which led to a plethora of fabric. He complained until I told him I used my savings from the Harvey House to purchase material to sew new shirts and blankets for him."

She swallowed the retort that Kane

should have no qualms about his new wife's simple purchase with Sophia's jewels and a thousand dollars in his bank account and more to come. "I wish I could make something like a braided rug," she replied as Nora made her way back to the kitchen.

"I've seen your embroidery work, so I am sure that you would do just fine making a braided rug." Nora reappeared with a wooden tray laden with her china teapot and a plate of scones and blueberry jam.

"This looks delightful," Sophia exclaimed as Nora set it on the table and proceeded to pour the tea. She took a sip and tried to suppress a gag. *How can this be so strong already? It barely had time to steep! Smile, Sophia. Smile.* "Mmm, nothing like a cup of tea with a friend." Sophia placed aside her cup and reached for the plate of scones.

Nora stirred her tea in silence before saying slowly, "You do know that Mr. Ashton was the reason that Kane and I were able to wed so quickly."

Sophia nearly dropped her scone into her lap. "Whatever do you mean? How could have Carver expedited your wedding?"

She blushed. "I'm reluctant to remind you, but I once told you that Kane's main motivation for marrying you was for money. He said he had always loved me and always would, but he needed your money. At the dance, he offered to keep me on the side as his . . ." Nora cleared her throat and pushed out her words, "his *second* family."

"Oh, Nora." Sophia pressed her hand to her lips.

"I refused his proposition, of course," Nora continued. "But then, out of the blue, he appeared for breakfast at the Harvey House, saying that he was ready, and we were wed at once. He has been most gentle toward me and his mother—oh, Mrs. Kane is the sweetest woman I have ever met and even asked me to call her 'mama.' I was so touched that I told her I was pregnant and she actually started weeping in joy."

Tears sprang to her eyes at her friend's happiness. What were her jewels in the face of someone so happy with her new life?

She cleared her throat. "But, back to the

matter at hand. This morning, while I was cleaning, I found these." She handed Sophia three telegrams from New Orleans. "Somehow, Mr. Ashton had found out about my plight and provided Kane with an incentive to propose, followed by a ghastly sum upon our marriage."

Sophia's fingers trembled as she read that the exact agreed upon sum had been wired to Kane upon the receipt of the marriage certificate. "I had no idea, but how? Carver had already been gone a month and I promise you, I *never* told him—"

Nora wrapped her fingers over Sophia's hand. "He discovered it from the withdrawal you made for Kane's first installment and after an inquiry, Kane sent him the signed contract." She nodded to the telegrams. "Mr. Ashton said the sum should be enough for us to move to a larger city if needed, or desired, and find a new job."

Had he used the profits from his first month at the store to secure her friend's happiness and therefore, her own? *Dear sweet Carver.*

"I know I should be ashamed of how our

wedding came about, but it gives me some consolation that Kane does love me . . . in his own way, and he will love our child." Nora rested her hand over her growing abdomen. "Although, I try not to think about what would have happened to me if Mr. Ashton had not been so kind and generous as to finish what you began. I want to thank you, Sophia. And Mr. Ashton, of course. He even mentioned that he knows of another city that needs a sheriff and has written to them, suggesting they hire Kane."

"But both of your families are here."

Nora met her gaze. "If I stay, I know my family will realize what we've done when I have such an 'early' birth. And I cannot live with that right now. I'm not strong enough, so I am encouraging Kane to move us within the month, and I'm hoping Mrs. Kane will sell her holdings here and come with us."

"And your moving will protect your reputation and the baby's future," Sophia nodded, understanding.

"I know Kane was angry at first with being coerced into marriage, but the money helped calm him down enough to where every day, he has been a little less grumpy at *having* to marry me, but he has been refocusing his resentment toward Carver and it concerns me."

"But Carver gave him so much!"

"Yes, he did, but Kane will always want more. He sees Carver's fortune as his own that was stolen from him. Thankfully though, Carver has given Kane's and my child a better future. Maybe, one day, he will be able to see beyond his bitterness and realize what Carver has done for us." She swallowed. "Carver is a good man. You should hold on to him."

"I intend to," Sophia smiled as she took a tiny, polite sip of tea. "I think I may send him a little book of poems to remind him just how much I love him."

Nora sighed. "A true hero you have found. A man who would rise to the defense of a nearly perfect stranger and who also has the ability to quote poetry to his lady love."

The door shut and the ladies turned to find Kane, hat in hand. "Sorry to disturb you ladies, but I was at the telegraph office getting updates on—well, it doesn't matter." He withdrew a telegram and extended it to Sophia. "This came for you, Miss Bird, and as I knew you were here, I thought I'd bring it over."

A telegram? She bit her lip and opened it, gasping at the contents.

"What? What's wrong?" Nora rose and moved about the table to rest her hand on Sophia's shoulder.

"It's Carver. He wishes for me to come to New Orleans." Sophia squealed as she jumped out of her chair and embraced Nora. "He says we can marry at once!"

Nora twirled her about. "Then I must fit your wedding gown right away!"

"I need to get to the telegraph office and tell him I will take the train tomorrow morn—"

"Nonsense." Nora nodded to her husband. "Kane will send your response. We have much to do."

CHAPTER 22

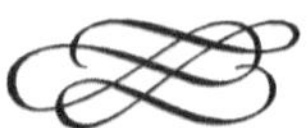

It had been difficult bidding her Harvey sisters farewell, but as the train finally pulled into the New Orleans depot, any remorse fled her body and only joy remained. Never, in her years in her sisters' shadows, did she imagine that she could marry the man of her dreams. Her sisters always told her that she only needed to wait for the right man to come along to find her beautiful, but she did not believe them . . . not until Carver.

She opened the telegram once more, reading over his instructions to meet her at the Commercial Hotel where he would have a preacher coming to marry them after she had a moment to freshen up. She almost felt like those mail order brides she had heard about in the West with marrying a man upon her arrival instead of planning a church wedding. But she and Carver had waited long enough. Her only regret was that Jane was not here to witness her happy moment.

Gripping her reticule, she stepped out of the first-class train car, signaling a porter to help her with her trunks into a hired carriage. She could almost laugh at the difference between the last time she had traveled alone to now. Her time at the Harvey House certainly had given her confidence.

She gave the driver the name of the hotel and settled into the worn leather seat of the carriage, taking in the sights of New Orleans—*her* new home. With its graceful live oaks dripping in Spanish moss and the humidity in the air, she at once felt at home.

The carriage halted in front of an impressive building in the heart of the French Quarter with beautiful stonework surrounding the first three floors and above the front entryway. A young doorman trotted up to the carriage door and held it open for her. She nodded her thanks to the young man and allowed him to lead her through the great doors into the exquisite lobby to the front desk, her heels clicking on the marble floor. She avoided the gaze of anyone in the lobby as they were no doubt questioning a lady traveling alone to a hotel, but she kept her head high and approached the front desk, inquiring after the set of rooms that Carver said he had arranged for her. As they found the reservation, she kept her attention instead on the ornate coffered ceiling and the massive marble columns reaching up to the second floor. Just as the grandfather clock along the wall struck six, the clerk finally released her key.

Following the bell boy, she climbed the stairs to the second floor and at the third door on the right, she inserted the skeleton key, her heart beating rapidly at the idea that the moment she was ready, Carver would be here to take her as his bride.

Humming as her trunks were lined in the corner, the bell boy departed as a maid appeared in the threshold, a stack of towels in hand. "Will you be needing any further assistance, Miss?" The maid asked as she set out the fresh towels in the bathroom, drawing the bath.

Carver must have left instructions, the dear. "I will only be staying a short while. Thank you." Sophia withdrew two coins, handing one to her and one to the bell boy in the hallway. Closing the door, she rummaged through her wicker trunk and withdrew her silk robe.

Stripping off her soiled clothing, she stepped into the tub, sighing from the luxury of bath salts and fine soap. While the guests from the Harvey House were given only the finest of soap, the staff were supplied with the less expensive, harsh lard soap of the general store. Having scrubbed the dirt of travel from her skin, hair, and nails, she immersed her hair and massaged the soap into her scalp for a second time, inhaling the sweet lavender scent as she rinsed it out.

Drawing on her robe, she used the comb from the vanity and slowly untangled her long locks, praying over her marriage to

Carver and thanking the Lord for His many blessings. While her time working had been difficult, she had discovered herself in the West, apart from the Fairfield name and all that society tied to it. She didn't know the amount of healing she had needed until she was away from her parents, and she prayed that one day her parents would not only accept her decisions but respect her for them as well.

Setting the heavy thoughts of her girlhood wounds aside for happier ones of Carver and her impending marriage, she slipped into the fresh undergarments and corset before lifting out her magnificent wedding gown. She shook it for scorpions out of habit and laughing at herself, she stepped into her dress and buttoned it with shaking fingers. She quickly draped a towel across her shoulders and sitting near the window, she arranged her long locks over the towel to dry them as quickly as possible when a knock sounded on the door.

Carver! She sprang up and threw open the door. "Carver, I—" She gasped, shrinking back, stumbling over her train. "You!"

"Sophia, my darling, are you well?" Prescott strode into the room as if he owned it and gently grasped her by the arms, helping her to her feet as if she were a child.

"Prescott? What in the world is going on?" She attempted to tug her arms away, but at the sight of the man joining them, she felt her knees weaken once more.

"Told you I could get her to come to you." Kane grinned at Prescott. "Now, where's my money? You said I could get paid before the ceremony tonight."

"Ceremony?" Sophia rasped as she attempted to free herself, but he only gripped her tighter, the stitches in her sleeve straining as he pulled her into the chamber.

"Calm yourself, my love," Prescott whispered into her ear, his face gently caressing her cheek as Kane shut the door behind them.

She leaned away from him, fear sending her body to quaking and her lungs to seizing. Unable to draw a full breath, any hope of screaming died. "What have you done to Carver?"

"Nothing yet, my dear."

Kane nodded, crossing his arms stubbornly. "That's right, but I want *all* of my money now. I didn't take the risk of being found out and quitting my job for pennies. I did it for the fortune you offered me."

Prescott rolled his eyes. "I told you *before* the ceremony, which is still a half hour away." He glared at him, his voice turning dangerous, "But if you ask again, I will not hesitate in cutting out a large percentage. There isn't anyone in New Orleans you can get to support you that I can't buy out, so I suggest you mind your greed, and do as I say if you know what is good for you."

Kane grumbled as he leaned against the fireplace mantel.

Sophia cringed as she felt Prescott's lustful gaze rove over her body. "Leave my room this instant."

"My, my. Quite the independent little woman you have become." He released her but cuffed her chin in his hand. "Careful,

Sophia. A little confidence is good for a woman, but too much makes her intolerable and distasteful. I don't want my wife to display such unfeminine characteristics."

She jerked her chin out of his hand, the scent of his cologne making her sick to her stomach. "I broke off our so-called engagement the minute I ran away. You have no claim on me now."

Prescott gave her a patronizing smile. "Ahh, my dear, when will you realize you never had a say in the first place? It was a contractually binding agreement signed by your father. By law, he has signed his claim of you over to me, so you belong to me upon our marriage."

"I belong to no one except the Lord Almighty. I am a free woman and I have a job with which I can support myself." *Well, had.*

Prescott shook his head. "Well, after the ceremony, no lawyer would ever side with the wife over the husband, so all I need to do is have the priest say the words and you belong to me for life and if you do not agree, I think there may be a vacancy in an asylum that I can dispose of you after you give me the sons I crave."

"I have promised my hand to Carver, and I will wed no one else for he loves me and I love him."

"I'm sure he does." He gently grasped her wrist, his hold tightening with every tug from Sophia. "But he will recover from your betrayal with a little help from his inheritance." He stroked her hair and slowly traced his finger from her temple to her lips. His gaze settled on them. "And so will you. Remember, you belonged to me long before you ever met Carver. You will be my bride whether you like it or not. It's up to you to decide to come with or without a fuss. Although, I would prefer it be without because otherwise, it will be quite an unpleasant wedding night for you." He lunged for her, catching her lips with his, pressing her to him.

Sophia clutched her fists and swung her free arm at him. He ducked with a laugh and caught her wrist, binding them together with his hand and stole another kiss, his fingers digging into her back. His intentions were all too clear.

"By the time Carver finds out you are gone, you will already be my wife. Wedded and bedded. No man would ever want to have you." He laughed. "My sloppy seconds, or thirds if you will." He squeezed even tighter around her wrists as if he could sense her rising outburst. "Now, now, you listen to me, my blushing bride. If you value Carver's life, you will follow me to the carriage now. After we are wed, we will . . . shall we say, *enjoy* ourselves for a few weeks in *my* hotel room before notifying my stepson that his parents are in the city and wish to visit with him before heading back to Charleston as husband and wife in *every* sense of the word."

Sophia cringed. "Why risk being discovered by Carver? Why bring me here?"

He shrugged. "I think it incentivizes you to behave."

She stiffened. "What could possibly—"

"Marry me and keep Carver safe or refuse my hand and forfeit Carver's life."

She felt the blood drain from her limbs, the room spinning. "You wouldn't dare."

His grin told her otherwise. "Why else would I feel the need to have Kane escort you here?"

"You would threaten your own stepson?" She whispered, her eyes widening in disbelief.

"If he got in the way, I wouldn't hesitate in taking him out."

She fought against her rising tears—tears of fear for Carver and anger at feeling fear when she had tried so hard to have courage. "How could you be so callous? Especially, against someone you were supposed to protect?"

"Allow me to tell you a story. My father re-married a woman named Louise Rawlings, but she died shortly after my fourth birthday, abandoning my half-sister and me. However, she was good for one thing as she left a large inheritance behind, which Father invested for us until my half-sister took after her mother by leaving our family and running off with her Mr. Kane, whom she claimed to love—apparently even more than she loved our family. She was disinherited, and I was able to claim both fortunes as my own. I've discovered throughout the years that, while people come and go and die, money stays as long as you nurture it. And I did all I could to nurture it with my first two wives. My accounts need more nurturing, and with your supple form that reminds me of my first wife, I think you would be a pleasant enough ticket, and Carver is all that stands in my way."

"Even without my promising to marry Carver, I would never marry you. I have tasted freedom, and I will never return to my old life. Your idle threats against Carver do not move me." She scowled at him, drawing out every word, "Let. Me. Go."

"Kane!" He barked, looking pointedly at Sophia, and with a grin asked, "How would you like to earn twice as much as I gave you for bringing Sophia to me?"

Kane's eyes gleamed, and he cast his cigar into the fireplace. "What do you need me to do?"

Prescott tightened his grip. "Create a deadly 'accident' for Carver Ashton."

"No! Prescott. No!" Sophia clawed at Prescott's face, screaming, "You leave him alone. You hear me? Don't you *dare* touch him."

"Gladly." Kane grinned at her distress. "Think I should make Carver's death a bit painful too?"

Prescott shrugged. "Well, now, it all depends on Miss Fairfield here. If she goes quietly, I don't think anything need happen to Carver, but if she struggles—" He left his threat hanging in the air.

"Prescott, you can't be serious." She whimpered.

"Oh, but I am," he replied, his voice rippling with suppressed anger. "Do you really think I would let *you*, a mere girl, treat me with such disrespect? You made me the laughingstock of Charleston society. I would never let a man get away with treating me with such flippancy, and I certainly will not take it from you. You *will* marry me, and you *will* be the best, most devoted wife I have ever had, and you *will* proclaim it from the rooftops that you begged me to take you back, and I graciously forgave your trespasses. Understand?"

She closed her eyes against his evil stare and remained silent, pursing her lips. *And if I don't, you will kill your own stepson? What kind of monster are you?*

He grasped her hand in his, pressing a gentle kiss atop, whispering, "Understand?"

She gave the slightest of nods, hating her tears for exposing her fear and weakness.

At the sight of her tears, his eyes softened. "I don't wish to be a strict husband. I want to love you and treat you like a duchess, but when you struggle, it makes it difficult to treat you with gentleness." He lightly stroked her hair in place with the tips of his fingers and bent down and kissed her forehead, releasing her at last.

"Now, be a good girl, fix your hair. I shall step into the hallway and give you ten minutes to make yourself the picture of a bride."

He turned away to speak with Kane in hushed tones as he shut the door between them.

Weak, she fell to her knees and lifted her

face to heaven. *Lord, I can't marry Prescott. I cannot believe that You taught me so much in the West only to let me marry Prescott and suffer in silence for the rest of my life. Show me the way out. I'm in New Orleans, so surely You have a plan for me. Keep Carver safe and send him to find me.*

She rushed to the window and looked below, hoping for an escape, but her room was too far from the ground. She would break her legs for certain if she leapt. She pressed her forehead on the cool glass when she spotted a young boy with a stack of evening newspapers passing under her window. She didn't have any money left after tipping the staff, but she did have Carver's locket.

She unlatched the window and threw it open. She leaned out and called to the boy, but her voice was lost in the noise of the street. "Paperboy!" She called again, only daring to raise her voice a hairsbreadth more. He looked around, trying to see who was calling. Sophia waved her hands desperately and dared to call out once more when he looked up and caught her eye.

His confused face shifted to a smile.

"Yes, Miss? You want a paper sent to your room?"

She shook her head as he came to stand directly under her window to hear her better. "I need to send a note to someone. I don't have any money, but I do have a gold locket as a promised payment. Give the gentleman the note and locket, and he will pay you a month's wages."

The boy's eyes widened. "A month?"

She nodded, trying to speak calmly. "Yes, but please, you must not tell anyone but the gentleman on this address that I gave you a letter. It's very important. Can I trust you?"

The boy nodded. "For a month's wages, I am your servant, my lady!"

"Just a moment then and I'll toss it down to you." She unlatched the locket from her neck as she hurried to the desk and hastily scrawled her warning.

At the Commercial Hotel.

Prescott forcing me to wed him. You

are in danger. Help me, my darling. Sophia.

She addressed it with a shaking hand and folded the locket into the note, securing her hair ribbon around it, making certain Carver's address was still visible. She rushed back and sighed in relief to see the boy was still there and watching for her. She held the package outside the window and released it, dropping it into the boy's hands. "The locket is inside the parcel, but it isn't worth as much to you as the money Mr. Ashton will give you if you deliver the package."

The boy nodded, glanced at the address, and took off running down the street.

With trembling fingers, she drew her hair into a stern bun as a light knock came from the door. Sophia's heart skipped and she dropped the final pin she was about to use to secure her low coiffure. She debated refusing for only a second before recalling Prescott's threat, in detail, against Carver. She tugged open the door.

Without a word, Prescott led her down

the hallway, and despite the stares of people in the lobby, he led her out into a waiting carriage. He stole another kiss, hungrier this time. She bit him.

With a growl, he jerked back, running his hand over his bottom lip. "If you are thinking of protesting at the ceremony, the priest won't listen. Even a man of the cloth, I'm sure, has his price that he is willing to forget his conscience for an hour . . . you only have to find the man who can be bought." He stroked her cheek with the back of his hand, wiping his blood onto her face. "And I will have your body. The question is, my dear, if you are going to give me yourself willingly, or by force. Either way, I will enjoy it."

Sophia's heart flipped, but she met his gaze. "I am not frightened by you."

"You should be," he hissed, eyes gleaming.

"The Lord has not given me the spirit of fear, but of power, and of love, and sound mind. I see you for what you are, Prescott Payne, and so does God Almighty."

His gazed wavered for a split second. He

clenched his fists and closed the distance between them, towering over her. "You think you can intimidate me with your little verses about your God?"

"My God will protect me, and *you* cannot harm me." She lifted her chin, confidence filling her that *this* was not how her journey ended. "You may think you have all the power in this room, but you are no match for Him."

Prescott threw his head back and laughed. "If you believe in all of that nonsense, you are weaker than I thought. If you recall the stories, my first wives died rather early. Take heed. If you come with me to the altar without a fight, I will treat you well, but if you cross me again . . ."

Sophia refused to react and shifted her gaze to the window. Had Prescott actually murdered his wives? Or was he trying to frighten her? She decided to put that out of her mind for now and leaned her head against the pane, watching, waiting, and praying. *Lord, send Carver. Please send Carver.*

THE MOONLIGHT STREAMED through the windows as Carver stood in his store, admiring the new shipment already lining his shelves, excited to share the customers' enthusiasm over the new goods in his next letter to Sophia, the letter that would ask if she would be willing to cut her time short with the Harvey House to come home with him after a wedding in New Mexico with her Harvey family.

He turned down the gaslights and headed to his office to lock up when he heard footsteps on the second floor. His skin prickled. All his staff had been sent home. He grabbed a silver candlestick, the weighted metal offering him comfort as he climbed the stairs.

"Hello?" He called in case it was a staff member. "The store is closed."

Glass shattered to his left as a masked man charged toward him. Carver swung the candlestick, catching the man on his jaw. He grunted, but seized Carver around the neck, throwing him to the ground. Carver whipped the candlestick back and rammed it into the intruder's skull. He went limp at once.

Carver glanced around him, grabbed a sash off the mannequin in ladieswear, and made quick work of tying the man's hands together and taking a second sash to bind his feet. Satisfied the bonds would hold, he tore off the man's mask, grabbed the crystal pitcher of water and threw it in his face.

"Who are you?" He roared as the man sputtered against the water.

The assailant glared at him, and Carver lifted the candlestick once more, bluffing, but the man's flinch was satisfactory.

"I will not ask again. Who are you? And why are you here?"

"I was sent because the lady wasn't feeling compliant." He mumbled in a thick southern accent.

Carver shook his head, confused. "What lady?"

"The one he is marrying at St. Louis Cathedral."

His heart stammered. "Are you speaking of a gentleman by the name of Prescott Payne?"

He shrugged. "He looked more like a cowboy."

A cowboy in New Orleans? Carver bolted for the door, praying he wasn't too late. He would send the police to deal with the henchman *after* he knew Sophia was safe.

CHAPTER 23

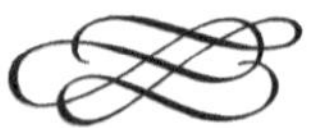

Moonlight pierced through her nightmare. The carriage halted at the stone steps of the massive St. Louis Cathedral, the clock in the center tower declaring it to be eight in the evening. With its three steeples reaching to the heavens as if in prayer, she too lifted a prayer to the Lord, knowing that whatever happened, He would be with her. She glanced about at the few people meandering in Jackson Square. If only she could scream, she could be free . . . but the threat against Carver wrapped about her neck, cinching her throat to any cries for help. She must give him a chance to read her letter. He would find her. He had to find her.

Prescott grasped her hand and fairly pulled her from the carriage. "Keep your head up and try to look like the radiant young woman I know you to be."

Sophia narrowed her eyes. "How can I possibly pretend to be happy about this? And besides, no wedding will occur tonight as our families are not Catholic. No priest would marry us."

Prescott rolled his eyes. "And why would I let on that we are anything but devout Catholics? Look happy, or I am *happy* to tell Kane to make certain Carver never walks without a limp again."

She lifted her head, feeling confident in God's hand in her letter that Carver would come for her. "You won't get away with this."

"Won't I?" He shoved his hand into his vest pocket and opened his palm, her gold locket dangling from his fingertips. "Nice try."

Sophia's heart sank into her stomach as he fastened the chain about her neck.

"If you don't choose to love me, then I will crush your spirit until it only does as I please." He patted her arm, "But I quite like your spirit, my darling, so please be pleasant, and don't make me be nasty." He motioned Kane forward. "Tell the priest we are here. I don't want Sophia to wait any longer than necessary."

The contrast of the coolness of the church to the heat of outside surprised Sophia. In spite of her circumstances, she could not help but be awed at the beauty of the church with its high arched ceilings and stained-glass windows lining the sanctuary and the ceiling murals of Christ's birth and resurrection. She pulled her gaze away, searching for an escape, but Kane returned to guarding the front doors as a priest entered through a side door, waiting by the altar for the couple to join him.

Prescott caught her hand and prompted her to move with a little jerk. Waves of nausea swept over her. *I'm doing this for Carver. If I don't, he will die.* She trudged down the aisle, tears trickling down her cheeks. She thought of Carver and how this was supposed to be their happy moment. She imagined it was him standing by her side, smiling down on her with love, instead of the lust exuding Prescott's eyes. She recalled Carver's and her time in Charleston in an attempt to drown out the heart wrenching words of the priest that were binding her to this horrible man.

The words ceased and Sophia jerked her head up to see the priest staring at her. "Are you quite all right, my child?"

Startled, Sophia didn't know how to respond. Prescott squeezed her arm, but Sophia couldn't bring herself to lie to a man of God, so she remained silent.

"Please continue," Prescott stated.

The priest closed his Bible. "The lady does not seem to wish this union. I cannot, in good conscience, bind her to you if she is unwilling."

"But I am willing," Prescott growled.

The click of a bullet being chambered sounded as Kane stepped forward. "Continue with the ceremony."

The priest narrowed his eyes as he rolled back his shoulders. "Your gun doesn't strike fear into my heart for I am confident where my soul will go if my body perishes by your hand."

He turned the gun toward Sophia. "Continue, or I will shoot her where she stands."

The priest's eyes widened as he turned to Prescott. "But you profess to love her."

Prescott shrugged. "Yes, but if I cannot have her, then no one else can either."

The priest sent Sophia an apologetic look and continued the ceremony with a shaking voice. "If anyone objects to this marriage, please speak now or forever hold your peace."

"I object," a deep voice resonated off the church walls, shattering her fears and filling her with warmth.

CARVER HALTED midstride in the aisle with his hands in the air as Prescott snatched Sophia by the waist, twisting her around with him away from Carver, giving Kane a clear shot.

Despite the terror of the moment,

Sophia was calm, trust shining in her eyes, as if she knew she would get through this trial.

"Take one more step and she will be shot," his stepfather shouted, digging his fingers into Sophia's waist. "Continue with the ceremony," Prescott growled as he jerked Sophia forward to face the priest.

Carver inched forward, his fingers itching for a weapon.

"I cannot. An impediment has been declared and we must first resolve the objection before moving forward." The priest closed his Bible and folded his hands around it. "Despite your threats against our lives."

Prescott narrowed his eyes at the priest. "Oh, I'll resolve the objection." He snapped his fingers.

Kane leveled his gun on Carver. At Sophia's scream, Carver hurdled backwards into the pews, the bullet digging itself into the wood. Carver grunted, painfully aware of Sophia screaming his name as a second bullet nearly hit him. Not waiting to be Kane's target practice, Carver crawled to the aisle and snatched a gilded iron candelabra, using it as a staff, swinging it into Kane, knocking the gun from Kane's grasp. Kane dove under the candelabra, their bodies slamming together as they grappled for the upper hand. Carver clenched Kane into a body lock and launched him over his shoulder, sending them both skidding across the black and white tile floors and into the sides of the pews.

From the corner of his eye, he was aware of the priest running to the door, shouting for the police as Sophia struggled against Prescott. She squirmed and managed to sink her teeth into his wrist.

"You little—" Prescott ripped his hand back, his release causing her to slip down the steps and slam into the ground, knocking her head against the floor, crimson staining the white tile.

"Sophia!" Carver yelled, but in his distracted concern for her, Kane landed a solid blow to his mouth, sending him staggering back into the aisle as Kane drew a knife from his boot, the silver glistening in the kaleidoscope of moonlight streaming through the stained glass. Gripping it with both hands, Kane plunged the knife toward Carver's chest as Carver snatched a hymnal and shielded himself. With the blade stuck in the hardback cover, Carver shoved Kane with all of his might into the pews.

Carver dove onto Kane and brought his head smashing into Kane's skull, knocking him unconscious. Spitting out a wad of blood, Carver pushed off of Kane and secured the weapons, glaring at Prescott as he pressed his hand to his side where Kane had nicked him. Carver's chest burned at the abuse coming from the man he had once admired. He limped up the aisle but stopped short at Prescott snatching Sophia from the floor, his fingers clutching her slender throat.

"Put your weapons down now, or I will end this."

He didn't dare question the man but reluctantly did as he was told, lifting his hands above his head. "Let her go, Prescott."

His grip tightened as he moved them down the altar to where a side door stood ajar from the priest's flight. "I don't want to hurt her, but you are making me. If I so much as see you following us, I will be forced to become the monster you all think I am."

Sophia panted, her glazed eyes half open. She gave Carver a sad smile as if already defeated. "It's okay, Carver."

No. No! He would not accept defeat when he was so close. "Prescott, don't hurt her. Your argument is with me. I was her escort. I could have let the matter be instead of following her to New Mexico." Carver lifted his hands, palms outward.

"She had as much to do with this as you did, Carver, my boy." He grinned. "It will give me immense pleasure to crush you by taking what you desire most. Sophia and I will be married, and you cannot stop it from happening. Kane!" He barked. "Get up and do your duty to protect us. I know a preacher willing to do the job in Charleston."

"Prescott, please!" Sophia whimpered, her hand trailing up her cheek to her bleeding temple. "Don't do this. Please."

He gripped her arm tighter and tighter until she gasped from the pain.

"Prescott!" Carver growled, taking a step closer as Kane rallied, gathering his weapons, aiming at Carver.

"Tell me I can shoot him, Prescott," Kane shouted, his chest heaving.

"Carver, please don't come any closer," Sophia whimpered. "If you do, you will die."

"And if I don't, then you will die slowly at the hand of this man and I will never allow that, not while I am still breathing."

"And I've heard enough out of you, but unfortunately, I need you alive to motivate my bride." Prescott jerked his head at Kane. "Tie him up, Kane."

"I could end him." Kane offered instead, his gun flashing in the moonlight.

"Yes, but then we would have no leverage. Hide him away and wait for my telegram to either kill him or release him." Prescott wrapped his arm around her waist, plucked the comb that was holding her torn veil in place and let it float to the floor as he lifted her in his arms and disappeared out the side door.

CHAPTER 24

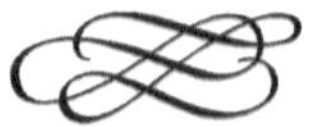

Sophia tucked herself into the furthest corner of the carriage away from Prescott, her hands trembling.

"Take us to the train station." Prescott called up to the driver as he joined her, Kane nowhere in sight.

"What's to stop Carver from telling my parents you have forced me to wed you?" She glowered at him.

"I've already received your family's absolute blessing to marry you, and I shall plead that I was crazed with love and that Carver's jealously has caused him to imagine things, and those imaginings have turned into exaggerated stories. My hands are clean. You came to New Orleans of your own free will as well as entered the church on your own. I held no weapon against you or Carver." He grinned at her victoriously. "Who do you think they are going to believe? Their wealthy, established business partner, or the man with a fraction of wealth and half the integrity as he fell in love with his future *stepmother* and tried to steal your heart when it belonged to me?"

"You don't really expect them to believe that nonsense?" Sophia scoffed as the carriage shuddered to a halt and the driver opened their door onto South Rampart Street where the sizable New Orleans Union Station stood.

"Money covers a multitude of transgressions, my dear," he replied, grasping her hand. He led her through the crowd and up onto the train platform, helping her ascended into his private Pullman car. Only when Prescott had closed the door firmly behind them, did he release her hand. Sophia, clutching her arms over her chest, took in the rich mahogany paneling, etched glass doors, and small, but beautiful, chandeliers. She sank against the velvet cushions and studied the people milling about through the window as they pulled out of the station. *If only I could scream without fear of losing Carver.*

Prescott handed a book of poetry to her while he opened his newspaper, settling back into his cushion. She cast aside his offering in favor of watching the landscape to distract herself from the need of using the necessary.

As if noticing her discomfort, Prescott smiled. "Feel free to use the water closet, my dear. I'll not bother you. The window in there is fixed, the exit doors are locked, and there's no way off the car, but don't even think about trying to pull something because I will not hesitate to send a telegram to have Kane eliminate Carver from the equation."

Sophia locked herself inside the lavatory, shaking from the day's turmoil. She leaned her head against the looking glass and sighed at the coolness of the glass. At the sounds of stirring outside the door, she hurried to meet her needs.

How am I going to get out of here, Lord? She prayed as she was washing her hands in the porcelain basin when she heard a voice. *Leap.* She whirled about and found the door still solidly shut. *You wish me to leap, Lord?* She peeked through the sheer fabric covering the narrow window of the water closet, the buildings blurring in the night. *Leap.* Drawing a deep breath, she wrapped her hands around the handle of the porcelain pitcher and poured out the remainder of the water into the basin and gripped the pitcher in her hands, waiting.

Sophia unlatched the door, calling out, "Prescott? The door seems to be stuck. Could you help me?" She lifted the pitcher and held her breath.

Prescott yanked it open with more force than necessary and Sophia smashed the porcelain pitcher down on his head and he crumpled to the lush carpet. She dropped the shard of the handle, and putting aside her fears over her actions, she rummaged through his coat pockets for his wallet and the Pullman's key. She removed the few hundred dollars, stuffing them into the bodice of her wedding dress as she charged for the door. She snatched up Prescott's dinner jacket that was hanging up along with her light cloak, and with trembling hands, unlocked the door.

The wind tore through her hair as the landscape whipped past. Unlinking the chain that blocked the small platform of the car, she studied the terrain as best as she could in the moonlight. The city was quickly fading away and now she was approaching a sparsely wooded area that she knew marked the swampland. She tugged on Prescott's jacket and tucked her cloak inside under her arm, knowing she was out of time. She needed to jump before she was too far from the city or, heaven forbid, Prescott regained consciousness and realized what she had done. She would rather take her chances of leaping than to allow that man to call her his bride. *God protect me.* She raised her arms to cover her face and leapt off the speeding train, crashing into the weeds and bushes below.

She hit the ground on her feet, the momentum of her body vaulting her down the slight incline from the rail ties. She rolled again and again until she gradually scraped to a painful halt. She sucked in her breath, slowly opened her eyes, and released her breath with a soft laugh.

Her shoulder throbbed and her arm burned, but thankfully, the jacket had saved her from getting cut by any thorns or sticks. She shook out her lopsided hair and freed it from pieces of leaves and dirt before taking a tentative step and biting her lip at the twinge that greeted her. *It's not too bad. Hopefully, I can hobble back into the station before it gets completely dark.* She dropped Prescott's jacket, pulled on her light blue evening cloak over the wedding dress, and sighed as she made her way back to the city that was only a speck in the distance.

Sophia squinted over each step, praying Louisiana didn't hold quite so many terrors in nature as New Mexico. *Please don't let me step on a sleeping snake or any sharp-toothed creature.* She grimaced remembering the tiny, yet powerful sting of the scorpion.

Within ten minutes, her delicate evening slippers were ruined. The hem of her elegant wedding dress, torn from the jump from the train, was now soiled beyond repair from trudging ankle deep in mud beside the train tracks. She stumbled over a railroad tie and cried out in pain as she fell to her knees, her hair tumbling from the last pins holding her golden tresses at bay. She groaned, picked herself back up, and plodded forward, terrified that if she paused for even a moment, Prescott would come running up behind her to spirit her away to Charleston.

The golden orb from a lamp glowed in the distance, urging her to safety, growing brighter and brighter until she finally stumbled up the wooden steps of the impossibly small home. *Lord, please let whoever is inside be friendly.* With shaking, filthy hands, she knocked.

The door jerked open to reveal an elderly man, his aged dark blue eyes widening at her disheveled state. "Miss! You injured?"

He rushed out from behind the door, and with a kind and withered hand, he helped her into the rocking chair on his dilapidated front porch. He poked his head inside and shouted, "Boy!"

A young fellow with a shock of red hair, no more than ten, appeared, a dinner plate full of beans in hand. "Yes, Grandpa?"

"Get this young lady a glass of water." He knelt in front of her. "Should I send a message to someone for you?"

"Please, find Carver Ashton of the *Ashton Department Store*. Tell him where I am," she whispered as the darkness overtook her.

The jostling of a moving train was the first thing she noticed, closely followed by the awareness that someone was holding her hand. She tore her hand from his grip and shoved against his chest, screaming, "Leave me be!"

"Sophia, it's only me." Carver's voice burst through her terror as he gently rubbed her hands in an attempt to soothe her.

She looked about and found she was not on a train, but a gig. She sank into the plush, leather seats and sighed. "I'm so sorry," she whispered, trembling. "I thought . . ."

"I know." His strong arm embraced her, offering her comfort and security.

She nestled into his coat. "I knew you would come for me, but how did you escape?"

He snapped the reins and filled her in on how he escaped from Kane with the priest's assistance as well as the police. "And what about you? From what I was able to piece together, you must have leapt from a train?"

She nodded. "I will tell you all about it later, but first, I must ask, where are we going?"

"Home."

"By carriage?" She blinked. "Or are we taking a steamboat to Charleston?"

Carver chuckled. "To our home on St. Charles Avenue, my love."

She spied his cheeks reddening even in the moonlight. "But it won't be *our* home until we are married."

"Which is why, uh, I thought we might be safer with you and I wed." He coughed.

"If you are willing, our first stop will be to my minister."

She wrapped her arms about his neck, giving him a saucy grin. "Willing? I jumped off a train for you, Mr. Ashton. I am *more* than willing to be your bride."

CHAPTER 25

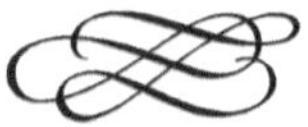

Sophia pressed her hands to her lower back, stiff after hours of arranging the library to satisfaction, but seeing her favorite titles lining the shelves in their new home sent a thrill through her. Half the shelves of the mahogany-paneled room remained empty, but Carver promised her that a lifetime of collecting books was in their future—a collection that would be passed down through the generations. Even though she had a hundred new titles to read, Sophia selected her now favorite poet, Keats, and settled into the chair before the stone fireplace, but the stillness about her made it rather hard to concentrate.

She flipped open the book once more. Tomorrow, she would begin tutoring the children in the orphanage. The noise of the children was just what she needed. Even after a week as Carver's bride, the quietness of the house still took some getting used to after living with her Harvey sisters and growing up in a houseful of children.

Upon her marriage, Sophia sent a telegram to her friends in New Mexico, letting them know she was safe and where they could write to her, along with the news of Kane's duplicity. He had thankfully been apprehended in New Orleans while Prescott had been excused already on grounds of passion after paying a hefty donation to the church—all of which Sophia had explained to her parents in a lengthy telegram.

Sophia rested her hand on the pocket that held their responding letter that arrived just this morning. Her parents offered stiff congratulations and a promise to visit next week to formalize her inheritance transfer and find out just what had truly happened with Prescott. She could not wait to tell Carver once he returned home from his meeting at the department store. Perhaps she could take a ride to tell him the good news that her parents were coming and might forgive her for running away.

With a gentle knock on the doorframe, Ruby, the young housemaid, dropped into a short curtsy. "Pardon me, Mrs. Ashton, but you have a guest. I showed her to the parlor."

"Oh? Did she give you her name?" Sophia inquired as she snapped her book shut and flitted through the names of the handful of women that she had met at her first Sunday service in New Orleans. Mayhap it was Mrs. Lennox who had three daughters that Sophia mentioned potentially tutoring?

"No, ma'am, but she, um . . ." she fiddled with her apron pocket, her freckles standing out in her distress in trying to find the right words. "She doesn't seem to hold herself as well as a lady of your status might, even though her dress is quite pretty."

Sophia nodded her thanks, calling over her shoulder. "If you could bring some tea for us that would be lovely." Her heels clicked on the hall's solid pine floors, her curiosity rising as she flung open the French doors. "Nora!"

"You look well, *Mrs.* Ashton." She smiled, holding out her arms.

Sophia rushed to her friend and embraced her, Nora's abdomen poking her in the stomach. "Are you well? Are you here to see. . ."

"When I discovered where Kane was being held, I had to come and make amends with you in person." Her eyes filled with unshed tears. "Between the actions of myself and Kane, I wouldn't blame you for hating us. I am so very sorry for what happened."

"I am sorry as well, but I could never hate you." Sophia embraced her friend and led her to one of the pale blue settees tucked in the bay window alcove shaded by the long, dipping branches of the live oak with its Spanish moss swaying in the light breeze just outside the window.

"I never thought Kane could be capable of such a horrid deed." Nora's eyes saddened as she sank onto the soft cushion. "When I went to visit him this morning, I learned that he's capable of so much worse than just kidnapping you." She dipped her head and wiped her eyes with her stained handkerchief.

Sophia gripped her friend's arm, concern and anger flooding her voice. "Has that man hurt you?"

"Besides breaking my heart? No." She gave a short, bitter laugh. "How could he when he is in jail? He would never physically harm me, nor our baby anyway, but he would do anything, *anything* to make our fortune. It seems with the impending arrival of our child, the need for more wealth has consumed him. He always wants more and that is why I am here. I know I said I came to apologize, but after my visit to the jail, I knew I had a much greater reason to see you. I came to warn you."

Sophia's heart thudded. "Warn me?"

Nora nodded vigorously, her chapeau in danger of tumbling off her head. "Kane seemed to think it was only a matter of hours or days before he would be free."

"How could he possibly think that? He will be in jail for a very long time. He has no friends or power in New Orleans."

"Yes, but they didn't lock away Mr. Payne, now did they?" Nora commented quietly.

Sophia bit her lip.

"You may want to check and see how well they are keeping an eye out for Mr. Payne in New Orleans." Her hand trembled as she pulled a wrinkled telegram from her reticule. "Kane slipped this to me through the bars."

Sophia unfolded it to read,

Isaiah 51:14.

Perplexed that the verses she had held dear were the sole message, Sophia looked up to Nora. "What's this supposed to mean?"

"Even the devil can quote scripture to suit his purposes." Nora scowled. "It's a verse about setting the captives free and how they will not die in the dungeon."

Sophia paled, knowing in her gut who sent the telegram. "Prescott would dare to use scripture as a means for evil?" She crumpled the note in her hand and threw it into the fireplace.

"It's rather brilliant of him because the jailer isn't going to look up a scripture reference. He will see it as innocent while Mr. Payne meant it for a message."

They paused at the sound of Ruby's soft knock at the door as she rolled in the tea cart. "Would you like me to pour, Mrs. Ashton?"

Sophia shook her head as Ruby set the tea and delectable Italian pastries on the alcove's small round table. "I can do it if you need to run to the market before dinner? Thank you."

"I'll be back soon, Mrs. Ashton." Ruby curtsied and closed the door behind her.

"I have to find Carver." Sophia rose, hoping to catch him on his way home from the department store. "I'm sorry to leave you, Nora, but help yourself to the tea and pastries and ring for the cook if you want anything else. I will return in under an hour after I let Carver know and we can continue our conversation."

"Let Carver know what? That Nora led me straight to you?" A deep voice called from the doorway, blocking their escape.

Nora grasped her by the elbow. "Kane!"

"Cry out and I'm afraid your friend will get very hurt." Kane warned his wife.

"But h-how did you—you were in jail!" Sophia gasped.

"Money can do a lot of things. . . even get someone out of jail who is on trial for abduction and assault. The only reason I showed my dear wife the note was for the plain and simple fact that I knew she would want to warn her dear little friend and thus, lead me directly to her instead of my wasting precious time and incriminating myself further by asking for directions." He patted his wife's arm. "That's what first drew me to you—your gentle heart, which is so predictable."

Nora jerked her arm away from him. "You are breaking my heart. We have all that we need and more. Can't you just leave Sophia and her husband alone?"

"It's all for our child, my sweet Nora. Don't you know that everything I do is for our future?" He gently wiped her tears away with his thumbs.

Sophia folded her hands in front of her skirt, praying she appeared without fear. "What do you want, Kane? More of our money? Because I haven't received my inheritance yet, and you have the lion's share of Carver's savings."

"You want to know what I desire? When Carver comes through that door," he opened his coat and took out a revolver, "I will kill him and take you back to Prescott for a fortune."

Sophia kept her face blank and her voice strong. "And what makes you think that you could take Carver when you couldn't the first time?"

"Why, because I have his precious little

wife, of course." He grinned. "Nothing quite motivates a gentleman to surrender himself without a fight like having the woman he loves being threatened."

"Carver and I will pay you more than what Prescott has offered you." She moved toward her writing desk by the window. She glanced out the window onto the street, spying Carver atop his horse. "I can pay you all that we have now and more later." She opened the drawer, finding the letter opener. Its sharp blade could prove useful.

Kane laughed as he leaned against the fireplace mantel, lifting the ornate porcelain and gold clock. "I know how much you can pay, and I'm certain Prescott will reward me more than you can ever imagine when I deliver you to him as a widow."

"Try me," Sophia replied as she leaned against her writing desk, her fingers grazing the silver piece.

Nora cried out and clutched her abdomen, sinking to her knees on the parlor rug.

Kane's nonchalant façade dropped as he

saw his wife's pain. "Nora?" He grasped her arm and helped her back to the settee.

"Kane, please stop this madness." Nora's eyes widened in panic. "Don't make me raise this child alone. We can run now. We can get away before it's too late and live a good and full life with our child." She grimaced, rubbing her stomach. "If you do this, you will be caught. I know it."

"Kane, you have to let me send for a doctor." Sophia interjected, grasping the handle of the letter opener behind her back, and reaching for the bell cord.

"Step away from that cord." He commanded, waving her back over to the desk with the barrel of his gun. He shook his head. "We can't send for the doctor. If we do, they will know where I am."

"Do you want to endanger the lives of your wife and child? It's far too early for her to be feeling such pains. Be a man and think of her for once in your selfish life."

"Kane, please." Nora whimpered.

Kane gritted his teeth against her pleas, throwing open the desk drawers were he found a stack of bills and stuffed them into his coat pocket before turning to Sophia. "Get me more and hurry."

"You have everything in my desk."

He seized her arm. "Well, then, go through your husband's desk and get me all the money in the house. My child won't grow up in poverty like I did. He will have his proper fortune, which was stolen from him by the Payne and Ashton families." He shook Sophia. "If you do anything to jeopardize me from getting my hands on that money . . . well, let's just say it won't be very pretty for Carver when he gets home."

"You'll leave us in peace if I do?"

"Fetch the money and be back in two minutes, or I will make you a widow and cart you off to Prescott for both of your fortunes."

Sophia ran to her husband's desk, retrieved a small chest from inside the deep side drawer, found the key hidden under his clock on the mantel, and brought it back to the parlor, setting it on her writing desk.

Kane snatched the key from Sophia's hand, along with the letter opener hidden up her sleeve, and gestured with the gun for her to stand by the curtain. "Stay where I can see you, and keep your hands in front of you."

Sophia risked a glance over her shoulder to check the window and refrained from gasping when she saw Carver climbing the steps. *Lord, help us!*

Kane lifted his gaze from the chest. "What? Does having your money stolen from you hurt?" He stuffed the dollars and gold coins into his money pouch and jammed it into his pockets.

"Sophia? I'm home!" Carver called from the front door.

Sophia closed her eyes against her tears, picturing him hanging up his coat on the hall tree, and with it, his pistol that he kept in his coat pocket.

Kane held his finger to his lips and stepped behind the curtain with his gun poised at her heart. "Call him in, but if you give me away—"

Nora groaned.

He glanced at Nora. "I am sorry this is taking so long, my love, but we will have you out of here in a few minutes after I have finished what needs finishing."

Nora clutched her abdomen and leaned on the back of the settee for support as Sophia called, "I am in the parlor, Mr. Ashton."

"WHAT? NO LOVING GREETING?" He laughed as he swung open the parlor door, his gaze fell on Nora, and Sophia jerked her eyes to the curtain. Carver whirled around as Kane stepped out from behind it with his sights trained on Carver.

"I didn't want to leave New Orleans without paying my respects to my cousin and the new Mrs. Ashton. That would have been *so* disrespectful," he drawled.

"Well, you have paid your respects," Carver replied, glaring. "So, I suggest you be on your way now before I retaliate for having a loaded gun in the same room as my wife."

"Yes, yes, I am going, but first, Sophia was going to give me a little gift."

Sophia gave him a puzzled look.

He nodded to her neck. "I think that a gold locket would be the perfect gift for my sweet Nora."

Sophia's hand flew protectively to cover her locket. "I've given you all the money you want. You don't need an old locket."

"But I know how much you love it, so you see, I do need it because it hurts you, and my bride could use a pretty bobble."

Carver nodded to Sophia. "Give it to him, my love."

Her heart tightened as she unfastened the locket, holding it out to the man when Nora moaned.

Kane glanced over his shoulder for a split second. "Nora?"

She grunted. "I just need to move a bit and distract myself from the pain." She shuffled toward a pedestal with an antique vase. She wrapped her hands around it and hefted it from the pedestal. "I have taken a fancy to this vase, so I think I will take it if that's all right with you, Kane."

He laughed, his eyes still trained on Carver and Sophia. "That's the spirit! You may have anything you want, my love. This wealth should have been ours after all." Kane drew back the hammer on his revolver with a click.

Nora slammed the vase over his head, and he crumpled to the ground. Carver bolted over to him and jerked his arms behind his back, yanking off his neckcloth to use it to bind Kane's hands as Sophia rushed to Nora's side.

"Nora, that was the bravest thing I've ever seen. Are you all right?"

Nora rested her head on Sophia's shoulder and shook her head, sobbing. "God help me. I-I love him so much, but he was going to hurt you. He wouldn't have let you two go without someone being killed."

Carver pulled the bell cord, praying aloud that Ruby had returned from her errands.

Ruby poked her head into the parlor. "I'm sorry my errands took so long Mrs. Asht—" Her jaw dropped as she took in the bound and unconscious Kane. "Oh, my word, is everyone all right?"

Carver nodded, raking his hand through

his hair as he rose with the gun trained on Kane. "Yes. Ruby, please send for the police, then I want you to find the doctor for Mrs. Kane and send him over straight away."

"Yes, sir!" She twirled on her heel and ran for the front door.

"Sophia, you see to Nora, and I will watch over Kane until the police come," he instructed, his gaze never leaving the man. "I don't trust him for a second not to twist his way out of those knots."

SOPHIA DREW Nora away from the horrid scene and showed her to the upstairs guest room, staying with her long after the doctor's departure until her sobs had abated into the deep breathing of sleep. Exhausted, she slowly made her way downstairs to join Carver just as he was showing the policemen out of the house after giving his report, detailing Kane's actions.

The moment he closed the front door, she flew into his arms, basking in the comfort and security of having his arms about her. “Is it over?” She whispered into his solid chest.

“I believe it is, and now the police are determined to take another look at Prescott’s case. Kane’s escape from prison was far too easy, and they know that if they can find out which officer was bribed, and by whom, they will be able to put Prescott away for his crimes against us.”

She pushed herself out of his arms. “Then it’s truly over? Prescott won’t attempt to separate us again?”

“I believe that his desperation in the end may have made him careless, leaving a trail for them to follow.” He pressed a kiss to her hands. “But I do wish to discuss the matter of Nora.”

Her stomach tightened. Nora couldn’t be without a husband *and* without funds—not with a baby on the way. “I know she has access to the funds we paid Kane, but please don’t ask her to return—”

“She must keep the funds, of course. I was thinking more along the lines that if she does not wish to return to a town full of memories of Kane, she should stay here and set up a business in New Orleans."

"Here, as in, with us?"

He shrugged. "If she wishes, and I know you have commented on multiple accounts of the house being too quiet. Besides, I remember from your letters saying that Nora wished to be a seamstress and—"

She threw her arms about her husband's neck and kissed him soundly. "Just when I think you can't possibly become more wonderful, you find a way!"

EPILOGUE

hristmas 1898

CARVER SIGHED as he settled next to Sophia on a cozy makeshift blanket pallet on the library floor by the fireplace. “After entertaining your family all of Christmas Eve, it’s nice to have a quiet moment together.”

“So much has changed in one year. Last Christmas, I didn’t even know you and now . . .” She cupped his face in her hands. “Now, I can’t imagine life without you.”

The fireplace crackled as he took her hand in his. “With you by my side, it feels like life is finally beginning. You were the one who gave me the courage to stand up to my stepfather—to break out on my own and open our department store." Carver tucked a loose strand of her honey blonde hair behind her ear.

She lifted his hand and kissed the top of it. "And what a wonderful life we have together, you and me and Nora and little Noah. I shall miss them when they move into their new flat above the dress shop with Mrs. Kane next week." She selected a tiny gift from the tree and laid the small package in his hands. She shifted her legs under her and rested her head on his shoulder to watch him open it, anticipating his reaction to the piece Nora had set aside her mound of orders at her new dress shop on Canal Street to create. Now that Nora's success was growing, Sophia had no doubt her friend would become famous for her work.

"What's this?" He smiled at her, his eyebrows rising suspiciously. He felt the package. "Did you make me a pair of socks? I've seen you sewing, you know, but I could never quite make out what it was before you hid it away."

Sophia giggled. "You won't guess, so you might as well open it. And no, I didn't make your gift. I gave up after a few tries and called upon Nora for her help, so you know the quality is lasting."

He tore open the package, and a knitted pair of yellow booties tumbled onto his lap along with a creamy infant's nightgown. He lifted them up and gaped at her. "Sophia?"

She gently pressed her lips to his and whispered, "Merry Christmas, my sweet, darling husband."

APRONS & VEILS
BOOK TWO

The Pursuit of Miss Parish

GRACE HITCHCOCK

CHAPTER 1

Nearing New Mexico
August 1898

WITH EACH BREATH, the stale air of the train and its malodorous passengers stuck in Belle Parish's lungs. *Am I doing the right thing?* She turned from the soot discolored window to Angelique, but one look at her friend's peaceful slumber, Belle knew she would only make light of their rather frightening situation. *Just remember every kind word Colt wrote in his letters. He shares your faith. How bad could a man be if he believes in the Lord?* Sighing, Belle leaned back on the stiff wooden seat and smoothed out the simple, pale pink skirt that Angelique had lent her for the journey to meet their future husbands for the first time. She tugged on the cream cuffs of her best and only shirtwaist and tried to calm herself by taking deep breaths, but the more air she gulped, the dryer her throat became.

If Angelique had not answered that advertisement in the paper on their behalf, Belle would not be here in the first place. But there was nothing left for her in Charleston. After Miss Fairfield had run away to become a Harvey Girl, life had grown unbearable, and she had been forced to quit the only position she had ever known. What else could a maid without a job do in the Wild West but follow through with the plan and marry? She shifted in her seat and tried to breathe in the air from the small opening in the train window, but the sun was melting her under her borrowed skirt, and, unlike her beloved city, there wasn't any dampness in the air to compensate for the heat. It was just plain hot.

Parched, Belle avoided the gaze of the

overly chatty woman in the seat behind them and wobbled down the swaying aisle to the communal bucket of water. Using the dipper, she trickled water into one of the tin cups and slowly returned to her seat, careful not to spill her drink. She sniffed it, her nose wrinkling. Taking the tiniest sip of the musty liquid, she fought to keep from gagging, but her thirst was not satiated. She pinched her nose and gulped a mouthful. Gunshots rent the air.

The passenger car erupted in screams as the train lurched, the wheels screeching and flinging Belle onto the floor of the car, her cheek striking the edge of a seat. She lifted herself on her elbow to rush to Angelique's side, but an elderly gentleman near her pressed a hand to her shoulder.

"Stay down. They may fire into the car, Miss," he whispered, his leathery wrinkled hands shaking.

"I have to get to her!" She crawled as quickly as she could manage in her long skirts to Angelique's side, clutching her friend's hand when the sound of the car door opening accompanied by the jingling of spurs chilled her to her core. A broad-shouldered man masked behind a scarlet bandana strode through the door, the barrel of his gun catching in the afternoon sun.

"Everyone keep your hands where I can see them. Your valuables are worth more to me than your life, so toss your jewels into my hat and we won't have no trouble."

And if one does not possess any valuables? What then?

THE STORY CONTINUES in *The Pursuit of Miss Parish* by Grace Hitchcock . . .

AUTHOR'S NOTE

Dear Reader, thank you so much for reading Book One in the Aprons & Veils series!

If this is your first time reading about the Harvey Girls, know that they did indeed exist. In the 1890s, there were not many respectable jobs for women, so when Englishman Fred Harvey created his chain of fine dining restaurants along the Atchison, Topeka, and Santa Fe railroads, single women without an education, or in need of earning their own way, were given a chance to earn an honest wage without the speculation that they offered anything else but food as a service. With Mr. Harvey's strict rules about the waitress's code of conduct, the women were given their independence while still maintaining their good name and place in society under the protective, fatherly arm of Fred Harvey. These extraordinary, brave women became known as the Harvey Girls, the ladies who tamed the Wild West with fine china, good pie, and exceptional service with complete propriety.

For the purpose of my story, I did take some small liberties with the Hotel Castañeda, such as the opening date. Sources claim different years, so I decided to begin this series the year the Castañeda was built. I also changed the dining room floor appearance. I did attempt to stay as accurate as possible with the Fred Harvey system and layout of the hotel based on the historical pictures and references available. This Harvey House is one of the few still standing and has been fully restored to operate once more.

If you enjoyed the story, I would love if you could please take a moment and leave a review or rating! Stay tuned for Book Two in the series, *The Pursuit of Miss Parish*. Happy reading, friends!

Grace Hitchcock is the award-winning author of multiple historical novels and novellas, including the American Royalty, True Colors, and Aprons & Veils series. She holds a Master's in Creative Writing and a Bachelor of Arts in English with a minor in History. Grace lives on the Northshore of New Orleans, with her husband, Dakota, sons, and daughter in a cottage that is always filled with the sounds of sweet little footsteps running at full speed. When not writing, or chasing babies, she's baking something delightful and can usually be found with a book clutched in her fist.

Sign Up for Grace's Newsletter!

Keep up to date with Grace's news on book releases and giveaways by signing up for her email list at GraceHitchcock.com

---

FREE from Grace Hitchcock

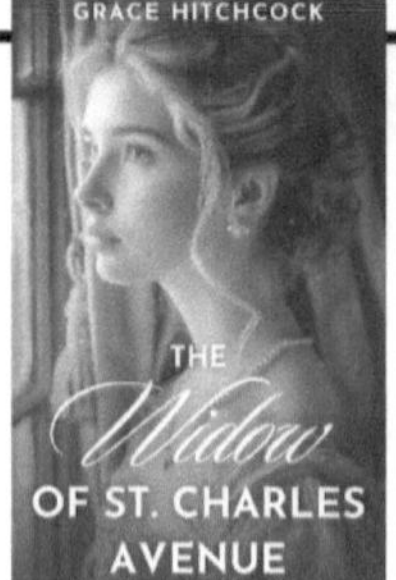

New Orleans, 1895

Colette Olivier, a young widow who married out of obligation, finds herself at the end of her mourning period and besieged with suitors out for her inheritance. With her pick of any man, she is drawn to an unlikely choice.

The Widow of St. Charles Avenue by Grace Hitchcock
a Second Chance Brides Novella
GraceHitchcock.com

Scan to Claim Your FREE Novella

More in your favorite series . . .

With a hope for belonging, Belle Parish leaves her position as a maid in Charleston to travel to New Mexico to become a mail-order bride. Colt Lawson's letters hold great promise, but something does not add up. Belle flees straight into the Castañeda Hotel Harvey House. Giving up the prospect of marrying, she focuses on her role as a Harvey Girl waitress until a strong Texas Ranger rides into her life.

The Pursuit of Miss Parish by Grace Hitchcock
Aprons & Veils #2
A Mail-Order Bride RomCom

Of all the dares Lorna Elliot had accepted, becoming a Harvey Girl waitress was by far the dumbest. And she had done it to herself in a fit of pique over a Texas Ranger who was mooning over another woman, but now that Ranger Reid is the new sheriff in her hometown, it's going to be impossible for her to move on unless she takes control of her heart—for better, or for worse.

The Enchanting of Miss Elliot by Grace Hitchcock
Aprons & Veils #3
A Friends-to-Lovers RomCom

Tanner Sterling has hunted his last bounty. As a new foreman, he wasn't expecting to rescue a sweet Harvey Girl from a raging river his first day. But, when he sees her on a wanted poster, he knows hunters will be coming for her. Despite wanting to hang up his past along with his gun belt, Tanner will do anything to protect her from the coming storm . . . even if he has to claim the bounty himself.

The Vanishing of Miss Victoria by Grace Hitchcock
Aprons & Veils #4
An Enemies-to-Lovers RomCom

You May Also Like . . .

Muriel Beau, country baker turned heiress, can't stop instigating outrage. She discards two arranged engagements, then further antagonizes Kent society by publicly proposing to a baron at a ball. His rejection leaves her with no choice but to flee to the city and to secure a coronet so splendid that her peers will forget her debacles.

To Catch a Coronet by Grace Hitchcock
Best Laid Plans #1
A Regency RomCom

While attending the Chicago World's Fair in 1893, Winnifred Wylde believes she witnessed a woman being kidnapped. She tries to convince her father, an inspector with the police, to look into reports of mysterious disappearances around the White City. He allows her to go undercover as secretary to the man in question—if she takes a pistol for protection and Jude Thorpe, a policeman, for bodyguard.

Miss Wylde in the White City by Grace Hitchcock
Heiresses of Adventure #2

An Italian lady's companion, a Charleston bridal shop seamstress, and a Harvey Girl on the run from her past . . . only heroes with hearts of gold will win their hands.

Hearts of Gold by Grace Hitchcock
3-in-1 Historical Romance Collection
GraceHitchcock.com

www.ingramcontent.com/pod-product-compliance
Lightning Source LLC
Chambersburg PA
CBHW031141050726
47495CB00018B/293

9798991270731